LAW OR JUSTICE

LAW OR JUSTICE

TERRA KRIS™ BOOK TWO

MICHAEL ANDERLE

DEDICATION

To Family, Friends and
Those Who Love
to Read.
May We All Enjoy Grace
to Live the Life We Are
Called.

— Michael

Captain Parker Garcia leaned back in the comfort of the plush armchair and rested his muddy boots on the glass table in front of him.

The table shook. A handful of drinks jittered off their coasters and splashed some droplets on the clear glass. The room was smoky. It stank of man and perfume. Music thumped loudly in the room, and the flashing colored lights cast Garcia into a hypnotic state of lust and pleasure.

Nearby, ladies danced on platforms, grinding their assets against the poles. There were others in the room—many others—ogling and watching the ladies, but the woman in front only had eyes for him, and that made Garcia happy.

She hadn't blinked in minutes. Each gyration was an invitation for him and him alone. Something stirred in his trousers, and the goofy grin that painted his face hadn't faded since the song began. In the nearby chairs, people chatted and laughed, although Garcia couldn't hear them properly. He was in his little corner of the world, and that was fine by him.

As long as she kept looking his way.

At the end of the song, the woman paused, one hand draped

lasciviously on the pole. Garcia reached into his pocket, taking a moment to let his hand rub against his swollen package, before removing his cell phone. He showed the screen to the woman, a number with too many zeroes written after it, and tapped to confirm.

A confirmation light flickered green at the bottom of the pole. A screen embedded into the platform's floor and facing the woman showed a message that she was happy with. The next song started, and she began her dance again.

She was halfway through her dance when Garcia was brought free from his bubble of filthy thoughts. The music thumped, but it didn't drown out the sound of a gunshot behind him. He glanced over the back of his chair toward the corner of the room and a booth sheeted in clear plastic. Blood splattered the protective barrier, and a group of men cheered and sneered at a bloodied corpse in their midst. On the table in the center was a black spiral where the spinning gun had been moments before the victim fell on his figurative sword. Russian roulette was a real man's game, and real men sometimes lost.

A burly man with a mop of dark curly hair that reminded Garcia of Weird Al Yankovic glanced his way with a smirk. He inclined his head. Garcia grinned and nodded back, a grin on his face. What other land in the country would let a Chief Officer for Justice enjoy the luxuries of murder, booze, and sex on the penthouse floor of a prestigious skyscraper overlooking the Atlantican coast?

Any other country in the world would force Garcia to stay on the straight side of the law, obey all the rules, live a life that was so squeaky clean he could eat off the floor. Not here. Not in Atlantica. As long as he remained in the arms of a private residence, he could do as he pleased. Hell, he could snort cocaine off a hooker's back, then blow a cap through someone's face without a flicker of guilt or remorse.

Ah, the good life.

Garcia returned his attention to the stage, but the dancer was gone. He glanced around the apartment, sweeping his gaze over the swath of assholes, crooks, and politicians all getting their rocks off until he found her.

She stood at the bar, topless and with only a thong to keep her warm. Garcia felt himself stirring again and rose from his chair. He was about to cross to her when he realized someone was blocking his way.

"Sir…" Antonio Francis stated, wary and a little cautious.

"Move." Garcia shoved him out of his way. He managed only a few steps before Antonio caught up. "Sir. You need to hear this. Something has happened. Something bad."

Garcia stopped with a grumble. He kept his gaze on the woman standing at the bar and waiting for the barman to serve her a drink.

I should be buying that woman's drink.

"It's about Cross," Antonio replied. He withered under Garcia's shadow. His thin mustache looked sketched onto his face. One of his eyes was milky and scarred from an old accident involving a knife fight with a former colleague. His Beretta was in his hip holster, but it had been some time since it had seen action. "He's…he's compromised."

Garcia whirled on Antonio. Annoyance and frustration surged through him. "What?"

"Cross," Antonio repeated. "He's dead."

"Dead?" Garcia repeated.

Antonio nodded.

Garcia's voice fell low, forcing Antonio to come closer to hear him. "By whose hand?"

"We don't know," Antonio stated. "All we know is that the AJS found him dead in the basement of the Laundr-O-Mat. Black was with them, but someone freed her."

Garcia gritted his teeth so hard that a small chip came off one molar. He swallowed it. "You're telling me the AJS found the den?"

Antonio nodded.

"Fuck." Garcia's face shadowed. "Cross is down?"

Antonio nodded again.

Garcia drew a long breath. "Tell me there was nothing down there. Nothing evidential to our cause."

Antonio nodded. "There wasn't. Cross managed to wipe the drives and servers before he died. It should have erased any link to you and your connections from existence." He stopped as Garcia's fist connected with his cheek. Antonio whirled, crashing into the glass table behind him. Drinks exploded and glass shattered. Still, the music played. No one batted an eye.

Garcia shook his fist, his face still grim and set. Antonio collected himself, working his way out of the shattered glass until he stood. His palms were bloody. A red lump rose on his cheek.

"How many did they get?" Garcia spoke as if nothing had happened.

Antonio raised his chin. "Sir...I..."

"How many?" Garcia repeated.

Antonio glanced around the room, his eyes imploring for help. He wouldn't get it. "They have thirty runners in custody."

Garcia's fist clenched. Antonio's eyes caught its movement. He held his ground.

"Thirty of our boys in custody," Garcia grumbled.

"And women." Antonio instantly regretted his decision to speak as another punch struck his cheek. He groaned in pain as the glass spiked into his body. This time he didn't rise, instead choosing to lay there and stare up at Garcia.

Garcia towered over him. "I don't care if they're space sharks with rockets up their fucking asses. Thirty of our guys are in AJS custody, and that puts us in a very vulnerable position, doesn't it?"

Antonio nodded, fidgeting on top of the glass.

Garcia continued. "Thirty men *and women* in custody means thirty opportunities for our guys to fuck up and let slip the truth. Thirty men and women in custody means we have thirty open loops we need to close before anyone lets slip the word 'Garcia.' Thirty men and women out in the wild, lowly fucking grunts with nothing more than cash in their eyes and ink in their skin, will start crowing the moment someone offers a better fucking deal."

A waiter passed with a silver tray of shots balanced on his palm. He stopped by Garcia. "Tequila, sir?"

Garcia took three and pounded them. The waiter, with no hint of irony or mirth, crouched to offer the same to Antonio.

He took a shot and drained its contents. The waiter held out a hand and helped him up before continuing on his way without a second look.

Garcia's eyes strayed over Antonio's shoulder to the bar, looking for the woman who got his loins stirring. She was gone. Instead, a morbidly obese man in a penguin-tailed suit threw his head back and gave a raucous laugh as the barman rolled his eyes and turned his attention to pouring his drink.

Garcia sighed. Antonio glanced over his shoulder, realizing what was on his boss's mind.

"Sir…I…" Antonio started.

Garcia held out a hand. "We have a problem to fix, don't we?"

Antonio nodded.

Garcia's eyes narrowed, his mind already moving to the solution. It wasn't going to be pretty. It would raise some attention. But, dear God, if he didn't act fast, his entire house of cards would come crumbling down.

CHAPTER ONE

Rain sleeted down the sides of the buildings, and a low rumble of thunder rolled in the distance. Above, the skies were as black as the shadows Terra clothed herself in, the only light the occasional glimpse of lightning that split the sky.

Terra rubbed the rain sting from her eyes, then buried her hands deep into the pockets of her black leather jacket. She was thankful that she'd put her hair in a ponytail before leaving the warm comfort of her parent's abode. At least it was out of her face.

Terra ducked through the alleys, the smell of Greek kebab and Italian pizza thick in the air. She shuffled past dumpsters piled high with trash bags. The occasional *thunk* against a steel container gave away the position of the homeless person inside, rifling around for scraps of food. Steam hissed from the vents at the backs of the brick buildings, and headlights grew and faded as traffic rumbled by ahead.

Terra turned left, heading deeper into the alley. The bridge lay ahead, a large, sweeping overpass that allowed Atlantica citizens to bypass the city proper. It was a veritable steel and concrete labyrinth of exits and on-ramps, the lanes often choked with bumper-to-bumper traffic.

Beneath the bridge, there was little to be found in the places where the trolls were supposed to hide.

Terra made for the cover of the underpass with her collar pulled high around her neck. With her black slacks and black boots, she was difficult to spot in the shadows. When she walked toward the group of vagabonds gathered around the glowing embers of an oil drum, however, there was little that could hide her from sight.

They barely lifted their heads to look at her, instead opting to rub their hands above the fire's warmth. Terra reached the umbrella canopy of the bypass and shook the residual water from her body. The rain had soaked her gloved hands and top. Her trousers were soaked too.

Yet, she'd been in worse situations. What was a little water, anyway? It would all dry in the end.

APRIL, watch my six.

Watching your six.

Terra continued onward, passing a large stone pillar that was easily twenty feet in width. She hopped over a narrow gully that filtered rainwater from the city out into the ocean and made for the farthest reaches of the darkness.

The ground began to rise. Terra forged ahead, the gap between herself and the road narrowing slowly. When she reached the top of the mound, she stopped. She couldn't go any farther. The chain-link fence topped with barbed wire prevented her from stumbling over onto the elevated railway tracks. She sat and waited.

Below her, the oil drum glowed like a beacon. The homeless few chatted among themselves, all of them bearded or skinny or sporting clothes that had seen better days. Somewhere in the distance, Terra made out the report of a gun, followed soon after by AJS sirens.

She wrapped her arms around her knees and rested her chin on her arms. Her skin broke out in gooseflesh, but only temporarily before APRIL stabilized her temperature and granted her the relief of warmth.

What's the time, APRIL?

00:48, APRIL replied inside Terra's head in a voice that managed to sound both human and robotic at the same time.

He's late.

That is correct. Shall I contact his telephone number and request his current location?

Terra smirked. *You know better than that.*

She gasped as the world slipped away before her. The hum of the bridge's traffic faded, the vagabonds disappeared, and instead, Terra was looking down at the streets of Atlantica through the fisheye lens of a security camera. A man exited the apartment building with his trench coat wrapped tightly around him. He lit a cigarette and paused before heading out into the stormy night.

The world lurched. Terra watched the man from the dashcam of a driverless cab. He was shadowed in the back, lit now and then by the strobe-like flash of the sodium lights as the taxi drove through the city. His eyes were dark, occasionally glinting like beetle shells.

The time on the recording read 00:41.

Another shift in lens as APRIL tracked through the city's data feed. The man exited the cab, running his fingers through his dark, damp hair. He stalked along the sidewalk, passing a building that flashed in neon signs which read "Denby's Desert Diner"—a business that was only a block away.

He should be here by now.

The world went dark. It took a few moments for Terra's eyes to adjust to what she was seeing. The security camera offered a view under a bridge and into the shadows. The nearest lamps had been smashed, according to APRIL's label reports in her vision.

Still, somewhere in the darkness, she saw the cherry of a cigarette glowing and fading.

Where is this feed? Terra asked.

The world reappeared. Terra's head was nudged slightly to the left by her internal artificial intelligence software. A hundred yards away, Terra made out the dark silhouettes of the broken lights. APRIL zoomed in to catch the flare of the cigarette.

Terra shook her head and scoffed. *Just like him to initiate a Mexican stand-off.*

You should go to him if you want to get the job done.

"He can come here," she whispered. "I'm not going to him first."

Perhaps he hasn't seen you.

"Oh, he's sure as hell seen me," Terra replied. "There's no way in hell that he hasn't."

I don't understand.

"He's playing games, APRIL," Terra explained. "You don't know this guy as well as I do. This is how he operates. It's all fun and games with him."

Unrequested information bubbles appeared around the man waiting in the darkness. They drew Terra's eyes to information such as Name: John "Dick" Chambers. Business: Private Investigator. Criminal charges: Zero convictions. Star sign: Aries.

Aries?

Aries: the first astrological sign in the zodiac. Aries are categorized by the individual's date of birth, applying to those born from March 20 to April 21.

I know what Aries is, APRIL. Terra shook her head. *You don't need to read me the Wiki entry every time I have a thought.*

Noted. However, it appears I know this man better than you.

Terra smirked. "No. You don't. You need to be human to understand this man. You need to have experienced him, have lived memories. You don't truly know a man until you've shot him in the ass and watched his pain."

APRIL pulled up a document in Terra's vision, a large piece of paper that listed Dick's medical history. It zoomed in to highlight the date of the operation and the extraction of Terra's bullet from the fatty tissue of his ass. **Is this what you're referring to?**

Terra chuckled. It had been a genuine accident, but a happy one, nonetheless. Served Dick right for crossing her path in the middle of a raid. "Yes, APRIL. That's what I was referring to."

Terra sat for a while, waiting for Dick to make the first move. After ten minutes, it became apparent that Dick wasn't going to play ball. Terra grumbled and rose to her feet.

She skirted the chain-link fence, making her way to the figure in the darkness. As she drew closer, APRIL engaged night vision in her left eye, and Dick's face and body came into view. She paused a short distance from him. "Still stubborn as ever, I see."

"Oh, Terra? I didn't see you there." The grin was evident in his words. "I thought it was unlike you to be running late."

"Running late?" Terra's lips thinned. "I don't have the patience to play your games right now, Dick. I still haven't forgiven you for the last time we crossed paths."

Dick took a drag of his cigarette. The cherry's glow lit his pale lips. His rash of stubble speckled his face. Although she couldn't see him properly in this light, she already knew of his outward charm and rugged appearance. It was what made the ladies swoon around him, though she had never fallen for his charms herself.

She knew Dick's type too well for that. A lone wolf, whose primary company involved the brown stuff in the bottle and the nicotine sticks that stained his clothes and fingers. You couldn't get close to a man like that. Not really.

Dick tapped the end of his cigarette. "You mean using you as female bait to catch an asshole who very much deserved to be locked up in jail?"

"That's the one." Terra glanced over her shoulder, casting a furtive look to ensure they were still alone. It had been almost three days since her scrape with Fernando Cross in his hidden drug den beneath the city, and she had yet to shake off the feeling that something bad was coming for her. She had disturbed a hornet's nest, and it wouldn't be long before they found her again. "As I recall, I did you a solid, then. I helped you catch your guy, now I…"

"Now you need *my* help?" Dick chuckled. The sound of it was irritating and cocky. He drew in a long breath. "I suppose I could help you, Terra. After all, fair is fair. The real question is, why does a self-proclaimed badass justice officer want help from a lonely PI? Don't you have the entire team at your disposal? Fleets of dogs and tools and gadgets and officers to help you round up the fuckers you want to catch?"

Terra's lips thinned. "You know it's not like that, Dick. Certain rules bind us. I still have to abide by the city code."

"So you need someone willing to do the dark deeds you can't?" Dick raised an eyebrow. "It's going to cost you."

Terra drew her GLOCK from the folds of her jacket and aimed it at Dick's crotch. Her face hardened, finger tensing on the trigger. "You can help me for free. Either that or I'll blow your goddamn cock off."

Dick didn't flinch. He raised the cigarette to his lips and took a long drag. When he lowered the cigarette, he turned so that the gun was pointing at his ass. "Or you could go for round two."

Terra thumbed the safety off. "Happily."

Dick turned, flicking the stub of his cigarette into the distance. He slid his hands into his pockets. "Relax, Kris. I'm only playing with you. You make it so easy. Besides, why wouldn't I help out to earn the favor of my favorite AJS officer? That way, I'll always have your support whenever I need it again in the future, won't I?"

Terra laughed. "I wouldn't count on it."

"I would." Dick fixed her with his gaze.

Terra lowered the gun, flipped the safety on, then slid it back inside her jacket. "I need your help, Dick. This is a big one, and I know that I won't be able to take it on alone."

Dick nodded. "Who's the target?"

Terra reached into her jacket and drew out a crumpled photograph of a man with a gray goatee, deep-set eyes, and ears that seemed double the size of how they should be. In the picture, he sported his pristine AJS uniform, his chief's hat a little crooked on his head.

"My old boss," Terra replied. "Captain Parker Garcia."

Dick raised an eyebrow, accepting the image. "Your *old* boss?"

"I have a lot to catch you up on," Terra replied. "You in or out?"

Dick drew a long breath. "I suppose you better catch me up first. I won't commit without the information."

Terra smirked. "I think you will. Knowing your constitution, this will certainly be one you don't want to miss out on."

CHAPTER TWO

Terra woke to the sound of her alarm clock.

Her eyes peeled open, the world a little blurry around her. Something moved beside her, and soon wet kisses were painting her face.

"Come on, Skooch." Terra chuckled, running her fingers through the Papillon's fur and gently encouraging her to ease off. "Mummy needs a shower, but not that kind of shower."

Skooch gave a happy little *yip* as Terra sat up in the plush king bed. Milky sunlight streamed through the window, and the curtains gently swayed in the breeze. Terra put a hand to her head where a dull throb was forming. "APRIL, what the hell? I thought you were supposed to balance my biochemistry and all that jazz?"

APRIL's voice was jarring inside her head, louder than she wanted it to be. **My programming insists on short breaks between vast bouts of biochemical manipulation. The body must be allowed to restore equilibrium for brief periods to maintain regular human bodily function.**

"Huh…" Terra mused. "Is that the reason I've been struggling to pee?"

Negative.

Terra laughed. "It was a joke, APRIL."

Ha. Ha. Ha. Good one, Terra.

Terra raised an eyebrow. "Yeah…it's going to be a while before they perfect humor in machines."

Humor. A human emotion.

Terra rolled her eyes. "That's enough out of you. Activate civilian mode."

APRIL fell silent.

Terra rose from her bed and stretched. She wandered over to the window and looked outside. The sleepy little suburb was picturesque. The patchwork of mansions and villas with their mix of white picket fences and golden gates wouldn't look out of place on the cover of *Home Owner's Weekly.* Perfectly manicured gardens showcased an array of flowers in bloom, hedges trimmed into the shape of animals, and water features on the brilliantly green lawns.

Terra chewed her lip. She would be sad not to wake up to this view anymore. Although it had only been a few weeks since her operation, she had enjoyed living at her parent's place again. Her old room cuddled her like an old friend. The smell was familiar and took her back to her childhood. There was also the added pleasure of having her cooking and cleaning catered for.

A thought crossed her mind. *I hope Mom managed to get the blood out of my clothes.*

Terra knew she needed to find somewhere else to live. As long as she stayed here, her parents weren't safe. Although they were high members of Atlantican society, having Terra in their vicinity would only cause problems. Terra had uncovered something big, and she could already hear the hounds barking on the horizon as they sniffed her trail.

Her mother waited for her downstairs, busying herself around the kitchen. She wore a clean, gray power suit and looked ready to do battle in the Diplomatic Office of Atlantica. "Morning, sweetie."

"Morning, Mom." Terra stopped at the kitchen counter. Skooch, who had been running behind Terra, tried to stop in time, but her paws skidded on the smooth tiles. Her nose butted into the back of Terra's leg. "Back at work today?"

"You know it," Marie replied. She took a parcel from the refrigerator and laid it in front of Terra. "That's for you today."

Terra picked up the plastic-wrapped tuna sandwiches. "Looks good. Thank you."

"You need your wits about you to choose the right place," Marie continued without looking. "I'm not having my girl putting herself in some dirty little hovel. You're a Kris. You're a *successful* Kris. You deserve something nice."

Terra's cheeks flushed. She had spoken to her parents about the need to get out and find a new place, although she hadn't gone as in-depth as she'd planned to. When sitting with Michael and Marie that night, all she'd managed was to say that she was in trouble and needed to remove herself from harm's way.

Her father had understood, holding up a placating hand. After nearly forty years in the AJS himself, he understood the risks. When Terra had insisted that they each take extra precautions, Michael had simply laughed her off. "Honey, you think that we've lived on Atlantica all our lives without learning to take security precautions?"

Terra cocked her head. "All I can see are the security cameras fitted to the exterior."

Michael and Marie exchanged a glance.

Marie finished, "Just because you can't see something doesn't mean that it isn't there. We can't count the number of times someone has tried to sneak onto this property. Do you know how many people have successfully made their way inside?"

"None," Michael stated.

Terra laughed. "Not sure that's true. I often snuck out as a teenager."

Michael grinned. "We know."

Nothing more needed saying after that.

Terra watched her mother move around the kitchen. "You'll be careful, won't you?"

"Always." Marie didn't bat an eye. "I hope you will, too."

"Always," Terra replied.

Marie finished packing her bag, then swept over to Terra. She kissed her forehead and smiled. "Go get 'em."

Terra met the housing agent in the center of the city proper.

The man was the definition of a slime ball. He'd combed back his receding hair in greasy streaks, and the bags beneath his eyes looked like bruises. His suit might once have fit a much more slender man but now stretched over his rotund figure, which he refused to accept. His palms were sweaty when he shook Terra's hand, and his gab had all the sophistication of an alley cat on crack.

"Shall we begin?" Edward Holmes of Edward Holmes' Homes asked.

Terra glanced around the busy streets and nodded. "We better."

The first few apartments were an instant no. Edward led Terra down a series of streets which Terra recognized from raids she had formerly been a part of. Although Atlantica liked to name its streets after founders or places of interest, it didn't take long for certain areas to gain street names based on their reputations.

The red light district was one such example, situated on Summer Lilly Avenue. What had formerly been one of Atlantica's prime spots for boutique flowers and perfumes now belonged to the ladies of the night.

Terra walked down Crosswind Boulevard, scanning the apartment windows that flanked her on either side. She had visited here regularly, had taken down several drug dealers and abusive partners the moment things got out of hand and their problems had spilled out into the streets.

APRIL, scan the surrounding buildings.

Scanning now.

Edward gave a rousing speech about the benefits of living on the street named after Sacha Crosswind. The woman had brought the green energy agenda to Atlantica—not that it ever properly took off. Many of Atlantica's vehicles and businesses *still* ran on fossil fuels in the absence of sufficient Atlanticore for the whole city. While he spoke, Terra's vision filled with thermal imaging of the scumbags who lived in the buildings.

Through the thermal imaging alone, she made out an orgy, several shapes gathered around a table and sniffing something off its surface, as well as a man holding a knife that appeared to be dripping blood.

"You're going to *love* this one," Edward informed Terra, stepping up the stoop of the nearest block. "It's a two-bedroom, with a spare office room, and at least—"

"Let me stop you there," Terra replied. She glanced around. "This is really the best you can do for my budget?"

Edward feigned offense. "My dear, these apartments are some of the best in the city."

Terra gave a derisive snort. She stepped closer, forcing Edward's grimy billboard smile to slip. "Then I up my budget."

"What figure are we talking?" Edward asked.

Terra told him.

His eyes lit up. She could see the mental arithmetic working toward its inevitable commission in his head. "Why didn't you say so?"

Terra shrugged. "Because I had the belief that not every

element in Atlantica wanted to suck your money from your wallet."

Edward laughed.

Terra held his gaze. It wasn't that she wasn't well off. Being the daughter of two highly successful Atlanticans and one of the fastest rising officers in the city—for a short time, at least—had gained Terra a significant nest egg. Still, the cash didn't drive her, and therefore she didn't see the need to spend unwillingly.

However, if she was going to get herself out of harm's reach while she zeroed in on Garcia and brought this shit to an end, she needed to invest in something better than this cesspit of filth.

"Got anything for me?" Terra asked.

"Oh, yes," Edward leered. "I have the perfect place."

***

Terra was confused as they approached the large, bubble-shaped building.

Originally an art installation by an architect forgotten in the sands of time, the Miriam Midnight Aquarium sat on the north side of the city, its glass front reaching out and over the waters of the Atlantic Ocean. From a distance, the building dazzled and sparkled on a sunny day, the best of the light catching the many globe-like shapes that constituted the building's design.

One entire panel on the building's west side was transparent, allowing city-goers a preview of what they could witness inside. Fish of all sizes and colors swam by in their schools, but that was minor compared to what featured inside.

Inside the Miriam Midnight Aquarium sat the world's great exhibition of deep-sea fish ever collected and curated. Darkness ruled in the recesses of the expansive rooms beneath the sea. Special lights set up in them allowed visitors to witness the monsters of the deep.

"It's not down below that we're going." Edward nodded at the only bubble on the structure that was entirely metal.

Terra frowned. "I'm not sure I follow."

"You better." Edward increased his stride, moving far in front of Terra.

He led her to a side door Terra had never noticed before and unlocked it with an ancient-looking key. The thick steel screamed against the hinges as it opened.

A dark stairway met them. Edward ushered Terra inside. She took one last glance behind before the door closed and darkness was total.

"I hope you haven't got any funny ideas." Terra activated APRIL's night vision mode and tracked Edward as he fished into his pocket for a light.

"Of course not. It would be more than my job's worth." His breath hitched, and Terra caught him staring in her direction, pausing for a moment. "Follow me."

The flashlight was an assault on her eyes. Edward led the way up the metal staircase, rising ever higher until Terra was sure they were at least six or seven stories high. At the end of the stairs, another door met them. Edward fiddled with another set of keys, then gained entry.

"Welcome to your new home." He motioned inside.

Terra's breath caught. She'd never seen anything like this in her life.

A cross between a high-class penthouse suite and a lighthouse, the large circular abode was overwhelming to process. She felt somehow under the sea and on top of the world at the same time. Port holes allowed light to seep in while granting a view of the aquarium. Nautical imagery decorated the curves of the walls, and pods led off to bedrooms, bathrooms, and an already furnished office. There was the sense of walking inside a giant submarine.

That wasn't all.

Light shimmered and danced around the room, and all Terra had to do was look down to discover where it came from. The floor was made entirely of glass. Dozens upon dozens of exotic fish swam beneath her, spiraling and waltzing in whirlwinds of color. Meters and meters below, fanciful coral dazzled the seabed of the exhibit. Enormous flying manta rays soared beneath her. Hammerheads and ocean sunfish made their way through the water.

"There are faces down there." Terra pointed at where children had their noses pressed to the glass. She spun to Edward. "You're selling me a peep-hole house? Lucky I'm not wearing a dress today." She advanced on him. "You're sick. Do you know that? Sick, sick, sick."

Edward laughed. "Relax, Miss Kris." He stamped his foot on the floor. "This is one-way glass. You can see them, but they can't see you." He stamped again. "Over three feet thick, too, in case that was one of your other concerns. It would take a wrecking ball to smash through this and have you sinking to your doom in the tank."

Terra relaxed a little, her gaze drifting back to the exhibition beneath her. "It is beautiful."

"Mesmerizing, huh?" Edward asked. "Within your budget, too."

Terra gave him a quizzical look. "How?"

Edward shrugged. "Fish freak rich people out. Well, most of them."

Terra examined the rest of the apartment. The place contained everything she'd ever need. It seemed as good a spot as any to hide out and undergo her detective work to track down Garcia. She returned to the main area to find Edward patiently waiting.

"Happy?" he asked.

"It's amazing." Terra's eyes strayed to the gaggle of people below, staring into the glass. Not one of them looked up toward Terra. "There is one more thing I want to check, though."

"The one-way glass?" Edward asked, a pallid grin on his face.

Terra nodded.

Edward moved toward a door that Terra hadn't noticed before. He stuck a key into the lock, then pulled it open. "Here's a shortcut for you. Your private gateway into the building." He put a finger to his lips. "Shhh. Don't tell anyone I told you."

"What is this place?" Terra asked.

"It was the owner's apartment many years ago," Edward explained. "They lived here while they put together the exhibits and made everything that you know and love about the Miriam. Sadly, they passed some years ago, and no one's picked this place up. I guess people don't see the true wonder of everything presented before you."

Terra narrowed her eyes. She slipped past Edward and made her way into the quiet corridor. After navigating her way past a series of bright yellow signs, she found herself at the top tank, a vast exhibition titled "Wonders of the Open Ocean."

She advanced to the massive glass window, waiting patiently for the buzzing crowds of children to thin so she could get closer. A sawfish swam past, met with a chorus of "oooh." A manta ray passed below them, where the exhibit trailed still deeper.

Terra glanced up at the roof of the exhibit, expecting to see the interior of the apartment.

The roof was black.

Terra grinned.

CHAPTER THREE

Terra shook hands with Edward, then transferred over the holding fee.

Edward glanced at his tablet. "Of course, this is all subject to references and background checks."

Terra waved. "I'm an Atlantica Justice Officer. I'll be fine."

Edward looked at Terra as though seeing her for the first time. "Oh."

Terra laughed, then signed her name on the papers. "I'll await your call."

She left the aquarium side door and instantly met a blanket of warmth. She hadn't realized the temperature drop in the aquarium but emerging into the bright, warm day gave her pause. She drew out her cell phone and dialed a number.

"Yeah?" the voice on the other end asked.

"I'm heading your way. You still at the meeting spot?" Terra asked.

"I am," the voice replied.

"Good." Terra checked her watch. "I'll be twenty."

Twenty-three minutes.

Terra ignored APRIL.

She hopped on her Ducati and kicked the stand back. She twisted the throttle and sped along the coastal road, the golden sands and glittering ocean on her left-hand side, a series of cocktail bars, merchandise stores, and deluxe apartments on her right.

The air whipping past cooled her. She snaked between the traffic and soon arrived at a small industrial spot on the southeast coast. She turned into the estate and slowed as she approached the factory building.

She parked her bike around the back, then skirted the steel exterior toward the front door. The last time she'd been here was under considerably different circumstances. Her mind flashed back to her encounter with Valentina and her surgical tools. That was when Terra's reality had shattered, and the truth came out.

Terra hadn't heard from Valentina since the day that she rescued Black from Cross's clutches. She hoped that Valentina had finally lived up to her end of the deal and disappeared for good. Terra was tired of knowing that others had access to the technology inside her head.

She made her way inside the trashed reception area and unlocked the door behind the counter. She ensured it was locked firmly in place as she descended the stairs and made her way into the AJS safe house.

She paused and grinned at the woman lying on the couch. "Well, you've made yourself at home, haven't you?"

Terra had never seen Corporal Leonie Black out of her AJS uniform. Today, she wore dark blue jeans and a Guns 'N' Roses t-shirt as she rested her head on the cushions. An empty coffee mug sat on the table in front of her, and the TV showed the news. Something strange scented the air, and only when Terra noticed the incense candles burning in the far corner did she realize why.

"This is my new home," Black snarked while sitting up. "What do you think? I've tried to make it hospitable."

Terra chuckled. She crossed to the kitchenette, took a mug from the cupboard, and poured the remaining coffee from the pot keeping warm on a hot plate. "It didn't take all too long. How are you finding life off the beat?"

Black shrugged. "I don't care for it much. Twenty years on duty sticks with you. I can't remember the last proper day off I took." She nodded at the cup. "Help yourself."

"I will." Terra sipped her drink, eyes narrowing on Black as she turned her gaze toward the news. Terra glanced around the safe house, remembering her visits with Dick to this place. She still wondered if this was the best place for Black to hide, but Black had insisted.

"The closer we are to danger, the farther away we are from harm," she had stated, misremembering the quote from her favorite movie.

Black shook her head. "This city is a disgrace. No matter how many of our guys are out on the street, there's always something happening in the news. If it ain't murders or sexual assaults, it's embezzlement, drug crime, or corruption at the highest levels. Do you ever sit back and wonder what we're doing it all for?"

Terra didn't hesitate. "No."

Black smiled. "You're a good one, you know."

"I know." Terra drained her cup, the heat from the liquid burning her throat. "Have you had any contact from the station?"

"No." Black crossed her legs. "Have you?"

Terra shook her head. "Only a couple of whispers. I'm going to do more digging today. It looks like they found someone to step into your shoes in your absence. Someone has also done a good job of finding an excuse for you not to be at work. There's no sniffing from the media or anything like that. As far as the AJS and the city are concerned, it's just another day."

Terra tried to recall whether there'd been anything else in the file Dick sent her late last night as he began his scoop of what the hell was going on in the outer city.

"It's impressive," Black mused.

"What is?" Terra replied.

Black sat forward. "Well, it goes to show, doesn't it? Someone along the chain is running the gambit and doing whatever they can to hide their trail." She sighed. "You were right, Terra. You were right from the moment you opened that line of inquiry toward Garcia. I'm sorry you got burned doing it."

"Not enough evidence," Terra replied. "I should have known better. When his goons surround a kingpin, you have to remove them first. Garcia has such a tight grip on his rungs of the ladder and all those below that we need to be smart with our approach."

"How did you find meeting with Dick?" Black asked.

Terra glanced at the countertop, aware that she didn't want to give away the fact that she knew Dick better than Black thought. "He's an interesting character."

"That's one word for it," Black replied.

Terra nodded. "He's a good guy. His heart is in the right place, and giving him the details of the case was like handing a fat kid a hunk of chocolate cake. His mouth instantly salivated."

Black smirked.

"What?" Terra asked.

"That twinkle in your eye," Black declared.

Terra frowned. "Puh-lease. I could do a thousand times better than that asshole."

"You said he was a good guy," Black replied.

Terra went quiet. She glanced around the apartment. "Are you sure you're going to be safe here?"

Black nodded. "If I'm not, you'll be the first to know." She held up her hand and waved her cell phone. "Download the app, and if anything happens, I can send you a signal straight away."

Terra nodded. Black gave the instructions. Terra pocketed her phone. They both turned to the TV as a reporter came onto the screen standing outside one of Atlantica's city parks. Behind them were several small white tents, the usually manicured lawn littered with holes and brown lumps of dirt. The ticker tape read, "Two dozen bodies found in Asheville Park."

Terra shook her head. "It's a good day to be working in justice, huh?"

Black nodded. "You know that *you're* off-duty, too, right?"

Terra smiled. "I'll let you know when I've tracked that asshole down."

Terra glanced over her shoulder as she strolled along the beachside promenade.

The sun was trying its best to break the Atlantica fog. The heat made it through, pulsing through the air in dry charges, but it blocked the worst of the sun's harsh rays. Men and women occupied patches of the golden sands. Some frolicked in the ocean. Speedboats, banana boats, and high-end yachts were visible farther out on the wavy surface.

Although none of them batted an eyelid as she walked, Terra couldn't help but feel exposed out here. Her thoughts strayed to her precinct, to the boys and girls in blue busy trying to mop up the shit Atlantica dealt. Dunston and Hewlett were likely out on patrol in some crack den somewhere, and though Terra had no clue who was there in Black's stead, she knew that she couldn't return. Not yet.

Terra Kris was AWOL.

It was for her safety. She knew that, at least. Besides, it gave her the chance to focus solely on the one goal she had fixed in her mind.

Satisfied that no one was watching her, Terra commanded APRIL to dial the number, then waited for the answer.

Slim's voice was soft and quiet. Terra made out the rumble of a car engine. "Hey."

Terra's eyes were drawn to a child screaming on the beach nearby, an empty ice-cream cone in his hand. "What's the craic?"

"Craic?" Slim replied.

"News. Updates. Gossip." Terra chuckled. "Anything new on the grapevine?"

Slim hesitated. "This isn't a secure line."

An idea came to Terra. *APRIL, can you encrypt this phone call?*

Examining protocol and technological networks. Terra's head filled with a sudden burst of static. She remembered once hearing the dial tone that crowed when the original dial-up Internet hit the mainstream, an awful assault on the senses. She wondered who had made that sound in the first place. What was wrong with a delicate tinkle of bells?

The sound caused her to grimace and stop. Slim must have heard it too because she cried, "What the hell?"

The sound stopped. **Call lines secure.**

Terra gave an approving nod, the dull thud in her head beginning to ease as APRIL got over their reluctance to manipulate Terra's chemical signatures once more. "I believe we're secure now."

Terra could hear Slim's skepticism down the phone. "How can you be certain? That's a thing you can do?"

Terra continued walking. "I'm never certain. I have to trust the computer that's in my head."

Slim gave a soft laugh. "Terra Kris trusting someone? A robot of all things? Now I've heard everything. Seriously, what have they done to you? How can you hear—"

"It doesn't matter," Terra interjected. "What matters is what's going on where you are. I want to come back to work."

"I'm not sure you ever leave work," Slim replied.

"I'm not sure I do, either. Update me," Terra requested.

Slim laughed, then filled Terra in on the events from the last twelve hours. Keen to fill the gaps vacated by Black's so-called "sick leave" and Terra's absence, the guys at the top HQ had installed a new figure to run the outer city precinct.

"Tobias Spencer," Slim announced. "Name ring any bells?"

It did. Terra had encountered Tobias on her dive into Garcia's dirty dealings. They were close friends, the pair of them often spending weekends playing poker in each other's houses. Tobias had a reputation for stepping over the line with his handling of delicate matters. He'd been on the business end of a court case on half a dozen occasions in the last two years alone.

"How does he keep rising through the ranks?" Slim asked. "He's bad news. I can tell you that from a mile away."

"That's the wrong question to ask," Terra replied.

Slim paused. "Oh?"

"The real question is, why has he been demoted to the role of corporal in the outer city?" Terra sat on a bench facing the ocean. "Last I checked, he was in Garcia's pocket, one below him in rank. Seems like a big demotion to suddenly be running one of the outer city stations."

"We both know the answer to that," Slim replied.

Terra smiled. It had been difficult to convince Slim of her situation. After the AJS cleared Cross's den, Terra had taken Slim to one side and unloaded the truth to her. Initially, Slim had been reluctant to accept what she heard until Terra utilized APRIL's internal video recording to email her footage of that night. Slim was skeptical, but she was also smart. She had a good heart and believed the best in people, which was the only reason Terra felt safe in trusting her.

Plus, she needed to have someone on the inside.

Again.

With Slim watching the action within the precinct, at least Terra could try to remain one step ahead of whatever was coming her way. Although Imani wasn't currently taking her calls—and for a fair reason—Terra knew she'd need to flank both sides of the AJS force if she was to stand a chance of finally bringing Garcia to justice.

"When does he start?" Terra asked.

Slim replied, "Already has. Clocked in at 5:00 a.m. this morning, all smiles and commands. Made himself quite at home in

Black's office. Gina's been pulling her hair out, attending to his wants and needs."

"Shock," Terra stated dryly. "I know the type. An asshole who swans around like he's the big business, but get him alone one-on-one, and he'll crumble."

"That so?" Slim replied. "Maybe I should try that."

Terra smirked. "Don't. I need you not to arouse suspicion. We already have our backs against the wall." She paused, pensively thinking. "Have they put a hit out on me yet?"

"Nothing public," Slim replied. Terra could tell she was holding something back.

"What is it?" Terra asked. "What aren't you telling me?"

Slim drew a long breath. "Hewlett and Dunston. Spencer's taken a particular liking to the pair, and they've had several meetings already this morning. I caught them walking down the corridor talking in whispers and heard your name thrown into the mix. They stopped the moment they saw me and shuffled on."

"Hardly known for their tact, are they?" Terra sighed. "So the pursuit has begun."

"Are you going to be okay, Terra?" Slim's compassion showed in her voice. "Are you going to be safe?"

Terra didn't know how to answer that. Was she going to be safe in bringing down a corrupt senior officer in one of Atlantica's finest justice institutions? All odds would have played against her had it not been for the AI living inside her head. As much as she hated to admit, APRIL was her saving grace, and she had every intention of pushing the intelligence to its limits.

"I'll be fine," Terra replied at last. "Just keep me informed of any changes, okay?"

Slim told her she would before ending the call.

Terra stared out at the rolling ocean. Waves rushed against the shore, foaming as they crested and crashed against the golden sands. The air was warm, and the chorus of children laughing played around her. The smell of barbecued sausages and burgers reached her nose.

Terra closed her eyes. Today was as perfect a day as you could get in Atlantica. For a moment, she allowed herself to drift and forget everything that waited for her out there.

For one moment, Terra allowed herself a modicum of calm and relaxation.

She held herself that way for an unknown amount of time, highly aware of the fact that the minute she opened her eyes, she had no idea when she would find this kind of peace again.

CHAPTER FOUR

Dick Chambers' nose wrinkled in disgust at the sight unfolding before him.

The man was a sight to behold. Sitting across the polished marble table, Ringo tucked into his pancakes in the same way Dick had seen pigs digging in shit for truffles. Ringo's wiry grey hair had no order to it, sticking out in all directions. Underneath the stains of maple syrup and cream that decorated his cheeks were oily gray smudges and streaks of dirt.

Not that this stopped Ringo from smacking his lips and ensuring that every last drop of sugary goodness was cleaned off his face and found its way into his stomach.

Dick sipped his bourbon, enjoying the way the liquor burned on its way down his throat. He narrowed his eyes, amazed and perturbed as Ringo finally sat back, his plate spotless before him.

"Thanks, Dick." Ringo was breathless as he patted his thin stomach. For a man who could eat more pancakes than an Olympic wrestling team, Ringo was stark thin. His cheekbones jutted out from the hollows of his cheeks, and his skin stretched tight across his forehead. "That hit the spot."

Dick nodded. "Now, what you owe me."

Ringo chuckled, a bright sound filled with the life that his body didn't show. "Right. Of course."

Despite the swanky decor of this cafe, each surface gleaming, the walls lined with golden frames set into the black and white tiles, Ringo slapped his ancient, fraying backpack onto the table. A nearby waiter glanced their way disapprovingly, then returned to cleaning a table.

"It's in here somewhere," Ringo muttered, rooting through the *clinking* items inside. A couple of stray computer chips and flash drives rolled out onto the table. "Ah, here we go." He withdrew a cell phone that looked as though it belonged in the 1990s. It was the length of Dick's whole hand, complete with an antenna that drew out from the top.

"It's a brick," Dick stated.

Ringo nodded with a grin. "It ain't pretty. But it'll do what you want it to. Basic cell-to-cell frequency with none of the Internet functionality from modern phones. You make a call on this, and the only person who'll receive it is the person who places *this* on their cell."

He handed Dick a chip the size of an aspirin tablet.

"What's that?" Dick asked. He wasn't ignorant of how technology worked, and he could handle himself when he needed to, but there was a ceiling to his knowledge.

"The receiver," Ringo replied as if Dick had simply asked what one plus one equaled. "There's an adhesive strip on the back. Stick that to your friend's cell phone, and they'll be able to dial in uninterrupted."

Dick thought about the job that lay before him. It wasn't so much that Terra needed convincing. It was that if Dick was to help her, he needed allies.

You couldn't buy allies with cash alone. Trust and evidential confirmation of honor were currency in themselves.

"Perfect." Dick rose from the table.

Ringo looked up, brow wrinkling. "That it? Thought we were going to catch up. You feed me just to leave me?"

Dick leaned over the table, face darkening. He shadowed Ringo, who retreated into his seat. "Be grateful you got your pancakes, friend. I could have taken what was mine and been on my way. I've done you a service here."

"Well, at least finish your coffee." Ringo arched his neck to look into Dick's empty coffee cup. "Oh."

Dick raised an eyebrow.

"I'm a bit lonely, okay?" Ringo chuckled. "You don't make a lot of friends in this kind of business. You're my nicest client."

Dick nodded. "Don't make a lot of friends in my industry, either. The difference between you and me? I accept this as a hazard of the job." He fished into his pocket and threw a couple of blue bills on the table. "Here. Maybe these guys can keep you company."

Ringo smirked and scooped the bills toward him. "Hello, old friends."

Dick exited the cafe.

Dick waited until nightfall.

He loved the city after dark. The way steam roiled out of the vents and rose to join the mothership of the fog veil above. The gentle rumble of car engines, the bright lights, and many places to hide.

Atlantica's citizens strode by beneath him. There seemed to be no order to the foot traffic, with each citizen involved only in their affairs. If one put their head down in the city, you could almost forget that this place was rife with the highest density of the world's criminal activity.

Which was where the Atlantica Justice System came in.

Ordinarily, Dick chose not to involve himself with the law.

His job as a private investigator took him outside the boundaries of the law, able to enter the dark spaces where no AJS may tread. He'd gotten twisted in the knots of justice on more than one occasion but always managed to separate himself and return, alone, to his apartment.

Dick looked down at the AJS station now. The building was monolithic, built of white marble with Grecian pillars erected at the entrance. A grand, sweeping staircase led to the door, with several officers coming to and fro. The building itself could easily have been the size of a football stadium, and it might have been if Dick could be bothered to take an interest in sports and measure the damn thing.

He brought a cigarette to his lips, then exhaled a ribbon of smoke into the air. She hadn't come out yet, but she would soon enough. He was sure of that.

He dangled his legs over the lip of the rooftop, sitting six stories high in the air. Occasionally he brought the binoculars to his eyes, and it was only when he finally spotted the mop of frizzy dark hair emerge that he knew he was on the right track.

Dick twisted until he dangled off the edge of the roof. He wrapped his hands around the drain pipe and shinnied his way down until he was at street level.

He sprinted to the edge of the shadows, barely spotting her as she disappeared around the side of the AJS station. Dick raised his collar, then dug his hands in his pocket as he crossed the road toward the alley.

A couple of officers glanced his way as he walked, but no one disturbed him. Why would they? He was doing nothing wrong.

He slipped into the alley where she'd disappeared and increased his pace. A parking lot came into view at the back of the building, half-filled with AJS cruisers and a row of motorcycles.

Two cars had their headlights on. Dick couldn't see inside the windows. One vehicle pulled out of its spot, and Dick took his chance.

He raised his pistol—a neat little gadget with a tiny mouth. He lined up the gun and pulled the trigger.

The projectile whistled through the air, finding its bed in the rear tire of the cruiser. Just for luck, Dick tracked the second vehicle, then pulled the trigger again.

The cars continued, undisturbed and unaware.

Dick gave a satisfied nod, then drew out his cell phone.

Imani Thomas glanced at her partner, Samson. "You ready?"

Samson nodded. He had none of Terra's charisma or personality, but Imani couldn't argue that he was a damn good cop. As far as substitutes went, she could've done a lot worse. The blinking lights from their HUDs confirmed that their glasses had synced with one another.

"Born ready." Samson's typical response.

They cut the engine and exited the vehicle, both officers' eyes tracking the nearby building. A large glass window made up the front, and they saw the silhouettes inside.

"Think they'll give us a warm reception?" Samson asked.

"Doesn't matter," Imani replied. "Not their choice to make. We go in there, and we shut them down quick. Element of surprise is on our side."

They stalked toward the building, its exterior made of smooth sandstone and carved with large replicas of Egyptian hieroglyphics. A sign above the door read Atlantican Historical Society.

Imani led the way to the front door. She nudged the glass and found it stuck fast.

She took a small instrument the size of a AA battery from her pocket, pressed it to the digital lock pad, and thumbed the button. A spark of blue light was followed by a *click* as the lock shorted and the door freed.

She nodded at Samson, and they made their way into the dark.

The moment they were inside, they heard the party taking place. There was a *whoop* of joy, followed by the *thuds* of bass music. A stink of weed lingered in the air. Imani tracked forward, Glock at the ready as she advanced on the nearest doorway.

"Ready?" she mouthed to Samson.

Samson grinned.

Imani counted to three, then kicked the door.

The panel swung wide open, revealing a couple of dozen party-goers waving their arms and jumping around to the music. Some of the women were topless. Several of the men were, too. All of their veins were dark gray from the copious amounts of ink they'd taken if the empty vials and syringes on the table were anything to go by.

"Freeze! Atlantica Officers for Justice," Imani barked. She trained her weapon on the woman closest to the stereo. "Turn that shit off, now."

The woman's eyes grew wide. She obeyed, fumbling to find the off switch until all that was left was silence.

"No sudden movements," Samson ordered. "This is AJS business now. Party's over."

For a moment, they rested in tense silence until one of the topless women stroked a lock of sweaty hair behind her head and smiled. "You've got nothing on us, pigs. This is private property."

"Yeah," the man closest to her replied smugly. A thick brown beard covered his chin. "We should call your superiors. Private property, bitches. We could shoot you where you stand."

As if the idea was infectious, a movement came from the corner. A man with a pot belly and a smattering of dark, thick curls on his chest raised the shotgun and pointed it at Imani.

Samson and Imani whirled.

"Shoot that thing, and you'll never see the outside of a prison cell," Imani warned. She held his stare, her heart steady.

A number of the partygoers closed in, grins on their faces.

Imani joined their smirks. "I think it might please the group to know that this is *not* private property."

Samson laughed as their faces turned to confusion.

"Yeah," Imani continued. "Afraid not, friends. The Atlantica Historical Society went public some years ago. Its governance aligns with private works, and the building closes on the weekends, but unfortunately, you're standing on public grounds. This building belongs to the city, which means you're all breaking the law right now." She turned to Samson. "Read them their rights."

The man with the shotgun growled, his hands trembling.

"This is bullshit!" the woman crowed. "You're lying!"

"Would we really lie?" Samson asked patronizingly. "Really? Do you think it's worth our jobs to lie?"

Imani straightened her back. "One last time, folks. Surrender, or we'll have to do this the difficult way."

The group growled, their panic collectively rising. For a moment, there was a blissful pause until the shot exploded.

Imani ducked, having sensed the man's finger tensing on the trigger. The back wall exploded drywall, and the room broke into chaos. A number of the partygoers ran toward nearby doors. Most were locked. Only one other was open. Imani pulled her trigger and sent a slug through the pot-bellied man's forehead. He went cross-eyed, a cloud of gore raining from his face as he hit the back wall.

The gunshot stilled the crowd once more. Many of the men and women fell to their knees, hands behind their heads. Some flopped to the floor in tears from the combined craziness of ink running through their veins and the reality of what they faced.

Three escaped.

Imani would get them later.

"Round them up," she instructed Samson.

They set to work, slapping cuffs on each of the perps as they read them their rights. Imani had been prepared for this to turn severely worse but was thankful it hadn't. Sometimes you needed an easier night.

When the majority were fixed and rounded into the corner, Imani tapped her HUD and called in for backup. Five minutes later, several cruisers appeared. Officers poured out to collect the rowdy arrested.

As the room emptied, Imani felt that smug satisfaction that came with a job well done. They wouldn't spend long in jail—that was a bona fide fact, with most of Atlantica's cell space already claimed. A few drug-using hippies would likely get a slap on the wrist and a few weeks in the slammer—but hopefully, they would learn their lesson. Half of good law enforcement was showing the gentle few the other side to deter them from further wrongdoing.

Still, ink was a hell of a drug. Although there was still a lot they needed to understand about the dark liquid, a raid like this likely wouldn't stop the substance's addictive nature.

Imani stood outside the sandstone walls and watched as the last of the cruisers exited the street and made their way back to the station. Samson appeared by her side, puffing on the plastic tip of his vape pen. The smoke smelled like candy floss.

"A job well done," he stated.

Imani nodded. "You betcha. Simple, for a change."

"I don't like it," Samson replied.

Imani looked at him.

"It's *too* easy," Samson continued. "I came into this business for a challenge, for danger."

"Take the easy days when they come," Imani advised. "Lord knows the harder days will find you. When they do, they don't let you go. You'll be wishing for simple when you're running on caffeine and adrenaline, and you know the whole damn world is out to get you." She turned back to the street, noticing something in the alley. She narrowed her eyes.

"Maybe for you." Samson chuckled. "I like the danger."

"Then go find it," Imani ordered, eyes not shifting from the alley.

Samson nodded. "Maybe I will." He looked at Imani, then tracked her gaze. Whatever she could see, he clearly couldn't. "You heading back?"

Imani dug the keys from her pocket and passed them to Samson. "You go ahead. I have to wrap up here."

Samson gave her a strange look. "I thought we'd finished."

"Go," Imani replied. "I'll get a cab back."

Samson waited a moment, then decided to comply. "Sure. See ya."

The cruiser's lights illuminated the way ahead. Samson revved the engine and took the cruiser out into the street. Imani waited until he was gone before walking back into the Historical Society's building.

She made her way up the sweeping stairs, navigating her way toward a back room. She entered the dark space and switched on a nearby lamp to cast a buttery glow around the walls.

There was a desk at the back of the room. She sat on its edge, faced the door, and waited.

She switched off her HUD.

The door handle turned, and a man slipped inside, all dark shadows and musk of alcohol.

Imani aimed her Glock at his chest. "What do you want?"

The man grinned, unfazed by the weapon. He stood straight, then fished a cigarette from his pocket. He lit it, then exhaled smoke into the room.

Imani didn't blink.

The man took another drag, his dark leather coat matching his dark…well, everything. "It's not what I want. But you already know that, don't you?"

Imani leered at Dick Chambers. "Who else would she have

sent to do her dirty work for her? I'm surprised it took her this long to start sending her carrier pigeons."

Dick chuckled, the sound gravelly. She had to admit, as rugged and careworn as he looked, something was appealing about him, something charming in the way he composed himself. "I wouldn't mistake my presence for the work of a mere carrier pigeon, and I don't often play messenger boy as a general principle." He reached into his pocket and took out what appeared to be a gray, plastic brick. "But desperate times, and all that."

Imani took the cell phone. It was basic and vintage. The screen was only slightly larger than her thumbnail. "What's this?"

"A way to communicate," Dick replied. "We're all going to need to work together if we're going to take this asshole down."

"I don't know what you're talking about," Imani replied flatly.

Dick nodded. "You play the part well. Kris filled me in. She's in a better state than when you two last talked. She wanted me to find a way to bring you that. It's a secure line. Custom-built by a friend of mine."

"Nothing's impenetrable," Imani stated.

"No," Dick agreed. "But some things are considerably harder than others." He turned to face the door. "Give her a chance. You know Kris. She's your girl. She needs to speak with you, and soon. That's your simplest method of communication. Take it if you want to take him down. Wait until I give you the signal, then call her. I need to secure the other line."

"How?" Imani asked.

"With this." Dick flashed the chip.

Imani chewed her lip. "Okay."

Dick made to leave.

"And you?" Imani asked. "What's your role in all of this?"

Dick contemplated this. "The usual. Justice." He met her gaze. "And coin."

Dick left Imani standing there in the gloom, cell phone in her hand.

CHAPTER FIVE

Terra awoke to the sound of something tapping against glass.

Terra Kris. Wake up.

She jolted awake, bleary-eyed and confused. APRIL's robotic voice combined with the weird tapping sent her into a strange spiral, her breath catching. Her legs thrashed under her covers as it took her a moment to remember where she was.

The walls came into focus, their nautical-themed images and the portholes showing glimpses of the dark world outside. She swung her legs out of bed, bare feet touching the cold glass. She glanced down and found the source of the noise.

A parrotfish pecked the glass, its hardened beak scratching and searching for shreds of algae. Terra let out a small sigh and pressed a hand to her forehead. "Not the wake-up calls I usually get. What's the time?"

She glanced around for a clock, but APRIL answered. **12:43 a.m. You requested that I wake you ahead of your meeting.**

"Meeting?" Terra thought. "Oh, right. Sure." She glanced at the end of her bed, a part of her wanting to find her AJS fatigues. Instead, she saw her civilian clothes: jeans, a black tank top, and a leather jacket.

She dressed, then tied her hair into a tight ponytail. Before heading outside, she examined her Glock, ensuring it was in perfect working order. It was. She made her way to the door, sparing one last glance at the brightly colored parrotfish still scratching away at the faint sheen of algae.

"I won't get used to that in the mornings," she commented, setting off down the stairs.

She made her way through the dark city, hands deep in her pockets. Half a mile away, Kingston Park stood in reverent silence, the gates locked and the lamps inside the small forest's pathways switched off.

Terra made her way to the gates. She paused outside, looking each way for any sign of someone watching, then climbed over.

She knew the pathways well and followed the hardened asphalt beneath her feet. The trees loomed over her like giant monoliths, the silvery moonlight struggling to break through the canopy. When she reached the center of the park, she came across the large basin fountain. A dark shape lay on its edge, the vagrant snoozing soundly in the dark.

Terra waited. "APRIL, night vision."

Night vision activated.

The world illuminated around her in shades of green. Terra discovered that there wasn't only one homeless woman in the park that night. Scattered around her were several of the city's unfortunates. Terra tucked herself into the dark recesses of the trees' shadows and waited.

And waited.

Every few minutes, APRIL gave her an update of the time. 1:30 a.m. approached, and as the clock ticked over and APRIL started talking, Terra found her.

Her shape snuck through the trees, using the darkness to cloak herself. Her steps were careful, and soon she was on the other side of the fountain, watching for Terra.

Terra grinned.

She set off into the trees.

Imani peered around her, the park cast in gloom.

She felt safe enough. The Glock strapped to her side and her AJS uniform protected her from monsters in the dark.

Still, she couldn't shake off the feeling that someone was watching her.

It was a risk, going solo into the gardens to meet Terra, but it was a risk worth taking if she could get back in contact with her best friend. She'd taken the cell phone and waited for Dick's signal. He'd texted her thirty minutes later, a simple message that read, **Now.**

Imani called Terra, glad to hear her voice once more. The two had only spoken briefly, their best efforts at remaining off the grid still never enough to evade the city's finest hackers. Imani wanted the call brief.

Terra wanted to meet.

Imani had been dubious, but she still trusted Terra. If Terra said she was no longer trackable, she would believe her...

For now.

Imani tucked herself against the trunk of the nearest tree. Somewhere nearby a homeless guy drunkenly called into the dark, baying like a slurring wolf. Imani checked her watch.

Terra was late.

The hairs on the nape of her neck prickled. Was this a setup?

A twig broke nearby.

Imani turned in the direction of the noise, hand hovering over the butt of her gun.

Another sound, nearer now. She looked around in the dark, seeing no one.

She listened.

Silence resumed. Still, that feeling...

She whirled at the same moment a mass of blackness came at her in the dark.

***

"Surprise!" Terra exclaimed, keeping her voice at a breathy whisper.

She wrapped her hands around Imani's neck, pulling her into an embrace.

Imani froze for a moment. Then she shoved Terra back against the tree.

Terra chuckled.

"What are you doing?" Imani scolded. "I could have shot you."

"But you didn't," Terra replied. "You wouldn't shoot me."

"Don't test me," Imani replied dryly.

For a moment, they stood in silence, a grin on Terra's face, a frown on Imani's.

Imani's face broke into a smile, relief flooding her features. "It's good to see you."

"It's great to see *you*," Terra replied. "Thanks for meeting with me."

Imani nodded, squinting a little. Terra could see all of Imani through her night vision, though she figured she'd be better off going to Imani's level. *APRIL, disengage night vision.*

Darkness took over, and for a moment Terra was blind.

Imani chewed her lip. "You said it's safe now. How do you know?"

"Because it is," Terra replied without expanding.

"But that…that thing in your head…" Imani stammered. "They have you logged. You live with an AJS AI system. How do you know they're not watching you?"

Terra half-shrugged. "It's a long story. Know that I wouldn't ever put you in the way of immediate harm."

Imani chuckled. "I know. It's the *delayed* harm I'm concerned about." She shook her head. "It's great to see you."

Terra choked a little as Imani's arms wrapped around her neck. "We should go somewhere a little more lit."

Imani agreed. The pair found a nearby spot where the canopy of leaves wasn't total. Moonlight spilled down into the little hollow where they sat on the grass and spoke. She asked questions about Terra's inbuilt AI, and Terra gave the truth.

Imani didn't flinch at the mention of Terra's involvement with Atlantica's most notorious assassin, but then Terra never expected her to. Imani was a solid friend, as well as her former partner. If there was something she couldn't trust Imani with, she hadn't found it yet.

Imani gave a thoughtful nod. "So there's no way that thing can link back to someone else's system and make them aware of your thoughts, movements, and who you're associating yourself with?"

"Nothing's foolproof," Terra replied solemnly. "Still, I trust the people involved who tell me that it's considerably harder."

"Why?" Imani asked.

Terra considered this. She remembered the restrictions APRIL had put on her not all that long ago. Now the toughest of those had lifted. Valentina had done something amazing to the system, and what reason would she have to fuck around with Terra in that regard? "Because I do."

Imani was silent a moment, eyes cast downward at the blade of grass she twisted between her fingers. "Well, that's good enough for me."

Terra smiled. Somewhere nearby, a vagrant stumbled through the trees. They both turned, decided they were no threat, then turned back. "What's happening on your side?"

Imani gave a small chuckle. "Not much to say. Garcia is keeping me pretty damn busy. I think it's so he knows where I am at all times and can guarantee that I'll be out of his way."

"He's suspicious?" Terra asked.

"Of course," Imani replied. "He might be dumb enough to leave breadcrumbs, but he's smart. He knows that I was in on your whole investigation."

She glanced down once more. "Honestly, I feel like all I'm doing is grunt work these days. Breaking up unlawful parties and hunting around the streets for drag racers. He's keeping the real work from me because he doesn't want me sniffing around his tail again."

Terra nodded thoughtfully. "That sucks."

"Yeah," Imani agreed.

They sat in silence for a while. The wind was cool, and the sky was a bleary white behind the fog. Bats swooped above them, darting toward the trees before wheeling back into the air.

"We need to bring him in," Imani offered at last as if this was the conclusion she'd been struggling to reach.

"Yeah," Terra confirmed. "But how?"

The last time Terra managed to get her claws into Garcia's trail seemed a lifetime ago. Memories of that time swirled in her head. She pictured drunkenly stumbling out of a club at two in the morning with Imani, all giggles and wobbles.

She remembered the dark of the alley as they made for the nearest all-night fast-food chain. She pictured the scuffle of something nearby in the dark, turning to find a group of druggies injecting their veins with ink. Among the group were three men in dark coats, collars drawn up and dark eyes glinting, nowhere near the stuff.

A fight broke out. Terra and Imani sobered up real quick as they stepped in to break up the scuffle, unable to turn off their justice switches that fixed their moral compass to their occupations. The fight was messy, but they all settled down. When the three men turned to flee, Terra noticed the tallest man's limp in his right leg and the wiry outline of his goatee.

It wasn't until the next day, head pounding, bags beneath their eyes, that they noticed the limp in their captain's step. Curiosity hit them like lightning, and out on the beat, they fell into a discussion about their captain's condition.

They kept a close watch on Garcia.

Over the next few months, any opportunity they could, they tailed him. First, Imani would tail him out of the parking lot. Next, Terra would watch from across the street. On one particular mission briefing, Garcia's breath struggled to catch, and as he reached for his tablet on the table before him, his sleeve slipped up to reveal veins that were more gray than blue. His wristwatch barely covered a little pockmark.

Their eyes met.

Words crossed unspoken between them both.

Garcia grew more cautious.

Terra grew more assured.

It was pure coincidence that brought Terra and Garcia together on that fateful Saturday night a few weeks later. Imani had been hard at work tracking calls and trying to find substantial evidence to present to their superiors, while Terra grew more and more anxious about what was to come. She had been walking home from work one night, making it a little over ten blocks from the station when she spotted Garcia across the street.

He loitered outside Kibble's Manor, a vast Victorian mansion complex set among the high rises and skyscrapers. The building looked ridiculous and out of place, as though a child had lost a tooth and this building was the stump. The architecture was gorgeous, a pure reflection of the classic houses Victorian aristocracy flaunted, but Terra knew it was far more than a simple residence.

Kibble's Manor had a history as a place of succor for the filth of the city.

So what was Garcia doing there?

More than that, why was he wearing all black, his face shadowed by a fedora.

Terra would have missed it. She might have walked by the group altogether had it not been for the raucous laughter that exploded as she passed. In that brief moment, Garcia lit a cigarette, and his shadowed face glowed in a swath of amber. Terra turned away, keen not to meet his eye as she tucked herself into the shadows and watched.

She monitored the place for hours. That night she made use of her cell phone camera, stalking around the outside of the building to try and get a glimpse inside. The air around the manor was cold. A faint stink of forgotten attics and bad memories clung to the walls.

Her boldness growing, Terra stumbled across an open window and let herself inside. She convinced herself that she wasn't on duty at that moment. She was a public citizen entering the premises.

That night should have been the night she got what she needed. She managed to get images and recordings. Twelve minutes and forty-two seconds of footage she captured from the manor, showcasing Garcia's transactions as he discussed his ink dealings with several characters who revealed themselves to be his top dealers. They spoke of coin and territory, although each one was shrouded in aliases and codenames.

When they'd alerted to someone inside, though Terra never figured out how they knew, she fled the scene.

"I've got it," she panted to Imani on the phone mid-run.

"Got what?" Imani returned.

Terra grinned. "The kill shot. Evidence. I'm going to Lewis."

Imani asked for an explanation. Terra relayed it to her. Excitedly, they both prepared to serve justice.

She sent the report to Garcia's senior, a phone call detailing all she had found. Major Sylvia Lewis asked for the evidence to be sent across. Terra obliged. In the morning, Lewis called them into her office—Garcia among them.

Terra sat there, excitement coursing through her body, wondering how Garcia would react at this sudden revelation.

Instead, what ensued was the most humiliating sixty minutes of Terra's career.

It seemed that Garcia had gotten to Lewis first. Calmly sitting across the desk, Lewis proceeded to detail Terra's role within the AJS system and how accusations against senior officers that were unfounded and wholly made up were unacceptable. Terra tried to argue. She checked her phone for the footage, asked Lewis to check her emails, but all that she could find were corrupt files featuring a large question mark in the center.

Terra was shocked.

Lewis brought Imani in for questioning.

Terra's cheeks flushed as Lewis grilled Imani, Imani doing a stellar job at pretending not to know a damn thing.

Garcia was silent for the most part, only answering the necessary questions. He didn't smile, but Terra felt his joy.

That day, she packed her bags and headed down to the outer city. Her only saving grace that night was the immense reputation she had built for herself working on the force. Even Lewis had to admit that it would be a blow to the AJS system to lose her.

Still, as she walked out of the office that day, she couldn't help but wonder if Lewis knew more than she was letting on and how the hell Garcia could have corrupted the files.

She had no question that it was him.

Imani rested her hands against the cool grass. "How? That's easy. We need to find substantial evidence. Physical traces and tracks that Garcia can't worm his way out of. We need binders, folders, *hard* evidence that even Lewis can't deny." Imani sighed.

"We've made a start," Terra replied. "Dick Chambers is sniffing into the case. Combine that with the fact that I'm currently on sabbatical, and there it is, a force to be reckoned with."

"Aren't you afraid of losing your job?" Imani asked.

Terra considered this. "Not if it means bringing an asshole to justice."

Imani smirked. "Good. I hoped that would be your answer."

"You did?" Terra replied.

"Yes," Imani confirmed. "Because I have an update on the case, and I think it's going to blow this sucker wide open."

CHAPTER SIX

Serena Temple sat back from her computer and rubbed her eyes.

The room was in a semi-permanent gloom. The only light sources were the six computers around the chamber and three small power-saving bulbs on the ceiling.

Today was warm, however. Today Serena and her team had been hard at work stacking the numbers and processing the orders. Their screens were black, for the most part, with the text written in neon green. Serena hated it. She didn't understand why the tech wizards who created the damn thing couldn't have made it friendly on the eyes.

She supposed it didn't matter. She got paid well for doing what she did, and that was all that mattered. She clocked in each morning, processed the orders, then clocked out on evenings and weekends. What more could she ask for?

Probably more time away from her husband. Probably some more time looking after her kids…

"Coffee?" Rosaline stood and stretched her arms. Rosaline was large. The only exercise in her daily routine was the short walk from the hidden parking lot to her desk. Their commanding powers had done a lot to ensure that the operation remained hidden, and even Serena had struggled to find the place when she first came to work and set her fingers to the keyboard.

"Sure," Serena replied, as did her other colleagues. Rosaline shuffled from the room, making her way out the door to a small kitchenette complete with a kettle and small pots for the drinks.

Serena rubbed her aching eyes again and returned to the information on the screen.

Twenty-one thousand units sold over almost two years. She swallowed dryly.

Twenty-one thousand units sold.

Twenty-one thousand vials of ink distributed through the city.

She turned away from the total number in the corner of the screen. She had learned early on that if she detached herself from the reality of what she was doing, it wasn't so bad. Keep your head down and get on with the operation. Take your pay check, and go home. That's all there was to it. The operation ran on private property, so what were the chances they'd ever get caught?

Zero.

Still… She tried not to imagine that her children were one of those twenty-one thousand. Max had recently turned nineteen and was already shying away from her confidence. Lisa was twenty-three now, and Lord knew she'd had trouble with substance abuse throughout the years. It was a hazard of the island.

A hazard that Serena was contributing to.

It's just a job. It's just a means to an end.

What was the end she sought? When she moved to Atlantica almost thirty-five years ago, she'd had dreams of wealth and power. She saw herself in a penthouse suite, sipping champagne by the moonlight, high above the Atlantica skyline.

Instead, she lived in a rundown apartment on the outskirts, and the cash she did make slipped through her fingers like sand.

At the desk behind her, Momchill sighed. A new addition to their team, hailing recently from Bulgaria, Momchill had found it difficult to navigate the new software.

"Problem?" Serena wheeled her chair to his desk.

Momchill ran a finger through his wiry black hair. "It doesn't make sense."

"What doesn't?" Serena noticed a few heads turn their way before returning to their respective screens.

"The whole thing." Momchill bit his lip. "I process like this?"

Momchill clicked on a flashing message that indicated a new order. On the screen was the information from the customer, an anonymized ID code, the quantity of the order, and the nearest drop-off point. On the bottom of the screen were several standard options. Among these were "Accept" and "Decline." There was also an order history so that, if there had been recent problems, they would know to flag these orders to the higher powers.

Serena sighed, once again explaining to Momchill their particular cog in the machine and how the system worked. It was simple, and she couldn't understand how he hadn't yet grasped this after almost three weeks of employment.

The chain was simple. Customers were able to download an encrypted, black market app onto their cell phones. The app would automatically deactivate when connecting to public Wi-Fi networks and only enable within secure locations.

Customers could then order whatever they wanted from the black market, tapping into vast quantities of substances deemed highly illegal in many parts of the world and some that were so experimental that they didn't yet have a street name.

Once the order was taken and paid for, the processing would begin. Serena and her team would confirm or deny the orders, then send the shipping instructions to the production team below. Dozens upon dozens of workers ensured the ink made it correctly into their bottles before being packaged and shipped out.

The drop-off points were the houses of notorious dealers in the city. Those dealers kept their affairs squeaky clean in public but lived in the thickest bogs of filth. They exploited the public versus private policy of the Atlantican government. It was a point of contention for all AJS crews but a point of celebration for those who benefitted greatly from its absurdity. The dealers spent their days allowing users to knock on the door and provide their secret passwords before collecting their gear.

Owners of these residences would receive a healthy percentage of the profits made from each sale. Their customers then resumed the responsibility of delivering their products without getting caught by the AJS. The moment they left the front door of the drop-off, they were entering public zones and therefore carrying illegal substances.

The AJS worked hard to identify these hotspots. At the beginning of the narcotic corruption of the city, they found them with general ease. As time passed, however, more drop-off owners made their residences comfortable abodes for drug users and charged those who came to their houses an extra fee for consuming on the property. Why wouldn't they want to make an extra buck for offering succor?

Once the customers collected the product, that was the end of the line of the producers. Serena and her team could tick them off the list and work on the next batch of orders.

"Make sense now?" Serena asked, flashing her tablet screen to show a flowchart of operation.

"Kind of," Momchill replied. "I don't understand still something, though."

"What's that?" Serena asked, visibly exasperated.

"How do people carry substance to drop off without being caught?" Momchill's eyes were young and curious. Serena saw herself in them years ago when she arrived at the island.

She stood. "That's a secret for the top bosses. It doesn't concern us."

She whisked her way back to her desk, leaving Momchill to wrap his head around the system once more. As Rosaline returned with coffees for all, Serena busied herself with her orders. She knew the answer to his question, of course. However, she was almost certain she was the only person in that room who did, and knowledge was a tricky thing to keep in Atlantica. Knowledge was currency, and currency was power.

As she focused on her work, the image of the carrier flashed through her mind. Magnetic rails and a long undercarriage speeding along the tracks.

She shook the thought away, homing in on her screen. Behind her, Momchill glanced over his shoulder, his bright eyes turning dark as he navigated to his encrypted email client and began typing.

Little did he know that he'd be found dead in his apartment twenty-four hours later.

CHAPTER SEVEN

The apartment building on Denizon Boulevard was swarming with blues.

The restaurant sat a few buildings down, its glass front offering a perfect view of the action taking place outside. AJS cruisers lined the curb, their lights creating a disco wall of the surrounding buildings. Officers spoke to witnesses and jotted down notes on their tablets, while others set up diversions to ease the choked-up traffic running up and down the street.

Dick Chambers tucked into his sirloin steak. The meat was juicy and tender. Just twenty minutes ago, he had received the phone call from Terra and sped into action to make his way to the scene of the crime.

How Terra knew about this murder, he didn't know. Still, Dick understood that this was important. He wanted to head straight inside the building and discover what he could, but he knew that wasn't the best tactic. As a PI, he had to wait until the buzz had died down, catch a cop on their own, then throw out his questions. With adrenaline and confusion racing, officers would be less receptive to strangers.

He finished his steak and washed the meat down with a black coffee. By the time he finished, one cruiser remained. Yellow and black crime tape sealed off the building, and Dick made his way toward this now.

He stopped at the stairs, glancing up at the building. He ducked beneath the tape and made his way inside.

The apartment was on the second floor. The door was open, another ream of tape marking the place as closed-off. He twisted beneath this tape, interrupting the two officers standing in the center of the apartment.

"You're not supposed to be here, sir," a fresh-faced officer announced, his keen green eyes boring into Dick. "This is a crime scene. It's an offense to trespass—"

Dick flashed his badge. "I'm a private investigator. My client's linked with the victim."

The female officer exchanged glances with Green Eyes and shook her head.

Green Eyes continued, "Afraid not, sir. Please leave the scene."

Dick held up his hands. "Fine. Fine. I just wondered if you could answer a few questions for me."

"This is a secure area, sir," Green Eyes insisted. "If I have to ask you again—"

"Can you confirm that the victim is Momchill Levski?" Dick interrupted.

The female officer's eyes flashed. "That is classified—"

"It is," Dick replied. "Good. That's all I need to know."

The female officer asked, "I thought you said 'a few' questions."

"And I thought you said you wouldn't give me any information." Dick exited without another word, leaving the two officers stunned to silence.

"Victim confirmed." Dick's voice reverberated inside Terra's head.

"Good work, soldier," Terra replied.

"Those days are long behind me," Dick corrected. "What's the significance of this guy, anyway? You seemed pretty eager to identify the body."

Terra stared out at the coastline from the porthole of her aquatic bedroom. Bright neons and dazzling lights lit up the restaurants, bars, and clubs facing toward the sea. "He's an undercover cop."

Dick was silent a moment. Terra was sure she could make out the metallic twist of the top of a hip flask. "Your point being?"

Terra examined the picture of Momchill that Imani had sent over to her cell phone. He was young, his face fresh and unscarred by years serving on the Atlantica Justice System. She tried to remember if she had crossed his path before but couldn't recall his features. "Imani informed me that Momchill was acting undercover for the AJS, working inside a suspected ink ring. He played the foreign fool, gleaning as much information as he could, and had started making good progress with those on the inside, particularly the administration team he had become a part of."

"Administration team?" Dick scoffed. "When did drug rings become corporate operations? What happened to the golden days of piss-soaked hovels beneath the ground and shadowed meetings on street corners? You going to tell me they've got a goddamn HR team next? The whole thing filled to the brim with bureaucracy and policy?"

Terra chuckled. "That's exactly how it is, Dick, and you know it."

Dick grumbled. "It takes the romance out of the capture."

"Romance?" Now it was Terra's turn to laugh. "You?"

"Not personally." Dick paused. "So what you're telling me is you had a mole on the inside, and now he's been taken out?"

"That's exactly it." Terra thumbed through the saved pictures on her cell. "According to Imani, Momchill had recently sent a communication outside of the internal servers, leaking certain information about clients that had been using the ring's phone app to order their product. With that information, members of Imani's squadron have been able to zero in on potential suspects and home in on the whole operation, gleaning enough evidence to make them nervous and, hopefully, slip up."

"Sounds interesting," Dick replied. "I'm always game for a raid and arresting a large volume of despicable staff involved in operations such as this."

"That almost sounded like a compliment."

"I wouldn't go that far. Keep going."

"What do you mean?" Terra playfully teased Dick.

"So your guys have a bunch of possible intel fed from the inside," Dick replied. "What does that mean for you? How does it help you zero in on your guy?"

"Because we got an address on the den," Terra replied. "The guys running the sting clearly didn't want Momchill to be of any further threat to them. Which means that their back is up, and they may be more likely to slip up."

"An address..." Dick chewed this over. "You're planning to storm the den single-handedly?"

"Not exactly," Terra replied. "But I do have an alternative idea..."

Dick Chambers worked the lock of the apartment door, then stepped inside.

The place was hauntingly quiet. The last officers had left a half-hour ago, leaving the area locked up and abandoned. There was an iron stink of blood in the air as Dick crept through the darkness and made his way toward the bedroom where they'd found the body.

The bedsheets had been taken for examination, as had the pillows. Likely DNA evidence could help narrow down the perpetrator of the crime—not that they'd bring them in. The murder happened inside a private space. The cops could do nothing other than identifying the victim and the killer and make a note of it on their files.

There was blood on the walls. It was likely that the murderer used a firearm. Small pink chunks of tissue mixed among the specs of blood, and a faint whiff of shit met Dick's nostrils.

His nose wrinkled.

"Same shit, different apartment." How many murders had he seen like this? How many people needed to lose their lives in Atlantica before the government reviewed that damn legislation?

He scanned the room, moving silently as he narrowed his eyes and hunted for any missed signs the cops might have left behind. There was a chip taken out of the chest of drawers, but that probably wasn't related to the attack. There were no visible signs of a struggle or break-in, so whoever did this must have either known Momchill on some level or been an expert in gaining access to the property.

"Oh? What's this?" Dick knelt to examine a small black scuff on the carpet. Somewhere outside, AJS sirens blared as they drove on to their next incident.

He ran a finger along the carpet, then examined the tip. Fine black dust coated his finger. He sniffed it, then rubbed his fingers together to clear the mess.

Taking a Q-tip from his pocket, he brushed the white head against the substance until black coated it. He placed the tip into a plastic pot, then secured the lid.

After a few more moments of scrutiny, he stood at the window, fingers laced behind his back.

Another cop down. Another body to add to the endless count of the Atlantican fallen. A city of freedom, wonder, and possibility? He scoffed, lip curling. *Bullshit. This whole place is a rats' nest. Its people are the illness and viruses that cause corruption and sickness.*

CHAPTER EIGHT

Dick Chambers' beat-up 2024 sedan choked along the bumpy roads of the outer city.

For the most part, the blacktop was smooth sailing. It was when you went into the outer perimeter of the city that things began to change. Single-track dusty dirt roads made their way to farms and forgotten residences, some leading directly into the heart of the dense jungle that surrounded the mountainous wilds of Atlantica.

Dick's sedan didn't like bumpy roads.

The suspension whined and groaned with each ascent and descent, dust kicking up into the air behind. On either side, crops grew as tall as two men, lush squares of greenery to feed the island's citizens. The alley of green enveloped Dick, the looming wilds of the jungle ahead.

He turned left as soon as he was able. A couple of miles down, he took a right. The watchtower came into view.

It was a beaten old thing made of rusting iron. Once, it might have provided a safe nest from the approaching jungle predators. Now it was a relic of the past. When the city swelled in the center of the island like a teenager's pimple, the need for shelter from your neighbors replaced the need for refuge from the jungle.

Dick parked the sedan and stared up at the tower. It was at least sixty feet high, its top beginning to blur against the fog. He lit a cigarette, then shielded his eyes against the strained daylight. After another drag, he headed to the tower's base.

He tested the ladder with one hand. The rung gave a little beneath his weight. He examined his palm. The pink skin had turned orange from the flakes of rust.

Dick shook his head. *Son of a bitch...*

He threw the cigarette on the ground and stamped it out. He set his hands and feet on the rungs and eased his way up, skipping the step that gave under the weight of his hand.

The journey was treacherous. A couple of times, a rung snapped and fell to the ground. Still, he continued, determined, using the outside bars to support him when the rungs failed. Halfway up, he looked out into the surrounding fields. He appeared to be alone.

He glanced up and continued his climb.

When he reached the top, he levered himself into the round crow's nest. The floor was dusty, strewn with debris carried in from the wind. He couldn't help but notice the floor swaying ever so slightly with the breeze.

"It's a protective measure," Terra announced.

Dick turned over his shoulder, unsurprised to find the Officer for Justice sitting with her back to the metal wall.

"Oh?" he asked.

"Helps with earthquakes," Terra replied. "Most buildings are given enough room to sway under extreme conditions. If you make a building perfectly rigid, one quake in its foundations, and the whole thing's toast."

"Good to know." Dick made to stand.

Terra scolded him. "Stay low."

Dick obeyed, taking a seat nearby. "So you're saying this isn't a social visit?"

Terra shook her head, her gaze thoughtful. "You think I'd meet you anywhere socially?"

"You're a hard woman to read," Dick replied. "I don't know what kind of things you're into. One minute you're shooting me in the ass, claiming I got in your way. The next, you invite me out to the middle of nowhere and nestle up nice and close in an abandoned watchtower."

Terra rolled her eyes.

Dick grinned. He wasn't sure why he derived so much joy from winding Terra up, but he did. He waited for Terra to speak.

"Did you bring what I asked you to bring?" Terra asked at last.

"Of course." Dick removed a small bullet-shaped device from his jacket pocket. "State of the art."

Terra took the bullet and examined its case. "It has 'Tr4ck3r' written in Sharpie on the side."

Dick chuckled. Ringo was a dab hand with electronics, but he wasn't exactly the best at visual design and marketing his products. Dick supposed that wasn't your priority when you ran your own underground makeshift technology hacking operation. "At least we know what it is."

"So will anyone who finds it," Terra replied. "So much for covert ops."

"Covert?" Dick smirked. "By the time anyone finds this baby, we'll be halfway up their tail. Relax, Kris. You seem tense. Maybe I can ease that pain with a little rubdown? I have the oils."

Terra theatrically dry-heaved. "I'd rather have a badger sit on my face and piss when I'm asleep."

Dick shrugged. "The offer's always there."

"That's the worst part." Terra examined the bullet again before taking her pistol and fitting the round into the chamber. "This better work."

"That part is in your hands," Dick replied. "Unless you want me to take the shot for you?"

Terra laughed. "I'm good."

They sat for a moment in quiet, the wind whistling through the ancient holes of the watchtower. After a few moments, Dick crept his way to the edge of the tower and peeked out over the forest. The leafy canopy stretched for miles, rising on a slow incline until the veil of fog claimed it. The brush and foliage were so dense that it was almost impossible to see where the dirt road that trailed into the trees went.

Dick spoke up. "You're sure this is the place?"

Terra nodded. "According to our intel, the den lies in a small cavern tucked inside the jungle. The road forks about half a click into the wilds. Take the left turn, and it soon trails down into a hollow beneath the ground."

"The jungle is public," Dick stated. "Why don't you call the guys to rush inside and take them down?"

"Because it's not," Terra replied. "The hollow is one of the few private pockets of jungle snatched up when The Powers That Be were claiming the island. The space itself is less than half a square mile, but it trails down—or so Momchill's intel tells us."

"Then wait until the guys drive out with the product," Dick shot back. "SUVs filled with ink on public property are an arrestable offense, or am I missing something here?"

Terra chewed her lip. "We don't know how they ship their product. Momchill spoke of some underground system, but we got no further information. I've been sitting here for three hours, and I've only spotted two vehicles come and go. There was no product inside."

Dick blew air between his lips. "You can't know that for certain."

Terra gave him a knowing look.

Dick met her gaze, then nodded and smiled.

Terra returned the smile. "Tell me what you think you know."

Dick raised his eyebrows. "I don't know what you mean."

"You're a smart man," Terra continued. "As much as that pains me to admit. What do you think you have on me?"

Dick's lips thinned, eyes filled with thought. "There's something new with you. A glint in your eye and a breath of knowing that you didn't have before. Don't get me wrong. You've always been one hell of a cop, but… When I look into your eyes, I see something there, something…inhuman. Sentient."

Terra grinned. "What do you think that is?"

"Your overwhelming ache to climb into bed with me."

Terra gave a derisive snort. "I give you too much credit sometimes."

Dick's laughter fell from his face. "What is it?"

Terra examined Dick's eyes, drawing a deep breath. Dick could tell a lot was happening behind there. He wondered if he'd imagined that slight green glint that flashed. "I was in an accident…"

Terra proceeded to relate her incident to Dick. She glossed over some of the details, choosing to focus on the main beats of her story. She told him of the fake footage and how she had linked everything back to Garcia. She told him of APRIL's capabilities and that she now had an artificial intelligence system permanently docked inside her skull.

The whole time she spoke, Dick sat there and listened. He showed no sign of surprise, anguish, mirth, or anything else on the emotional spectrum. For all she knew, she was outlining her journey to a cyborg.

When she finally reached her conclusion, she sat and waited for Dick to respond.

He took his time, reaching for a cigarette and lighting it. He took a long drag, then breathed the smoke into the air where it joined the dense fog above. "You're telling me you have a robot living inside your head?"

"Yes." No two ways about it. Straight and to the point.

Dick nodded thoughtfully. "Can you believe we live in a time where that kind of shit is believable?" He chuckled. "And you're saying that it gives you abilities beyond human?"

Terra nodded. "That's how I could see within the vehicles as they went by. The AI—APRIL—can scan the vehicles in several modes and see what they're holding. We can detect heat signatures, night vision, touch into public—well, and private networks, now—and use the systems to glean our intel."

Dick smirked. "Superpowers."

"I wouldn't go that far." Terra's ears pricked up as she imagined she heard an engine in the distance.

"What does it stand for?" Dick asked. "APRIL?"

Terra recited, "Advanced Police Relationship Intelligence Liaison."

"That's a mouthful," Dick stated.

"Hence the abbreviation." Terra chuckled. "There was another name at some point."

"What was that?" Dick asked.

"OSCaR. Officer Security Companion and Report."

"Dryer than a saltine in the desert," Dick confirmed. "I like it."

"Of course you do," Terra shot back.

Dick smirked. "Has a nicer ring to it. OSCaR is better than APRIL."

"You sound like Valentina," Terra replied.

"She's a woman of great tastes." Dick met Terra's eyes, then turned away. Was there a slight flush to his cheeks?

"You only like it because it's a guy's name, and you love the idea of a guy claiming a woman's mind," Terra dealt back.

Dick frowned. "That really what you think of me?"

"Does it matter?" Terra asked.

"Not really." Dick stroked his chin, ears pricking up as the engine became unmistakable. "You hear that?"

APRIL, enhance and track audio, Terra thought.

APRIL obliged. As Terra crept to the far side of the watchtower, she looked out onto the jungle. APRIL zoomed in to the noise source, identifying a blip that appeared in Terra's left eye. She tracked the vehicle as it drove through the forest.

Dick was beside her. "You see something?"

"APRIL does," Terra replied. She readied her pistol, resting the barrel against the top lip of the guarding wall. She closed one eye, letting APRIL help to line her up as the vehicle neared.

She counted down. "Ten. Nine. Eight…"

Dick puffed on his cigarette. Terra coughed as smoke reached her lips.

"Three," Terra continued. "Two. One…"

As she finished counting, the vehicle emerged from the tree line. It was a camo SUV with tinted windows. APRIL revealed the shapes of three people sitting inside. Terra lined up the shot, waited until the SUV was as close as it was going to be, then pulled the trigger.

The bullet sped silently through the air. It found its bed in the rear tire, APRIL identifying the thick rubber as an anti-blowout measure that prevented gunfire from blowing out the tires and forcing the vehicles off the road.

The shape of the rear passenger showed their head turning. Other than that, there was no acknowledgment of the attack. Terra gave a satisfied nod as the vehicle kicked up dust and sped along the old dirt track, following the lines toward the cornfields which would eventually lead out to the city.

"Nice shot, Kris," Dick stated. "It's like you've done this before."

Terra coughed, then gave Dick a hard shove. "Get that cancer stick away from me."

CHAPTER NINE

Terra emerged into the city a short while later, her Ducati's engine rumbling, a beaten old sedan not too far behind.

The *blipping* had stopped on Dick's cell phone, showing a fixed location where the tracker resided. Terra took the long way round, avoiding the known roaming routes of her precinct division to remain out of sight. Only once did they narrowly pass a fleet of AJS vehicles, all too occupied with their current mission to notice the woman hooking a sharp right and moving out of their path.

Terra wondered if they were actively looking for her. According to APRIL's infiltration of the AJS database, there were no public hits out on Terra Kris, which only made her anxiety worse. There was no way Garcia and his cronies wouldn't be out looking for her.

Who were "they?" When would they appear on her radar? There were too many unknowns, and Terra didn't like it.

When they were only a few blocks away, Terra parked her motorcycle in the depths of an alley, then climbed into Dick's sedan. The air was warm and stale inside the car, stinking of old booze and nicotine. The car itself was tidy—which made a nice change, judging by what Terra knew of guys' cars—and he'd tuned the radio to a jazz station where a saxophone softly played its solo over the airwaves.

"I'd have had you down for a rock man," Terra stated.

Dick grinned as he turned right onto the street where the tracker led. A holder cradled his phone on the dash. The screen showed two icons, one with their current location, one with the static tracker.

Dick slowed as they passed the building.

Terra's lips thinned. "Kibble's Manor."

It shouldn't have surprised her, but somehow it did. There stood the manor where she had lost it all. The place where she'd crept in and tried to glean evidence of Garcia and his criminal activity. It was in that manor that her world had fallen apart, and life had grown incrementally shittier.

"You know it?" Dick asked.

"You could say that." Terra couldn't peel her eyes from the front door. From the outside, the place looked vacant and unassuming. "Keep driving. Find somewhere nearby to park."

"Aye-aye, Captain," Dick replied.

Terra growled. "Don't call me captain."

Dick pulled into a small lot at the back of a nearby 7-Eleven. He left Terra in the car while he went inside to grab a fresh carton of cigarettes and a brown bag with a glass bottle inside. When he climbed back into the car, he put the cigarettes in the glovebox, then handed the bag to Terra. "Here."

She raised an eyebrow. "Thought that'd be for you."

Dick chuckled, pulling his hip flask from his pocket. "I'm always set. This is your game, now."

Terra reached into the bag and took out the bottle. It was ribbed, filled with a fizzing black liquid. "Coke?"

"Figured you'd need your caffeine fix." Dick raised his flask. "Cheers."

Terra smiled, despite herself. She had envisioned wine or gin or some other useless alcoholic beverage she didn't need right now. "Thanks."

Dick glanced down at the flick top. "Need a bottle opener?"

Terra smirked. "I got it." She placed the tip of her metal thumb against the lid, then flicked it off.

"Nice," Dick approved.

"Thanks."

They sat in the car and enjoyed their drinks together. Terra rested her head against the back of the seat and sighed.

"Problem?" Dick asked. "Penny for your thoughts."

Terra's brow creased. "This isn't where I saw myself at this point in my life, y'know? A couple of months ago, I was an elite member of the AJS, kicking ass and taking names. Now…"

Dick interjected. "Now you're a part-cyborg sitting in an old-fashioned dumpster on wheels, sipping Coke from a bottle with a man who has more bad habits than a self-destructive inker who can't control himself?"

Terra laughed, a genuine chuckle that felt good at the moment. "Kind of."

Dick looked out the window. "For what it's worth, I don't see you staying down for long. You're a tough kid. Probably one of the only folks in blue I have any sort of respect for. Despite the scar you left on my ass, I know you've got good in you, and that's something to hold close. The good triumph in this place, Kris. You still believe that, don't you?"

Terra thought about this. "I honestly don't know."

"Yes, you do." Dick sighed. "Atlantica is a cesspit of shit, but that doesn't mean good doesn't live here, too.

"All around us are people trying to make this place better. All they lack is money, influence, and power. But if enough of the little people rise and band together, they can make a hell of a change. People like you, you're the beacons of this city. You shine bright so others have permission to shine their lights."

Dick went quiet for a moment. "I mean, couple that with the

fact you've got a cyborg inside you, and you're goddamn unstoppable."

Terra smiled. She didn't know how to reply to that. She'd never witnessed Dick be sweet and genuine before—if that's indeed what this was. Eventually, she settled with, "Thank you."

"Don't mention it," Dick replied.

Terra nodded.

"Seriously," Dick added. "Don't mention it. I'm not sure my ego could take me hearing that back on replay."

Terra tapped a finger to her head. "Shame that I got it all on camera."

Dick chuckled. "Shit." He went quiet. "What's the plan then, Kris? Wait until nightfall, then raid the premises?"

Terra nodded. "Precisely, Dick... Precisely."

Night fell. The parking lot emptied.

"Time to rumble?" Dick asked.

Terra nodded, then exited the sedan.

They stalked the darkness, clinging to the alleys as they worked their way toward the manor. Dick tucked behind Terra as she activated APRIL and scanned the surrounding areas.

The buildings lit up with thermal readings of hundreds of individuals, shining bright like Christmas lights on a tree. With this foresight, she was able to identify and target the cluster of three individuals gathered near the back of the manor, a fourth body stretched in the air between them, the thermal reader registering them cold and lifeless.

Terra held out an arm. Dick paused in his tracks.

The three figures tossed the body into a nearby dumpster, one of their number proceeding to bury the body in heavy trash bags.

"Good riddance to bad news," one of the group stated,

brushing their hands as if to erase the final dregs of dirt from their task.

They shut the lid, then returned in the direction of the manor.

Terra crept closer, Dick following behind. The pair were silent, not a word spoken as they closed in on the dumpster. Curiosity got to Terra and she turned her attention beside her.

"Raise the lid," Terra whispered.

"Why?" Dick replied, having not seen the picture as clearly as Terra.

"Just do it," Terra commanded.

Dick raised the lid of the dumpster. Terra shifted the bags until the pale face stared emptily back at her. "APRIL, identify the body," she muttered.

Dick glanced skeptically at Terra.

Charles Bronswick, APRIL stated. **Age sixty-two. Male. Registered address...**

APRIL went on until Terra commanded it to stop. She turned to Dick. "You know a Charles Bronswick?"

Dick considered this a long moment, struggling with something inside. "Name rings a bell..."

Terra shifted the bags a little more. She drew out her cell phone and shone a light inside. Dick gasped. "Holy shit."

"What?" Terra asked.

"Chuck..." Dick replied.

"So you do know him?" Terra replied.

Dick's eyes darkened, composure fixing his face. "Yes, and no."

Terra nudged him. "A friend of yours?"

"Not really." Dick took a breath. "A colleague of sorts. The less I say here, the better. We're currently standing in public terrain, and I'm aware that though you're currently off-duty, your allegiances will return to the AJS when this is all said and done."

"Intriguing."

Dick drew a long breath. "Rest in Peace, Chuck." He pulled the bags back over his face. "You goddamn son of a bitch."

Terra asked no more, and Dick offered nothing further. They closed the dumpster in silent agreement, then turned their attention to the manor. The alley they were in traveled for another thirty feet or so before reaching the back entrance to the place. The three individuals had slipped back inside so Terra and Dick crept closer.

"Hold on," Terra stated as they reached the edge of the shadows. She examined the surroundings, then spotted the security cam hidden above the back door, perched a little higher than the security light fixed to the wall.

APRIL, show me the feed, Terra ordered.

Initiating data jump.

Terra's world shifted. The alley disappeared beneath her feet. Now she was suspended above the door, looking out from the back of the manor. She turned her attention to the alley to her right, her stomach queasy as she examined the darkness, unable to see herself or Dick standing there in the shadows.

A sudden thought occurred to Terra. The events at the Laundr-O-Mat had been harrowing enough that she hadn't fully processed what Valentina had told her about APRIL's new settings.

APRIL, how did we jump into this camera? Isn't this networked to private property?

Private property protocol missing, APRIL answered. **Manufacturer's coding modified. Executable file: Red Countess Override.**

Terra grinned. *Valentina, you goddamn goddess.*

"What's going on?" Dick's voice came from right beside her, making Terra jump. Her body leaned into a wall that wasn't there from the viewpoint she looked out from.

"Just wait," Terra replied.

APRIL, is there a way you can shut out this camera feed?

System lacks capacity to override the security feed.

Shit...

However, I can alter the camera feed's directional input.

Terra's viewpoint began to spin, moving away from the alley until the camera looked to the left. It happened slowly as if it was a part of the camera's programming. Soon there was no chance of it spotting Terra and Dick as they approached.

You have approximately twenty seconds to make the distance before the camera turns again.

"Move," Terra ordered Dick. "APRIL, exit data jump."

I cannot exit data jump while controlling networked hardware.

"Shit," Terra grumbled.

Dick knocked into the back of Terra. "What are you doing?"

"Running…" Terra took off.

It was a strange sensation, coordinating her body while her mind was inside the camera. She ran blindly forward, estimating where she should place her feet and where she would stop. At one point, Dick grabbed her arm and guided her toward the door, though Terra saw none of this as the camera feed pointed at the far wall. She had never left the island, but Terra imagined this experience wasn't all too dissimilar from running on a boat riding over choppy waters.

At last, Dick's hands gripped her shoulders. "Terra. Focus."

APRIL, exit data jump.

Exiting data jump.

The world twisted around Terra, turning from the camera feed to a wall of red brick. She gasped. "Shit."

"Terra?" Dick urged.

Terra shook her head, attempting to shake off nausea. "Not now. APRIL, thermal scan inside."

Activating thermal scan.

Terra looked around the inside of the building, identifying several targets either sitting or wandering around the house. There was no one in the immediate vicinity, so she turned her attention to the lock. There was a keypad set into the stone. Terra took a chance. *APRIL, can you unlock this pad?*

Negative.

Can you get us inside?

Terra's vision zoomed in on the keys, where fingerprints glowed like hot irons. **Identifying order of pressure input.**

The numbers throbbed in color as APRIL showed Terra the most recent keys pressed in the correct order. Terra followed her instructions and the door unlocked.

Terra slipped inside with Dick behind her.

They entered at the back of a long hallway that crossed the entire house. Terra scanned nearby to determine the safest route to pass through the building.

Two doors away, there was an office with only a single entrance in and out. Terra opened the nearby door and discovered a long dining room with a table that ran along its center. The dust settling on the placemats showed that this was a room that was hardly ever in use. She ran to the other side of the room, Dick in tow, and passed through the second door.

They entered a forgotten office.

The man stared back at her.

For a moment, Terra froze. The man's eyes were dark, fixing her with a terrible gaze. The smile was crooked and unnatural, and it was then that Terra realized that the man wasn't a man at all. Not anymore. He'd been dead for some time.

The smell hit them both in full force.

Dick eased the door closed behind them. "Friend of yours?"

Terra shook her head.

Dick lit a cigarette and exhaled a cloud of smoke into the room.

Terra raised an eyebrow. "Smoking? Now? Really?"

"It's not like it can smell any worse in here."

Terra had to agree. She'd rather the smell of smoke over the stench of this guy. "APRIL, identify the body."

APRIL scanned the man's face, returning a moment later with **Marcus Tellerone.**

Dick confirmed he had no idea who this man was, and neither did Terra. According to APRIL's database, Marcus had a history of violence behind him. He ran with some nasty circles, never quite seeing the inside of a cell but forming a name for himself on the west side of town, a trail of bodies behind him.

"Good riddance to bad news," Terra stated.

"It's no way to die, though," Dick countered.

Terra gave him a strange look.

"What?" Dick replied. "You like the idea of your family not knowing you're dead? Of not being able to claim your body and put you at peace in the grave?"

Terra considered this. "I like the idea of not unjustly killing and hurting people. You live like shit in life; you deserve shit in death." She turned her attention to the rest of the house, using APRIL's thermal scan to gain a lay of the land. Inside this house was something that she could use. There was a reason the vehicle had made its way here, she was certain.

"What happened back there?" Dick asked.

Terra ignored him.

"Terra." Dick's voice was firm.

Terra asked APRIL to switch back to her regular vision. "We don't have time for this, Dick."

"Yes. We do." Dick waited patiently.

Terra sighed. "I told you about the abilities that APRIL has… the abilities that are within me. APRIL can enter databases and manipulate technology. Back then, with the camera feed, I was *inside* it."

"You were beside me," Dick corrected.

"Yes, in body," Terra replied. "But my *mind* was inside the feed. Looking out at us."

Dick scoffed, mirth disappearing when he realized Terra was serious. "Shit. That's a hell of a gift you've got there."

"And a large portion of the AJS database, too," Terra replied. "I can scan civilians and pull up their information, lists of criminal activity, medical information. It's all here."

"Jesus." Dick scratched his chin. "That's dangerous."

"Tell me about it."

"Wouldn't the AJS shut it down?" Dick asked. "If you've gone AWOL, one of the chief cops is after you and knows what you think you know, why wouldn't they intercept and shut it down?"

"Beats me," Terra replied. It was something she'd certainly thought about. The only reasonable explanation to that question was that they hadn't realized yet, *or* Garcia couldn't make those kinds of changes without arousing too much suspicion. "Doesn't matter at this point. All that matters is that we get some real evidence of what the fuck is going on here."

Dick nodded. "Where to begin?"

Terra motioned at the dusty files in the cabinets around them. "What about here?"

CHAPTER TEN

Slim drained the last dregs of her coffee, then rose from her desk.

The bullpen was near empty—the emptiest it had been for some time. While Corporal Tobias Spencer certainly had a way of rubbing people the wrong way, he knew how to get things done. Nearly every officer was out on the beat, attending to some issue in the city.

It was quiet.

Slim didn't like the quiet. It gave her time to think. She couldn't help but notice that the station had also dropped several degrees in temperature since her crew's body warmth was absent.

Slim shouldered her pack, then headed for the door. The lights were dim. One fluorescent in particular flickered and *hummed* above her, its plastic casing filled with dead flies and spiders. She wondered what it would be like as she rose through the ranks, whether she'd ever make it to the big leagues where the coffee was hot, and the lights were unobstructed by dead insects.

She strode through the corridor, boots clomping on the floor and echoing around her. The offices to the corridor's side were empty, and Slim started to get a bad feeling. Where the hell was everyone? They couldn't *all* be out.

As she made her way to reception, a voice rang from behind. "Officer Newman," Gina called.

Slim turned to find Gina standing a distance down the hallway, a tablet clutched to her chest like a schoolgirl holding her books on her first day of elementary. "Yes?"

"Corporal Spencer would like to see you," Gina replied.

"Now?" Slim asked. "I'd just finished up. Was thinking of heading home and heating up a Hot Pocket. *Jeopardy!* starts in thirty minutes."

Gina smirked, a strange look on her face Slim hadn't seen before. "Now."

Slim nodded and headed off after Gina. The thought of winding down for the night was appealing, but Slim couldn't smudge her perfect record on the force. She had given too much time and effort to her job.

Since she joined the precinct nine months ago, she'd taken every assignment and delivered. Those still open kept her up at night, and she knew the higher Powers That Be had noticed her work. Black would often set her assignments that were above her station, just to test her. Every time, Slim would deliver, no matter the partner she was given.

Slim paused at Gina's office, detecting the faint whiff of something strange in the air, a scent that she hadn't experienced in some time.

Sweat and pheromones.

Gina motioned toward Spencer's office. A makeshift sign created from duct tape and permanent marker covered Corporal Black's embossed name, now reading "Corporal Tobias Spencer."

Slim glanced at Gina, noticed the flush in her cheeks and the small nest of ruffled hair at the back of her usually perfectly groomed head. Papers were on the floor that Gina now collected and straightened as a hand tugged her pencil skirt down into place.

Slim didn't need to be a detective to know what had happened here. The greasy ass marks on the wood of the table were a dead giveaway.

She opened Spencer's office door.

"Ah, Jenna Newman," Spencer bellowed as Slim entered the room. Her skin prickled at the sudden drop in heat. Gloomy darkness filled the room, only lit by the monitor of the computer screen on the desk.

"The other officers call me Slim," Slim replied.

Spencer chuckled. "Of course they do. Look at you. Six-five and as thin as a bean pole. You'd think you'd snap at a small gust of wind, but you don't, do you? One of our stellar superstars on the force." He grinned, a predatory show of teeth, then motioned to the chair. "Take a seat."

There was no "please" in his words or actions, nor was there a chance to refuse. Slim sat across the desk and waited.

Spencer sat back, lacing his fingers behind his head. He wore a gray checkered shirt—which defied typical AJS uniform guidelines—and the underarms were dark with sweat. His brow looked sticky, and what remained of his thinning brown hair was combed firmly back, slick with what Slim could only presume was wet-look hair gel fresh from a nineties boyband video. He was still a little breathless, and though he had a strong physique, he was clearly tired from his little rodeo with the girl next door.

He studied Slim for a moment, eyes exploring her body before settling back at her face. "You're a good kid. You know that?"

"No offense, sir. I'm no kid," Slim replied.

He smirked. "Spunky. I like that. You have a reputation behind you." He turned his attention to the computer screen, fixing a pair of broken glasses to his face. "Almost a one hundred percent completion rate on your assignments. More individual arrests in your nine-month tenure than any other cop and one of the most promising individuals to have graced this precinct. Well, outside of Terra Kris, that is."

His gaze darted to hers, searching for ruffled feathers.

Slim kept her cool.

"Next in line for promotion," Spencer continued. He peeled his eyes away from the screen and rested back in his chair, hands back behind his head. Slim's gaze zeroed in on those dark pits, clammy, wet messes beneath his arms. "You're in line for great things, Officer Newman. I've seen your type before. I was one of your type…still am. Always exceptional, you know what I mean?"

Slim nodded. *Sure...exceptional.*

"People like us, we're destined for great things," Spencer stated. "We want the best. We give the best. We're the shooting star soaring across the sky. We're the gleaming diamond among all the coal. We're the rose between the thorns." He sat forward, bringing with him a scent of something stale and adolescent. "It's because of people like us that change happens in this cesspit city."

He stared at Slim as if waiting for a reply. After a moment, she returned, "Of course, sir."

Spencer grinned, the mention of "sir" having some kind of effect on his heart rate. "Good." He nodded, pleased. "Good. So we're on the same wavelength."

He reached into his bottom drawer and pulled out a thermos. He unscrewed the lid and placed it on the table, then proceeded to fill the cup with the flask's contents. It was steaming, the smell of coffee filling the room. There was also a hint of something else in that coffee that took Slim back to nightclubs and sticky bar floors.

"I have a job for you, Newman." Spencer brought the steaming cup to his lips and slurped loudly. "An offer that I don't think you'll be able to refuse."

Slim waited patiently, not liking the look he was giving her.

"My buddy Garcia is looking for talented folk who are ready

to transcend to the big leagues. Ivy League. The Super Bowl. I'm talking the crème de la crème of the AJS system." Spencer paused dramatically. "We want you to take your ticket and fly."

Slim tried to keep her cool, though her face twitched. It didn't go unnoticed by Spencer, who offered a cool smile in return. Slim controlled her breathing, wondering if she was merely getting confused in all of Spencer's metaphors.

Spencer leaned back once more, a splash of coffee spilling on his shirt. "You seem oddly quiet for a woman who just received everything."

Slim straightened in her chair. "Excuse me, sir. I'm not sure I understand what you're asking of me. Are you saying that you're reassigning me to the inner city?"

Spencer's smile didn't slip. "That's exactly what I'm saying. At this time on Monday, you could be walking through the stone arches of our premium division, joining the likes of Garcia, Snowdon, and Telemarney at the top of the chain."

Slim swallowed.

"Could?" she asked. "I assume this offer is conditional."

Spencer's smile darkened. "You *are* as smart as they say. Of course, we're not going to accelerate you without one final trial. Those who have gained the seats of the giants have proven their worth, and though your track record is pristine, you've yet to show us something…exceptional."

"What do you need me to do?"

Spencer's eyes narrowed. He leaned so close to Slim that she smelled his musk. She became aware of Gina standing in the doorway, with her steaming mug brought to her ruby red lips. "We want you to bring in the exile."

"The exile?" Slim asked innocently, knowing exactly where this was heading.

"Yes. The exile." Spencer's gaze intensified. "Bring us Terra Kris, and we'll unlock the door to your wildest dreams."

CHAPTER ELEVEN

While the filing cabinets stationed inside the crypt—a nickname that Dick found it appropriate to title the room they were currently situated inside—were informative, they didn't give Terra much to go on.

"It's just receipts," Terra complained. "Hundreds of receipts and invoices. All anonymized, nothing to link back to Garcia at all."

Dick, elbow-deep in the cabinets across the room, nodded. "I say we pack this one in. Move on. This has yielded nothing other than a headache from the stink lingering in the air."

He sniffed his jacket, nose wrinkling. "I've got dead stink in the fabric of my clothes. Do you know how much it costs to get this shit dry cleaned?"

Terra rolled her eyes although she had to admit she desperately wanted to leave the room, too. "Fine. We'll stop there. APRIL, did you record all I found?"

Search documented. Performing background analysis.

"What did she say?" Dick asked.

"She?" Terra replied.

"APRIL. It's a girl's name," Dick returned.

Terra frowned. "It's an AI."

Dick raised an eyebrow. "Fine. Where to next?"

Terra glanced at the walls. "APRIL, thermal scan."

Terra's vision filled with red and orange outlines of people roaming around the house. For some reason, this side of the manor was nearly empty, with most of the activity concentrated in a far room on the property's top floor. A group of a dozen or so figures stood or sat around a table.

Terra looked nearby, gaining a perspective of the lay of the land. She spotted a lone figure a few rooms over. "Follow me."

"Do I have a choice?" Dick secured his grip on his pistol.

They exited the crypt, arriving back at the large, abandoned dining room. They closed the door behind them, and both instantly sucked in deep lungfuls of clean air.

"Reckon they've abandoned this side of the building because they don't want to deal with a dead body?" Dick asked.

Terra considered this. "They didn't have any problem disposing of that guy in the dumpster outside."

"It's different though, isn't it?" Dick asked.

Terra gave him a questioning look.

"Well, taking out a fresh body is one thing," Dick explained. "Letting one rot, then taking it out is another. Maybe they didn't get to that guy in time."

Terra frowned. "You're telling me they didn't know he died, and by the time they'd stumbled across him, he was already melting into the furniture?"

Dick shrugged. "Anything can happen in Atlantica."

Terra left it there. There was no defense against that truth.

They made their way into the hallway, sticking to the shadows as they snuck toward the lone figure in the other room. Terra guided Dick through several rooms with boxes stacked high, unique ID codes stickered to the corners. They opened a few to find quantities of ink and needles and other paraphernalia packed neatly in decorative boxes with a company logo on them.

"APRIL, what do you know of this company?" Terra asked softly.

APRIL reeled off a string of information about "Ink & Quill" —probably some "clever" spin on the needle-like quality of the quill and the ink that flowed from the tip—detailing the company's relevance on the black market apps that the AJS had been trying to close down for years. Terra echoed the information to Dick.

"So it's not a public company?" Dick asked.

Terra shook her head. "According to April, it's all for show. People working on an operation of this magnitude wouldn't make the mistake of registering something like this with the IRS or the state government. It's all underground."

They left the boxes and continued toward the lone figure. The closer they got, the clearer they were, and Terra could now see that they were slumped over something, possibly fast asleep.

Terra placed a finger to her lips as she turned the door handle. The room was dark. They tiptoed toward the figure, Terra taking her position behind, Dick pointing his pistol at their head.

Terra scooped the figure into her hands, one hand clamping her mouth, the other easing her back and holding a tight grip. "Wake the fuck up," she whispered into her ear.

The woman gasped, unable to take a breath. Her hands flailed. Terra held her firmly as the woman slapped Terra's hands. "Keep the fuck still. Stay the fuck quiet. I'm happy to let you go if you cooperate. You're in no trouble as long as you comply, got that?"

The woman continued to flail.

Terra continued. "My colleague has a pistol aimed at your temple. My recommendation is you stop resisting unless you want to join your ancestors in whatever place you call heaven."

The woman slowed, knowing when the fight wasn't worth it. Her arms slumped. Terra felt her soften beneath her grip.

"I'm going to let go now," Terra stated. "Any funny business, and it's game over for you. Got that?"

The woman nodded. Terra asked Dick to turn on a nearby lamp.

Terra stepped back slowly, releasing the woman's mouth. In the dim lamplight, Terra saw why this woman had been sleeping. The table was a mess of paraphernalia.

Plastic needles coated with the last dregs of the thick black substance that had been running rampant through Atlantica lay nearby. A box that had once stored the equipment had been torn open without care, the woman eager to get at the substance inside. She had dilated pupils, hair knotted in tangles, and dark veins beneath her pale skin.

Terra exchanged a look with Dick.

"What do you want?" the woman asked, her voice soft, her words slurred. "You some kind of cops?" She chuckled weakly, unable to hold Terra's gaze.

Terra sat beside her, moving directly into her line of sight.

"It doesn't matter what we are," Terra replied softly. "What matters is that you need to answer our questions. Give us the information we're looking for if you wish to go unharmed and without incident. You got that?"

The woman's head wobbled on her neck as though it weighed two hundred pounds and she was struggling to keep it up. "You're awful pretty for a cop."

Terra looked at Dick, then instantly regretted it when she saw his grin. "She's not wrong."

Terra's expression hardened. "What is this place?"

The woman waved around her as if the answer was obvious. "Utopia." A string of drool escaped her lips. "Heaven. Mecca. I don't know what you want to call it, but it's safe, and it's home…" she drew a deep, wet intake of air. "All the ink, and none of the danger of the outside world." She smirked. "You want some?"

She tapped the table, hands searching for the syringe that was right in front of her. "I've got a little spare." She brought a vial to her eyes and examined the drops inside. "If you like, you can get a taste. A buzz. Enough to get you started, honey."

"I'm not interested," Terra stated firmly. She glanced around the house, APRIL keeping their threats highlighted for her. "Who are the people here?"

The woman gave her a look as if she'd only just seen her for the first time. "You're pretty."

Dick moved closer. "Terra. This is a lost cause."

"No," Terra replied firmly. "What's your name?"

"You're pretty," the woman replied, attention turning to the needle as she tapped her arm and looked for a good place to prick. There was nothing in the tube. Terra snatched it off her before she could do damage. "Hey…"

"What's your name?" Terra insisted.

The woman's eyes half-closed, her head lolling. "Sabrina."

"Sabrina," Dick interjected. "Who are these people here? Are you in danger?"

"Only danger is if you're a cop." Sabrina chuckled. "Cops get shot." She turned her hands into a gun and aimed at the door. "Pow, pow, pow. Private property, bitch. Cops get splattered, thank fuck." She drew a deep breath. "We're a family here, guys. Family is for life. Ink is for life. Family is…"

"What's your family's name?" Dick pressed on. He waved the gun barrel in Sabrina's face. She straightened slightly, fixing her gaze on the dark hole of the gun's muzzle.

"I don't want any trouble," Sabrina stated. Her voice was soft, her demeanor showing a sudden lucidity that hadn't been there before. Eyes sparkled as she looked at Dick. "Please, sir."

Dick leaned closer, the metal barrel only half an inch from Sabrina's face. "Then answer our fucking questions."

Sabrina looked at Terra, then back to Dick. "El Justicia."

"Justice?" Terra replied.

Sabrina shrugged. "El Justicia."

"Yeah, repeating words isn't going to help us," Dick replied. "You're going to have to elaborate."

"That's all I know," Sabrina replied, though Terra could tell that wasn't the whole truth. "El Justicia provides, and us mere servants bathe in the riches he showers."

Sabrina did something that surprised them both, then. Her tongue crept between her lips, and she licked the barrel of the gun. She giggled, head wobbling once again as the clarity in her eyes faded.

APRIL, is she telling the truth?

Negative. Subject is lying.

Subject? Terra asked. *This isn't a science experiment.*

APRIL chose not to answer, instead turning Terra's attention to something orange and glowing. **Warning. Strangers approaching. Threat level unknown.**

Terra glanced at the corridor, shocked to see that another figure was approaching. Dick leaned in to ask another question, but Terra cut him off. "Someone's coming. Quick. Lights."

Terra shut off the light. Sabrina grumbled, something plastic rolling onto the floor. Dick grabbed Sabrina around the mouth and hushed her as the door opened at the far end of the room.

Terra moved quickly, sneaking through the dark until she was an arm's length away. A male voice crooned, "Baby… Where d'ya go? You ready for me?" before the light switched on to reveal a man with a sparsely populated beard and long dark hair.

His eyes showed the same dilated pupils as Sabrina's, and they widened as they took in the sight of Terra standing a few feet away. A moment of stillness passed before his face curdled, and he reached for his weapon.

Before he could aim the gun, however, Terra grabbed his wrist and twisted it behind his back. The weapon slipped from his grasp, clattering on the floor. Terra spun behind him, pistol held to his throat. "Any sudden movements and you're going to have a real problem."

"You fucking pigs?" the man replied, eyes fixing on Sabrina.

Dick chuckled. "Strange way to ask if we're into bestiality."

"No," Terra replied. "We're not pigs. You see an AJS uniform?"

"You smell like cops," the man replied, growl turning into a smirk. "Either way you're fucking dead."

"Now we're necrophiliacs," Dick shot back.

"Let us go, if you know what's good for you," the man instructed. "This place isn't for the likes of you. We're armed to the nines. One wrong move and this whole place comes down like a ton of bricks."

Terra glanced around the room. "Well, so far we're doing okay. Just a couple of loose ends to tie up and we can continue our search, can't we?"

The man spat on the floor. His skin was greasy and pallid. Terra felt as though she were holding a waxwork. "You asked for it."

The man wriggled, trying to escape Terra's grasp. She held firmly, grip tightening around his throat. When the man realized he'd met more than his match, his eyes widened. He tried to holler, but Terra squeezed his windpipe. She held him close, Dick and Sabrina watching silently from the far side of the room as the man's consciousness slipped from his body. His eyes closed and he went limp in her arms.

"Fuck," Dick stated.

Terra hooked his arm over her shoulder. "APRIL, confirm vitals."

Vitals stable. Status, unconscious.

"Good." She glanced at Dick. "He's fine. Just gone sleepy bye-byes."

Sabrina laughed, a manic sound that echoed around the room. "You two are funny. You should stay." She leaned down and grabbed the needle from the floor. Before Dick could react, she spun and stuck him in the leg.

"Son of a bitch," Dick grunted before smashing the pistol against Sabrina's head.

Sabrina's eyes rolled back as she slipped from the chair. Dick reached down and drew the needle from his thigh. "Are you kidding me?"

"Are you okay?" Terra asked.

"I don't know," Dick replied, examining the syringe. "There's barely anything in there."

"Let's hope so," Terra replied. "We've got to get moving before these fuckers wake again. You got any rope?"

Dick tossed the syringe on the table with his eyes fixed on his thigh. "Not really. I hadn't prepared for a hostage situation."

"It's not a hostage—" Terra left the sentence unfinished. "Whatever, just help me get these two somewhere where they're not going to be an issue." She dragged the man to the far side of the room and opened the door to a vacant closet containing only a bucket, mop, and broom. "This'll do."

She set the man inside. Aiding Dick, she dragged Sabrina in there, too.

"You got a key?" Dick asked.

Terra raised an eyebrow. "Do I look like I'd have a key?"

Dick rolled his eyes. "Here." He shut the door, then drew out a series of tools from his pocket. He played with the lock until something *snapped*, then straightened and gave a satisfied nod. "That might hold for a bit."

"At least until they start screaming," Terra replied. "Come on. We need to get a move on."

"Where to?" Dick replied. "You got a plan to get whatever you're after?"

Terra glanced up at the room populated with people. She sighed. "I have a bad feeling that El Justicia is upstairs, and the answers lie with him."

Dick followed Terra's gaze. "Promise me you're not leading me into a shootout situation."

Terra shrugged. "That's one promise I'm never going to give. Be prepared, okay."

She turned to Dick and saw him rub his eyes.

"Getting tired?" She smirked.

Dick shook his head. "No. No, I'm fine. Let's go, Captain."

"Don't call me that," Terra replied. Garcia's image popped instantly into her mind.

As they made for the door, Terra wondered about Dick's eyes, unsure about whether his pupils had begun dilating or she'd imagined it.

CHAPTER TWELVE

Climbing the stairs was tricky.

Each floorboard protested as they made their way up. Terra kept her thermal gaze fixed on the moving blobs around her, cautious that any advance would immediately set the whole hive alight.

She clutched her pistol tightly in her hand as she stepped the last three in one. Dick trailed behind her, alert, keen, and unblinking.

She waved Dick toward her, hunting for a safe space among the occupied rooms. Most of the activity stayed concentrated in a room at the far side of the manor, but nearly all the rooms had a minimum of one orange blob occupying them. Most were lying down, clearly asleep, while a few showed small groups gathered close, possibly injecting each other with ink.

Terra's lip curled. Why would people do that to themselves?

The truth was, she knew the answer. When you moved to the cesspit that was Atlantica with dreams of greater things, gold and riches, and power, then realized that not everybody could be top dog, you searched for other forms of happiness—ways to forget and create artificial happiness.

Terra still remembered the first time she'd ever entered a drug den. Two of the lords running the operation had a dispute, and gunfire had spilled onto the street—as well as the two perpetrators.

When you ran a business on top of a stack of precarious tinder, one flame could set the whole operation alight. Dispatch had sent Terra and several team members to quell the situation. They ended up in a showdown that saw twelve dead and two cops injured. When the guns lowered, she'd been one of the few to rifle through the den and saw what was going on behind closed doors.

Compared to that place, this manor was a friggin' palace.

Terra ducked into the nearest room as two figures emerged into the corridor ahead. Dick followed swiftly, the pair finding themselves in another space stacked to the brim with boxes. On the far wall was a square door set in the center.

Terra watched the figures, ensuring they didn't follow them. When they zeroed in on the room, she instructed Dick to hide.

For a moment, they hunted for a good spot, both finally finding a place behind a stack of boxes.

The door opened.

Two men entered. They turned on the light.

One of the men wore a stained white sleeveless shirt, his skinny arms highlighting his dark veins. The other had taken a different method of numbing himself, it seemed, a few sprinkles of white powder caught in his thick blond mustache.

"…told me she'd leave me if I come here again," White Shirt continued, unaware of the two figures hiding in the room. "Piece of shit. Knew I should've taken Dad's advice. Ain't no woman can make an honest man of an Ashton."

"You got it good, man," Mustache replied. "Least you got someone keeping your bed warm at night. I'd rather sleep here than stay in that flea-ridden piece of shit I call home."

White Shirt paused, eyes lighting as if the best idea in the world had come to him. "Maybe we could swap for a couple of nights. I get alone time. You get the headache that is the wife."

Mustache chuckled. "Don't make deals you won't want to shake hands on."

White Shirt offered a hand.

Mustache took it.

They both laughed. White Shirt closed his eyes and drew a long breath. "Man, that ink don't hit as hard as it used to."

"You growing a tolerance?" Mustache sawed his hand across his nose and sniffed.

"Maybe," White Shirt replied. "That a thing?"

Mustache shrugged. "Top it with the white stuff."

White Shirt chewed his lip. "You got any?"

"Got a ton," Mustache replied. "El Justicia hasn't figured out yet how I'm supplementing the folks in this place. Ink is good, but it doesn't beat the classics, y'know? Dollop of coke on your finger keeps you going all night."

"Better up the chute, though, right?" White Shirt tapped the side of his nose.

Mustache laughed. "Yeah. Exactly."

White Shirt approached the square at the far wall. He slid open the doors to reveal a dark chute leading down to somewhere below. A pulley system hung on the right-hand side.

"Or better down," Mustache added as White Shirt pulled the ropes and brought the dumb waiter's carriage into sight. A box was sitting on the platform.

White Shirt removed it and added it to the stack.

"Is this necessary?" Mustache asked. "Can't you take one of these here?" He motioned to the other boxes.

White Shirt shook his head. "They're all assigned to customers, man. You never seen how this works? Justicia will fuck us up if we take what ain't ours." He pointed toward Terra, and for a heart-stopping moment, she wondered if he'd seen her. She turned her head to the side, noticing the splatters of red-orange on the walls. "Take someone's shit, and you get dead. Honor among thieves."

"I thought the phrase was 'no honor among thieves?'" Mustache asked.

"Probably," White Shirt replied. "Who knows?" He took a box cutter from his pocket, then sliced through the tape sealing the top of the cardboard.

Mustache rubbed his nose again. "Fair enough. So, what about it? Want some Charlie?"

"Nah, I'm good." White Shirt reached into the box. He stood sharply, drawing out a gun fixed with a long silencer. Without hesitation, he pulled the trigger. Mustache's head exploded in an instant. The sound was a *hiss*, followed by the wet *smack* of tissue staining the room around them.

Mustache's body crumpled. White Shirt didn't flinch. He knelt and took a large clear bag of white powder from Mustache's pocket. "You fuck with Justicia; you get fucked right back."

From across the room, Terra caught Dick's eyes peeking through the boxes. He held up his pistol.

Terra shook her head slowly. She wasn't sure that Dick got the message.

Dick jumped a little at the gunshot.

Dick never jumped at gunshots.

He felt a little strange. The world blurred a touch around the edges of his vision, a peculiar lightness creeping into his body. He smiled, although he wasn't sure why, and when Terra caught his gaze, he wasn't sure he could see her properly.

She moved a little slowly, out of focus across the room.

He raised his pistol, signaling that he was ready to take this fucker out, but she shook her head.

Was she trying to send some message? Why would she say no, when the guy in the room had blown his comrade's head off?

Dick blinked, his eyelids suddenly heavy. A dull throb in his thigh reminded him of Sabrina and her syringe.

Shit.

He glanced at his hand, carefully moving it in front of his face. He examined the backs and found that his veins were a fraction more prominent than before.

Had there been more in that syringe than he thought?

Dick turned his gaze back to Terra, the intensity of her stare almost comical. He felt the laugh creeping up his throat. He bit his tongue, but it was rising, rising like a bubble in the ocean, searching for release on the surface.

He moved his hand to cover his lips. Terra's eyes widened. The man in the white shirt kicked the body on the floor before shaking his head and exiting the room.

He left the door open behind him.

Dick snorted, unable to hold back the laugh any longer.

White Shirt's footsteps paused, then grew louder.

What the fuck is Dick doing?

Terra shrank against the wall as Dick let out a strange, choked snort. As he laughed, his shoulder banged against the wall. Terra watched White Shirt pause in the hallway, then turn and head back.

Great. Nice going.

The door opened fully, blocking Dick from view. Terra relied on her thermals.

"Who's in here?" White Shirt aimed his gun around the room. He approached the boxes. Dick shrank back, but he couldn't hold his chuckles. "Well, hello there."

Terra's heart pounded, knowing she had to act fast. She

slipped out from her hiding space and shouldered the door shut. With fluid swiftness, she kicked the back of White Shirt's knees and sent him buckling forward. He slammed into the boxes, the cardboard crumpling around him. Dick drew a sharp breath and continued laughing.

Terra stamped on White Shirt's hand, his grip releasing from the pistol. She came down on him, jamming her elbow into the back of his neck and knocking him senseless.

"Dick, get out, now," Terra barked.

Dick exited his hiding place, although not with grace. Boxes toppled, crashing to the floor. Many of them buried the two men, and as Dick emerged with a broad smile on his face, Terra spotted the dilation of his pupils. "You've got to be kidding me."

"Sorry." Dick didn't look in the least bit sorry. "I can't help it."

He scoffed again as APRIL alerted Terra of the approaching threat. **Chances of discovery increasing. Sound levels above desirable. Group approaching.**

Terra glanced around, finding a group of at least six individuals heading their way. *Shit.*

She looked around the room. *APRIL, find us a way out.*

Examining surroundings. Cross-referencing blueprints for Kibble's Manor.

Wait, you can do that? Terra asked.

Affirmative.

Terra's vision turned into a strange 3D grid from a 2000s computer system. It homed in on the dumb waiter, and a weird feeling settled in Terra's stomach. "You're not serious?"

"What?" Dick replied.

"Follow me," Terra instructed, sounding resigned. She made for the hole in the wall, which was at least three feet wide and three feet high. She glanced down, staring only into blackness, the carriage already lowered by whoever waited on the other end. "Why is it always down into the dark with these missions?"

Dick scoffed. "I'll never fit down there."

"Bullshit," Terra replied. "You're going first." She grabbed Dick by the shirt collar and propelled him toward the wall. Sensing her seriousness, he levered himself into the opening and used the ropes to begin his descent.

His progress was slow, and Terra needed him to hurry. She eased herself inside, the ropes creaking as they bore the weight of both of them. The glow of orange bodies flared, only meters from the doorway.

Terra drew the doors to the dumb waiter shut, then continued to climb down, foot occasionally catching Dick's head.

"Ouch," Dick muttered, humor in his words.

"Shut up and go."

Terra fixed her gaze on the room above, the glow of orange bundling around the doorway. Half a dozen bodies entered the area, examining the two men lying on the floor. Voices were muffled above her, raging and crying out. A gunshot fired. Terra knew without being able to see that White Shirt was dead.

By the time the group above thought to examine the dumb waiter, Terra and Dick had reached the bottom. They trod on the dumb waiter platform, then clambered out the opening.

Dick dusted himself off, the smile still fixed to his face. "That was a close one," he stated, unaware of the irony of it being his fault.

"Yeah…" Terra replied. "*That* was." She had already noticed what Dick had seemingly not. A woman waited in the small room they had entered, a pistol in her hand, aiming directly at Terra's forehead.

CHAPTER THIRTEEN

Regina Tubbs pressed her back to the wall and gasped for air.

Her brow was slick with sweat. The evening was dark, and the air filled with the scent of cigarettes and sewage. Vents expelled warm plumes of air, and sirens wailed.

Shit, shit, shit. Regina shrank into the shadows as a series of gunshots fired. A group of dark figures sprinted past the gap between the buildings. She closed her eyes, praying to God that they didn't see her.

Not tonight. Not tonight. Not tonight.

Regina had a bad time of it. Arriving on the island of Atlantica a little over two years ago, she had found herself immediately thrown into the ink trade. They spotted her at the airport, tracked her to her apartment, and before she could throw a housewarming party, she was employed.

The money was great. The hours were long, but she knew that one day she'd be able to claim back her time. Atlantica was the golden island, a land of riches. Everyone had told her so.

Another burst of gunfire. Someone screamed. The sirens grew louder. Above, the Atlantica City Railroad passed with its strange magnetic hum, a beast of a vehicle levitating two feet above the long steel tracks. Regina poked her head around the corner, then ducked back.

"Over there!" A voice shouted.

Regina slipped farther into the shadows, squeezing between gaps she shouldn't have been able to fit through. Dumpsters and trash bags blocked her path, but she fought her way through, clothes tearing, stomach scraping against brick. There was no light down here to guide by, only her other senses, and they told her to flee.

She was right. Goddamnit, she was right.

Regina received the phone call only an hour ago. One of her closest colleagues in her time of working underground in the Laundr-O-Mat's den. They had both been quality testers, working with the production line, sampling the products, and ensuring only the best ink made it onto the market. At least, until the AJS raid only a week or so ago.

Nadine had warned Regina to run. Regina had laughed her away. They had managed to talk their way out of criminal charges with the AJS. Some benefactor up top paid their way out for all those involved in the operation—it was good to have friends on the inside.

But now…

"Check down there," another voice exclaimed.

Flashlights erupted at the end of the alley. Regina ducked to the side, taking a hard right. She pumped her legs, then twisted her ankle on a stray tin can. She went down hard, face smashing into the dirt. She let out an involuntary scream, then heard their footsteps coming after her.

She pushed herself to her feet. Red and blue lights flashed ahead, bouncing off the brickwork. Although she couldn't see the car, she knew safety was there. All she had to do was make it to the end of the alley and call the AJS. That would save her. She was in public, after all.

Shots fired. Bullets *pinged* off the brick. Regina grunted but made it to the end of the alley.

She emerged into the quiet street. This side of town was comprised mostly of local businesses, all with their doors shut to the night. She turned to the AJS vehicle, her smile slipping as she stared into the face of someone she'd only heard about in rumors.

Streetlight bounced off his bald head. Dark eyes glinted as the man pulled the trigger. Everything Regina knew disappeared as the lights went out, and all that remained was darkness.

Parker Garcia growled, and his lip curled at the corner. A handful of men and women emerged from the alley, pausing only when they saw that the woman was dead on the ground.

"Sir?" one of the women offered.

Garcia turned his back to the group, his AJS uniform hidden beneath his dark jacket, protecting the fabric from the woman's blood splatter. He climbed into the passenger side of the car and closed the door. The window rolled down, and he reached up to pull in the AJS lights and switch them off. The Saturn Vue was as plain a vehicle as any, and no one would suspect the deception it carried.

Tobias Spencer shifted the car into gear, then turned his head to Garcia. "Happy?"

Garcia grumbled, looking out the window at the shithole around him. The magnetic railway line was the only part of this side of town that matched the outside world's expectations of what Atlantica offered. Everything else was black, grim, and empty. Many areas of the city had received heavy investments, but some sections fell to the dogs. The rich didn't always take care of their toys.

"No," Garcia replied.

Spencer raised an eyebrow. "Sir, we've rounded up twenty-eight of the thirty. We're on track."

"We haven't finished," Garcia snarled. "Antonio is tracking the last two." His phone lit up. He scrolled through his messages.

"Still," Spencer offered. "We're making progress. Soon the fuckers will all be silenced, and you'll be able to breathe a sigh of relief."

Garcia paid no attention. His eyes stayed fixed on the screen. He'd hoped for better news, believing that soon he would receive the update that informed him they'd re-enabled tracking in the APRIL system and he'd be able to bring that bitch in once and for all. Still, some news was better than no news.

"Motherfucker," Garcia muttered.

"Problem?" Spencer asked. "The wife giving you a headache again?"

Garcia shut the phone off. "One of the last two has been spotted."

"Oh?" Spencer asked, turning right onto Sickle Street. "Where?"

"Kibble's Manor." Garcia shook his head.

"That's not far from here." Spencer's eyes lingered on a woman walking down the street, her red dress barely below her ass cheeks. "Wanna visit?"

Garcia narrowed his eyes. "Don't you have a station to run?"

Spencer offered a half-shrug. "Place is a ghost town. Did as you asked, sir. Assigned all the officers to the locales away from those we were searching. Consider me Moses and the AJS your Red Sea."

He looked at Garcia for laughter and found none.

"What do you want to do?" Spencer asked

Garcia considered this. "I suppose we could divert for a brief visit."

"On it." Spencer nodded, turning right at the next junction. "Who's the target this time?"

Garcia narrowed his eyes. "Joshua Ashton."

"Ashton?" Spencer laughed. "He should've stayed hidden."

"That's not a problem anymore," Garcia replied.

"Oh?" Spencer raised his eyebrows. "How come?"

"Because he's been shot dead," Garcia answered, not a hint of emotion or remorse in his eyes.

CHAPTER FOURTEEN

"Who the fuck are you?" The woman was lean, wearing a white tank top that showed off her defined muscles. She wore her hair in a tight ponytail and looked almost the spitting image of Terra.

Terra and Dick raised their hands.

"We're no one," Terra replied.

The woman cocked her head, eyes narrowing. "A couple of no ones dropping down the delivery chute. Seems a bit suspicious to me." She glanced at the dumb waiter. "Any more of you waiting to come down there like juvenile Santas?"

Dick chuckled.

"Shut up," Terra warned him.

The woman gave them a strange look. "One more chance. Tell me who you are and what you're doing here."

"My name is Terra Kris," Terra admitted. "This here is John Chambers."

"My friends call me Dick," Dick added.

The woman raised an eyebrow.

"What are you doing here?" the woman asked. "Seems a strange place for a friendly visit."

APRIL, scan target, Terra instructed.

Words popped up in her vision, floating around the woman's head. The woman was Harley Crawdad, a thirty-five-year-old daughter of two deceased parents. Her criminal record was murky, having spent several months at a time in prison on charges of extortion and possession in public. Terra also spotted something that caught her curiosity, and as she read the information, the woman nudged them on.

"Speak," she stated, jabbing the gun their way.

Dick answered for her. "Honestly? We came for our product and got waylaid. There are some assholes up there, and the minute we were about to claim what was ours, they tried to steal it. Inkers without conscience. We lost our product and nearly lost our lives. This was the only safe route out."

As if to highlight their point, another gunshot rang from the dumb waiter, followed by raised voices.

The woman's lips thinned. "Why should I believe you?"

"Why would we lie?" Dick asked.

Terra was impressed. Perhaps his momentary flare of ink had faded. Or maybe the adrenaline coursing around his body was beginning to combat the worst of it.

The woman nodded at their weapons. "Hand them over."

Terra was reluctant.

"Now," the woman urged.

Terra did as she instructed, as did Dick. They laid their weapons on the floor in front of them.

"Kick them away," the woman continued.

They obeyed.

"Good." The woman holstered her pistol and took a step closer. "I don't know what kind of shit you got into up there, and I'm not sure I want to. If you want to get the fuck out of here, you've got one of two options. Take the hard route up, or follow the yellow brick road."

She jerked her thumb over her shoulder, where a crude yellow line painted on the floor disappeared through the doorway. "Emergency exit protocol," she explained. "Glows luminous in the dark. Helps people in case of fire."

"You get many of those?" Terra asked.

"More than we'd care to admit," Harley replied. "You leaving, or what?"

Terra and Dick exchanged a glance, then nodded. They reached for their pistols as they passed. To their surprise, Harley allowed it to happen. She kept her gaze fixed on them until they got to the door. When they were gone from sight, Harley turned her attention back to the boxes, scanning the labels and setting the correct packages on the dumb waiter.

Thirty seconds later, a loud *thump* sounded as something landed at the bottom of the chute. She clicked her tongue and shook her head as the dead man's arm flopped from the small gap remaining around the boxes. She called up, "We're not a fucking crematorium down here."

Laughter was the response.

The underground hallways were a hive of activity.

Carts ferried boxes around, men and women walked the halls with headphones blaring music as they lost themselves in their work, machinery sounded that Terra couldn't identify the source of.

"We're in the thick of it now, Dick," Terra muttered softly enough so that only he could hear.

No one batted an eyelid as they passed, each worker stuck in their head, eyes down, performing their duties. Terra and Dick followed the yellow line, passing several rooms with closed doors. As they passed one door that happened to be ajar, Terra poked her head inside.

Sticking out of the far wall was a conveyor belt from which boxes were slowly filtering into the room. A long pipe disappeared into the wall, a blowing sound accompanying the packages as they arrived down below, rolling along the conveyor belt into the hands of the worker.

A man with a large Afro and tiny headphones bobbed his head as he scanned the boxes before placing them in the piles behind him.

"Excuse me," a voice called from behind.

Terra and Dick shifted out of the way as a woman appeared with a pallet truck. She levered several boxes onto the truck, then wheeled out of the room again.

"Where are they headed to?" Terra asked aloud.

The person continued without a second glance.

"Come on," Dick encouraged. "Let's not linger."

They continued down the line, taking a turn away from the delivery receptacles and entering a corridor where several bedrooms branched off. Terra couldn't believe there was this much activity beneath the city. She wondered if these guys weren't just supplying ink to Kibble's Manor but a whole raft of distribution locations. For years, the AJS had been trying to figure out how the ink networks managed to get their product across the city. Had Terra and Dick stumbled across the answer?

At the end of the corridor, a set of stairs led them down and farther into the city's depths.

"Deeper?" Dick asked, his eyes beginning to return to normal. "Seriously?"

"She said it was the only way out." Terra looked over her shoulder. "You see another way?"

"Nope." Dick started down the stairs.

Terra followed.

Garcia looked down at the two figures below him.

One of them still slept. The other was wide awake with a drunken grin on her lips. "El Justicia…"

Garcia frowned, glancing between the pair. He was already pissed about the mess that they'd made upstairs and the blood splatters on the product that his entire operation relied on. It would take a fair bit of cash to clean everything up. Now he had two customers slammed in a locked cupboard. Sabrina's voice was hoarse from the screaming she'd done to grab their attention.

"Who did this to you?" Garcia asked.

"El Justicia…" The woman laughed. "In the flesh. I grovel at your feet."

She folded, her lips covering Garcia's shoes in saliva. Garcia kicked her away. A red mark appeared on her cheek. "Who did this?"

Sabrina gave him a quizzical look, tilting her head as she strained to answer the question. "A man."

"A man?" Garcia asked. "What man?"

"A sexy man." Sabrina glanced at her companion on the floor as if she might offend him. "Gave him a taste of our medicine. A little drop of ink."

Garcia growled. "You wasted product?" he spat.

Sabrina looked offended. "It was mine to give. I pay fair and square."

"So a man locked you in the cupboard?" Spencer asked, emerging from behind Garcia. "Why?"

"The woman?" she answered, uncertain as she glanced at the floor and side. "A pretty woman. Bet those two were fucking." She giggled, then bit her lip.

"What did she look like?" A bad feeling settled in Garcia's stomach.

Sabrina described the woman, matching Terra's description to a "T." "Fuck," he grumbled.

"What is it, sir?" Spencer asked.

Garcia growled, looking around as if he could see her running through the house. "Widen the search. The bitch is in the nest. We have to find her before she stumbles across something big."

Spencer made to leave. "Not you, though. Back to the station with you. You disappear too long, and people are going to start getting suspicious. Got that?"

Spencer confirmed that he did.

Garcia ground his teeth together, then made his way upstairs. He had some fuckers to question about what the hell happened here tonight.

And a nosy-ass cop to find.

Imani Thomas lowered her binoculars with a coy grin on her lips.

Across the road, Kibble's Manor stood, smaller than all the surrounding buildings. The lights were on in the upper rooms, but the occupants had drawn the curtains. She could make out activity inside but had no specifics about who or what she was watching.

Apart from Garcia, of course. She had trailed him from the moment he left his office. As he drove around in his beat-up Saturn, she followed him, collecting pictures as she went. Always just out of sight, Imani logged his movements and tracked him on the map, hoping to stumble across something significant at some point.

When she heard the gunshots earlier that night, she thought she had him nailed, but she was too slow to move into sight without alerting him to her presence. Something big was going on. She just didn't know exactly what or why.

Now she stared out the window and watched the manor. Garcia had arrived here a short while ago, and he had yet to leave. Imani had heard rumors about Kibble's Manor, had heard

Terra's part of her tale from the last time she was here, and couldn't quite believe that Garcia would return after such a near miss before.

Then again, what happened in private stayed in private. What did Garcia have to fear behind closed curtains?

A short while later, the Saturn appeared from the meager parking lot. Imani adjusted the binoculars, finding it impossible to see inside the car now that it was dark. She snapped a picture with her camera, then hurried down the apartment stairs toward her AJS bike. As the car slipped back to the outer city, Imani silently followed.

The stairs led them to an underground road.

The surface was hard-packed mud. A fleet of pickup trucks with canvas sheets strapped across their beds sat parked to the side. Workers unloaded boxes from a couple of vehicles freshly arrived in the tunnels.

"Holy shit," Dick muttered.

Terra had to agree with him.

She asked APRIL to scan the workers. All of them had minimal convictions and accusations, though every one of those convictions centered around drug trafficking and possession. A couple of heads turned as they continued on the yellow line, which led to a small bank near the road then stopped.

They stood there, looking around. Terra couldn't help but feel they both stood out like sore thumbs.

"Y'all looking to head on out?" a man asked. His skin was dark, his face kind. There was a horseshoe of silver hair around his crown and heavy bags beneath his eyes.

"Yes," Terra replied. "We've finished for the night."

The man cocked his head, eyes unblinking as he stared

intensely at Terra. "Shuttles headed out twenty minutes ago. Same schedule every night." His eyes narrowed. "Like always."

Shit.

Dick tapped his watch, throwing a frustrated hand in the air. "I knew this fucking thing was broken." He showed the face to Terra. "It's thirty minutes slow."

Terra played along. "That means we have to wait for the next one."

The man chewed his cheek, a box balanced in the crook of his arm. He wore stained denim overalls and a claret shirt. "Next shuttle ain't come 'til morning." He spat on the floor. "You folks new here?"

"Yes," Dick replied. "Fresh-faced on the job. Just want to get back home to rest up for a bit, y'know?" He stretched. "Been a long night."

"They don't get any shorter." The man set his box down. He rubbed his palms on his overalls, then offered a hand. "Willy Junior. Most of the guys call me Bill."

"Nice to meet you, Bill." Dick took his hand. Terra offered hers, but Bill ignored it.

"You folks want a ride out? I can fire up one of those trucks and get you into open waters." He sniffed, then hocked a mouthful of phlegm. "What d'ya say?"

"Sure thing," Terra replied.

Bill cast a suspicious glance Terra's way. "Gots to be quick. My shift don't get off for another six hours. Y'all ready to go?"

They told him they were. A moment later, they were sitting cozy in the cab of a green pickup. The headlights shone, the truck revved. Bill hit the gas pedal and took them onto the road.

The road was bumpy, and with every knock and turn, Dick thumped into Terra. She grimaced against the constant nuisance as Bill turned up the radio and blared country music into the truck.

"Nothing boosts morale like some song of the soil, don't you agree?" He grinned. "Reminds me of my paps. Played in a band, y'know? Had killer fingers for the banjo."

"Anything we would have heard?" Dick asked.

"Likely as of not," Bill replied. "Played a couple of things that went on Spotify and iTunes, but nothing in the big leagues. He ain't no Delilah Sampson."

Terra and Dick exchanged a glance.

"Sampson?" Bill looked hurt at this revelation. "Dewright? Jonesy? Oh, you folks ain't lived."

The tunnel twisted and turned, the road only wide enough for two vehicles to pass with inches between them. Once or twice they slowed to allow the other vehicle to pass, each one laden with more boxes of product.

"Quite the operation going, don't you think?" Bill tracked Dick's eyes as yet another truck faded into the tunnel behind them. "Folks need a way of getting this shit to their customers without AJS finding out. Smart operation, really. Tunnels and byways beneath the dirt. Private residence in, public tunnels between, private residence out.

"Unless those blue shirt motherfuckers drill down into the core, they ain't gonna find no way to block this shit. Not without a warrant to search private, and we all know what the law says about that shit."

He fixed his gaze on Terra for such a concentrated amount of time that she worried when the vehicle started to drift toward the wall. Dick opened his mouth to speak, but before he could, Bill continued.

"Man, this city is fucked up." He shook his head, looking out the window at the earthen walls. "My pap used to clear out infestations before he became a country music star. Cockroaches, termites, rats, flies, anything that can buzz and hum and make a woman jump onto a chair. Still, in all his years, I bet he ain't never seen a rat's nest as large as this one."

His eyes glazed over. "I wonder what Pap would think about

his darling boy devolving to a simple greasy cog on the wheel of chaos this city wrought."

Terra cleared her throat. "Bill, you talk as if you have no other option."

"Do I?" Bill half-shrugged. "I suppose I must have once. Made my bed now. I lie in it. Dishonest work for honest pay.

"Least I don't stick myself with any of that ink shit. Happy to clock in, take my coin and go. Not like half the workers on this force. They get paid in the Devil's elixir, drain it, then come back for more. Least I gots me a little savings, y'know?"

"How much farther?" Dick stared ahead at the seemingly endless tunnel.

Bill smirked, then cast a knowing glance their way. "You don't belong here, do you?"

Terra's hand moved instinctively to her pistol. Dick's moved to his. Bill's moved to his.

"None of that in the truck, thank you," Bill stated. "Let's get somewhere a little more…private, first."

Terra couldn't work out whether Bill was joking or not. All she knew was that this man was not to be trusted, and now they were trapped inside his ride.

CHAPTER FIFTEEN

The earthen walls gave way to a concrete underground parking garage. Pillars held up the thick floors above, and strip lights flickered and bathed the space in their fluorescent glow. Vehicles of all different shapes and sizes packed the place.

Bill navigated around them, heading up three levels before the world opened before them. He flashed a badge at a barrier, and the arm raised to allow them to exit.

"See what I mean?" Bill stated. "We on private property now. Only one way into the tunnels, and that's through private land either end. This place is four square acres. The moment people cross onto this land, they're safe from you AJS types. God, the rich know how to exploit the rules here, huh?"

Terra remained tight-lipped, her mind lingering over the fact he had somehow worked out her connection with the AJS. She didn't know if he was guessing or if it was an educated decision.

"We'll hop out here," Dick instructed as Bill continued across the plot of land. Now that they were outside, they could almost make out the canopy of stars through a thin layer of fog. Surrounding the right side of the property were the jungle's limits, great trees arcing over the three-meter-high chain link fence that surrounded the compound. Behind them, a stately manor stood like a freight liner on a lonely ocean.

"You ain't going nowhere," Bill replied. "Get your asses down, now."

Before Dick could argue, Terra grabbed his head and dragged him down until they were both ducked in the footwell. Thanks to APRIL's thermal scan, she had already glimpsed what lay ahead.

Two guards blocked the way out, AR15s in their hands. They wore combat boots and desert camo, which seemed a strange choice for this kind of environment. They walked inside the fence, keeping to the private property limits.

They stopped the truck when Bill approached.

"Morning, gents," Bill cheerily announced. "Just forgot a couple of things at home needed by the boss."

From her position in the footwell, she couldn't see their reaction, but Bill was a good actor, indeed.

"Memory's slipping, Bill," a voice called. "You'd forget your head if it wasn't attached to your shoulders."

Laughter came from the other.

Bill chuckled. "I may be getting old, but I ain't senile yet. Come on, fellas, you going to let me pass or no? Boss will be getting mighty itchy if I'm not back and clocked in soon."

"Sure thing, Bill," the second voice called.

Bill's foot eased down on the gas pedal, and the vehicle rumbled forward. It was five minutes later before he informed the pair they could get up.

Terra expected to see rolling fields and the city limits coming into view but instead discovered that trees surrounded them. Bill drove confidently through the foliage, following a single dirt track as it wound and snaked ahead.

"Where are you taking us?" Terra asked.

"Somewhere private," Bill returned, choosing not to elaborate. "Hope y'all ain't got a problem with that."

Dick and Terra glanced at each other, silently communicating.

Terra had an uneasy feeling in her stomach, but Bill had helped them so far. He seemed to be able to pick up more than they were willing to tell, and she was secretly glad to be out of that compound, even if she hadn't quite found what she was after.

The trees parted briefly on the right, revealing a small lake, curls of mist rising from its surface. At the far side of the shore, Terra saw a candle of tapirs splashing about in the waters. A few parrots and colorful birds took wing as the engine rumbled past.

After another twenty minutes, mostly taken in silence, Bill nodded ahead. "Almost there, kids. Don't get too angsty."

Terra rested her hand on her pistol for comfort. She asked APRIL, *Where are we?* and was pleased to receive a set of coordinates that tracked their location.

Despite how long they'd driven, they still licked the edge of the jungle's borders. Terra zoomed in on a single-track road that approached a large villa surrounded by trees.

She blinked away the digitized information as the trees parted and the villa came into view.

The place was simple but elegant. The villa was built mostly of woods and clays and blended in well with the jungle's surroundings. They passed a large rectangle of land that had been dug about two feet deep. Bill explained, "Working on a pool. Ain't got the cash to buy outright and get help, so doing it ourselves."

They parked near the front entrance, the sudden silence of the engine dying pressing in on their ears. Although they were only a short distance into the jungle, the humidity from the surrounding trees made their skin clammy, and Dick removed his jacket.

"Out," Bill instructed.

Terra gave Dick a "be prepared" look, then exited the vehicle.

Bill strode ahead, a slight limp in his step, his back a little weighted by time and gravity.

"Juniper!" Bill called. "We gots company."

Terra entered the house, confused by what she saw. Despite

the magnitude of the property, there was barely anything inside that she would expect in a home. Only a couple of pictures hung crookedly on the wall. The stairs were ancient wood, the floors dirty and scratched. There were hardly any doors in place, and the only furniture Terra could see in the living room were a couple of beaten-up La-Z-Boys, facing a boxy seventeen-inch TV screen.

"Welcome, welcome," a woman announced, appearing from the kitchen as she wiped her hands on a faded rag. She was thin, her clothes hanging off her, but her smile was coat hanger wide. Terra performed a quick scan, surprised to see that there were no convictions associated with Juniper Huckman. She slapped Bill's arm. "Billy, don't be rude. Introduce me to your friends."

Bill laughed. "Tells you the truth, I don't know, myself."

Juniper rolled her eyes. "Hello, dears. I'm Juniper, and in case this dopey old git hasn't mentioned, he's Willy Jr."

"Bill," Bill corrected.

"And you are?" Juniper asked.

"Terra," Terra replied.

"Dick," Dick stated, meeting a strange glance from Juniper.

"John," Terra clarified. "John Chambers."

"Dick," Dick insisted.

Bill and Juniper laughed.

"Welcome to our humble abode, Dick and Terra," Bill replied. "Now, are you both ready to tell me the truth about what it is you were doing inside the facility?"

Terra glanced at Dick.

Dick smirked. "He's observant."

"I mean, it wasn't hard," Bill replied. "Wearing clothes like that and wandering around like lost puppies. I'm surprised no one stopped you before I did." He touched his chin. "Scratch that. That facility is full of hard workers doing their jobs. I'm surprised I spotted you both."

"Tea?" Juniper asked.

"Please," Terra replied.

"None for me, thanks," Dick added.

Juniper disappeared into the kitchen. "Come into the lounge. I don't have long, but Juniper will take good care of you if you both need it."

Terra sat on one of the La-Z-Boys while Dick remained standing.

Bill narrowed his eyes. "You're both cops, correct?"

"Half right," Terra replied. "I'm AJS. He's PI."

"Make a mighty team," Bill replied. "Don't AJS have rules about not coming on private property? You know I could report you?"

"I'm not on duty," Terra replied.

Bill chuckled. "Still, you're a cop. That's enough to have you suspended, I bet. What you doing risking your career by jumping into an inkers hellhole?"

Dick answered. "We're looking for El Justicia."

Bill's humor left his face. "Oh."

"You know him?" Terra asked.

"Of course," Bill replied. "Not exclusively, mind. But enough to know to be scared."

China rattled on a plastic tray. "Tea."

Juniper placed the cup in Terra's hands. She also handed Dick a glass with amber liquid inside. "You seemed the type."

"You're a good reader," Dick replied.

Bill studied Terra with a wary eye. "To track down El Justicia is a fool's errand. You know this."

Terra nodded. "I do. It's of vital importance that we bring the whole damn ring down, though. AJS can't have drug rings of this magnitude running through the city, poisoning the veins of our people."

Bill gave a thoughtful nod. "How do you plan on tracking down the kingpin? How do you expect to bring El Justicia to justice? You think people haven't tried before?"

He gave a derisive exhale. "Terra, many have tried before, and many have failed. When you got the law on your side, you don't stand a chance at toppling the towers."

Terra's eyes narrowed. "What do you mean he has the law on his side?" She knew what she wanted Bill to mean. She just wasn't sure if she was reading him correctly.

Juniper shuffled uncomfortably.

Bill looked down at his lap. "I have a suspicion that you know."

"A name," Terra stated. "Give me a name."

"El Justicia," Juniper replied, looking worried.

"A *real* name," Terra pressed.

Bill met her gaze. "You know."

"I need to hear it from your lips," Terra insisted, blood growing warm as they danced around the subject. Terra needed to hear it. She needed to know that someone else knew. How they knew would come later, but for now, all she needed was confirmation that her theory was true—

"Garcia," Bill replied.

Juniper looked down.

"Parker Garcia," Bill finished. "Captain Parker Garcia, to be specific."

CHAPTER SIXTEEN

Terra pressed Bill further. "How do you know his name?"

Bill looked at his watch. "I've got to go." He stood.

"How do you know his name?" Terra repeated.

Bill walked to the door. Dick moved in front of him, blocking his path.

Bill looked into Dick's eyes. "Son, I suggest that you move. Unless you want to arouse suspicion and really kick up a stink, it's best for us all if I get back to work. He watches. He knows. And if you want to keep me here, you'll end up having to beat up an old man. I think you're more honorable than that."

Dick looked over Bill's shoulder at Terra. Terra nodded.

Dick stepped to the side.

"Thank you." Bill headed for the front door. "Juniper will take care of you. If you want answers, you'll have to wait until I'm back. I clock off at 11:00 a.m. There are spare beds upstairs if you require rest, and Juniper's a hell of a cook. I highly recommend her homemade breakfast waffles."

"Thanks, dear," Juniper crowed.

"You're welcome, honey." He blew her a kiss. "See you soon."

In the wake of Bill's exit, a strange silence fell over the house.

Terra wondered what the hell she was doing here. She had planned to snatch information from the manor, and now she was in some stranger's house in the jungle. Judging by the look that Dick was giving her, he was thinking the same.

"So…" Juniper clapped her hands together. "Waffles?"

They sat around the kitchen table while Juniper busied herself in the kitchen. With no other transport to make an easy escape, Dick and Terra sat quietly and drank their drinks. Juniper presented two plates filled with mountains of waffles, complete with lashings of syrup and dollops of cream.

"Eat up. It'll make you strong." Juniper sat at the table, coffee in her hands, staring at the pair.

Terra asked, "Aren't you having any?"

"No, thanks." Juniper offered a warm smile. "I'm not one for calorie-rich breakfasts. Folks like you must need it, kind of professions you're both in." She nodded at their plates. "Please, tuck in."

Terra did. It hadn't been that long since living at her parents' house, but she had never eaten quite like this in the morning. The waffles were divine, the syrup and cream a perfect accompaniment. At first, Dick seemed unsure, then soon his plate was empty. He patted his stomach with two hands. "Outstanding."

"Thank you," Juniper replied, a strange look in her eye. She leaned forward, resting on her elbows. "You know that Bill's a good guy, right?"

Terra frowned. "What makes you ask that?"

"Well," Juniper half-shrugged. "Your kind is a suspicious lot. But, trust me, ain't no cleaner man than Willy Jr. Sure, he gets involved in some dodgy corporations, but what choice is there out on this island? Everything that man or woman touches is instantly rusted and tarnished. That's the nature of things. Power comes in knowledge, and knowledge helps the world go around."

Terra fixed Juniper with her gaze. "How much do you know about your husband's dealings, Juniper?"

Juniper laughed. "Everything, child. Ain't no secret kept between us two. We as thick as thieves."

Dick sipped his drink. "So why are we waiting for Bill when you can tell us what we need to know. Garcia. What do you know of him?"

Terra leaned forward. Outside, birds squawked.

Juniper sipped her drink, composing her thoughts. "Probably not half as much as you'd like."

Dick shrugged. "Anything will do."

Juniper nodded. "When we came to the island—oooh, some years ago now—we came with a vision of hope. Bill's father and mother, the original owners of this house, bought themselves into the booming economy, working their backsides off as laborers in the city. The hands of our folks, of greater, elder people who first migrated to the city shaped many of the skyscrapers now staining the island's skyline.

"Me and Bill were kids at the time. My folks lived in the city, founded the slums. Yeah, slums in a futuristic metropolis…crazy to think about, right? But not all folks can grow up rich. Everything gets dealt in balance."

Terra glanced at Dick, giving him a "are we going to get her life story" look.

"When me and Bill met," Juniper continued, "I was just nineteen. We both interviewed for the same job—a cleaner in the Atlantica National Bank—and though neither of us got the job, we stayed in touch. By then, Bill's parents had played enough of the stock market with their savings to grow a kind little nest egg —Atlantica grew so quickly you couldn't help *but* make money if you had it—and they moved out of the city and into the wilds." She motioned her hand around the bare, stripped villa. "Paradise, at last."

"Why here?" Dick asked, curiosity getting the better of him. "If so much was going on in the city, why come out here?"

"Because the city was darkening," Juniper replied. "Rates of crimes were rapidly rising. Murders were up. Drugs filled the holes and cracks in the pavements. We had to get away—especially after the island introduced the public versus private rule."

She muttered beneath her breath, something that sounded like, "Executioners." "The world fell to shit, and Bill's father—an honorable gentleman—was almost murdered one night when walking home."

Juniper drew a long breath. "The jungle seemed like the ultimate getaway. A small portion of paradise. At the time, only small sections of the jungle were up for grabs—rumors have been flying around for years about ghosts and haunting monsters in the trees, but we've never seen them. Bill's parents managed to grab this plot of land before the laws changed and the jungle became a protected reserve. Now we've got one road in and one road out, and it's ours. Our private pocket of paradise."

"What's all this got to do with Garcia?" Dick asked, a tad impatient.

Juniper sighed. "When mine and Bill's parents passed, we needed a new source of income. We searched all around for a job that suited us, but most of what was available was frontline working in guard duty or dealing drugs. Our skills don't lend to all that much. We're not as educated as our parents would have liked us to be.

"One night, Bill and I had a terrible argument. I won't bore you with the details, suffice to say that living on the breadline can aggravate a person's soul, and Bill found himself drinking alone in the city. He got talking to a man who promised him income with almost zero risk. He didn't like the 'almost,' but the offer sounded too good to refuse. He's been working the underground ever since."

Terra thought about all that Juniper had told them. "That doesn't line up. Ink has only been hitting the city for the last couple of years. You say it like he's been doing this for a decade."

"It hasn't always been ink," Juniper replied. "But it has been

Bill and the guys for a long time." She got up and boiled the kettle again, nodding to ask if the others wanted more. They declined.

"Bill is a loyal soul. He's worked his ass off for the last six years and made his way safely home each night. That doesn't mean that he doesn't hear and see things he shouldn't. Bill knows more than most what goes on at that place."

Dick shuffled in his seat, impatience on his face. "Garcia?"

"I'm getting there," Juniper replied. She returned to the table with a scalding tea. "When the product switched to ink, things changed. Manufacturing increased, and demand rose exponentially. Many moguls in Atlantica noticed the sudden demand for the city's latest craze, and the guys at the top of Bill's operation got hungry. The one thing they didn't have: someone from the inside able to help them.

"Bill was there. Late one night he went to speak to his bosses to discuss time off. It was then that he saw his first glimpse of El Justicia in the boardroom, standing with his benefactors. They told him to wait. He snatched glimpses of their conversation and spotted the blue AJS uniform hidden beneath the man's jacket. Their handshake sealed the deal. The AJS became integrated with the ink trade."

Terra looked at Dick as she asked, "Why wouldn't they be more careful? Why wouldn't they send him away before they discussed their business?"

"Why would they?" Juniper replied. "What have they to fear from a lowly grunt? If they discovered he said anything, they'd find him and kill him. Fear is a powerful weapon and keeps a lot of mouths shut.

"Bill knew better than to blab. Not only that, but who would believe him? You can't take anyone down in this place without evidence, and even if you have it, the laws and regulations on this island are so confusing that it's almost impossible to get a clean grab."

"You're telling me," Terra replied.

"Anyway," Juniper continued. "Over the years, Bill has seen increasing sightings of the one they call El Justicia. It wasn't until Bill got curious one night and looked up public AJS records to find out who the man really was. Captain Parker Garcia. A real piece of work."

Terra leaned forward, ideas stirring in her mind. "Juniper… You and Bill…you can help."

Juniper offered a weak smile. "I don't think you understand, Terra. By helping you, it would be to the detriment of our family. This job has been good to Bill. He gets paid on time, and he gets paid well. We'll soon have enough for our retirement, and that's just fine for us."

Dick returned the smile. "Oh, I don't think that's exactly true."

"Oh?" Juniper asked.

"No," Terra took over. "If that was the case, you wouldn't have told us half of what you just did."

Juniper gave a knowing nod. "You're keen observers."

Terra reached across the table and took Juniper's hand. "Juniper, whatever it is they're paying you and Bill, I'm confident we can find a way to subsidize your income. If you can help us bring down a corrupt cop and straighten the system, the city will have no choice but to reward you richly."

Juniper withdrew her hand, then moved to the window. She stared out at the trees. "Nearly five decades we've been living in this city, and all we've seen is trouble. It would be nice to know that we've done something positive to make Atlantica shine just that little bit more brightly. It's been years since I've felt anything like that hope in this place."

"So, you'll help?" Terra asked.

Juniper offered her a kind look. "You two must be exhausted. Why don't you settle down for a bit. You can discuss with my husband when he arrives back from his shift."

Terra looked at Dick.

Dick shrugged. "I could do with a nap."

Terra nodded. "Sure. Why not."

They headed upstairs and were soon asleep in twin beds with plain white cotton sheets. Dick snored soundly, mouth hanging open. Terra, on the other hand, found that she couldn't rest.

That worked out to her advantage when the hum of a dozen engines rumbled through the jungle.

CHAPTER SEVENTEEN

For a short while, the house was quiet.

Juniper had pottered around downstairs in the kitchen, cleaning up after her guests, though silence soon came. Dick's snores were the only accompaniment as Terra struggled to sleep, using the time instead to speak to APRIL.

What information have you that can confirm Juniper's story?

No specific information available. Extrapolating the information received by Juniper, one can assume a level of truth. I detected no falsity in her statements, and her record and her husband's are clean. The pair of them tell true, so one can assume that their stories will corroborate.

What about Garcia? Is there any information that can confirm his part in any of this?

APRIL was silent for a moment, then CCTV footage appeared in Terra's vision, displaying a montage of clips that showed Garcia arriving and leaving Kibble's Manor. The first entry was over a year and a half ago, around the time that Juniper had told her that Bill had first seen him. Though the footage didn't explore inside the manor, relying mostly on public CCTV footage from outside the place, it was clear that Juniper's story had an air of truth to it.

Can't you examine the CCTV footage inside the manor? Terra asked, already knowing the answer.

No CCTV footage is available inside the manor.

Because he's smart, Terra thought. *No weak links inside his industry. The moment you enter that building, all is blind, and anything can happen.*

She thought about the man dumped into the dumpster and the dead man in the chair.

How do we nail him? Terra asked.

I have no current answer, APRIL replied. **Garcia shows decorum and composure in public spaces. Evidence will have to be taken in private and brought out into the public domain. Garcia must slip.**

What are the odds of this occurring? Terra asked.

Seven thousand, six hundred eighty-nine to one, APRIL replied.

Wow. I didn't expect specific odds. Terra considered this. *Still... It means there's still a chance.*

She rested her head on her hands and stared up at the ceiling. A door was wide open nearby, leading out onto a small balcony that overlooked the trees. A couple of insects buzzed around on the ceiling, engaged in some primal dance.

The engines hummed.

At first, Terra thought it was more of Dick's snores. She glanced over, seeing him still fully dressed, asleep on top of his sheets. He looked peaceful, sweet. It was a side of Dick that Terra never thought she'd see.

The hums grew louder.

Approaching vehicles, APRIL announced before Terra could ask. **Twelve cars approaching.**

Terra sat up. She moved to the balcony and looked right,

where the dirt road trailed into the jungle. Dust kicked up in a steady cloud, and several cars rolled toward them.

"Shit." Terra crossed to Dick and shook his shoulders. "Dick. Wake up. Now."

"Huh?" Dick grumbled, rubbing his eyes. "What is it?"

"We've been outed," Terra announced. "Get up."

Dick sat up straight away, bags beneath his eyes. He strained his ears and caught the sound of the cars. "You sure that's not Bill coming home?"

Terra pointed at the balcony. Dick leaned out and saw the cars himself. He sighed, shoulders softening. "Just once, I'd like to sleep in a stranger's house without getting ambushed."

Terra readied her pistol and approached the bedroom door. Dick followed.

Warning, APRIL stated. **Enemy outside.**

Terra's vision switched to thermal, and outside the door, she spotted the form of Juniper, the shape of a revolver in her hand. Terra groaned. Dick almost bumped into her.

"Get going," he hissed.

Terra put a finger to her lip and indicated a threat was outside.

Dick scanned the room. The only exit outside was the balcony. He grumbled.

"Go," Terra whispered.

Dick strode over to the balcony. Terra waited a moment behind, long enough that she could slide a nearby chair beneath the door handle. She retreated quietly, meeting Dick outside, his fingers clutching the rail as he lowered himself.

Terra vaulted over the railing and twisted. She caught herself on the decline and hung for a moment, swinging. Dick worked his way to the top lip of the next window down, then shinnied. Terra followed. The grumble of cars grew louder as they approached the front of the house. Dust clouds flew around, large enough to mask them and provide cover.

Dick coughed. "Son of a—"

"Keep going," Terra warned.

Dick dropped to the ground, landing heavily on his feet. He stretched his back out, then offered hands to help Terra.

Terra, who was far leaner and more agile than Dick, swung to the window, then hopped down beside him. She crouched to absorb the impact of the landing, then threw a cocky smile his way. She patted his stomach. "You wanna lay off the booze, old man."

Dick smirked. He was larger, but he was by no means less fit. "Just get going."

Terra looked around them, finding it hard to see the jungle through all the dust. "This way. Come on. Into the jungle."

They ran toward the place they knew the trees to be. Something *crunched* around the dirt nearby, an engine suddenly exploding in sound beside them.

A mud-colored SUV appeared through the dust cloud, pulling up beside them. Their feet pounded against the dirt, racing for the trees, but the SUV was faster. The driver yanked the handbrake and drifted the vehicle until it spun and blocked their way, facing them head-on.

"Split up," Terra shouted, following with a wordless instruction. *APRIL, help me out here.*

APRIL obeyed, lighting up several bodies surrounding them both. Terra realized far too late that it had been a trap, spotting several vehicles with silent engines blocking the way in the dust cloud. "Dick!"

She spun, heading in the direction she'd sent Dick. She raced on, knowing that the minute the dust settled, the newcomers would catch them. She looked ahead and made out the shape of Dick running head-first into a group of people. A fight broke out. Dick swung, took out one person, then another. Someone attacked him from behind and cracked him on the head with a pistol, but still, he fought on.

Terra advanced, closing the gap until they came into view. Her eyes stung from the dust, but adrenaline coursed through her body and spurred her on.

Dick fell to one knee, a man beside him with a gun aimed at his head. Terra leaped at the man, raising her foot to strike him in the cheek.

The man went down.

A woman lunged at Terra. Terra spun. She struck the woman in the ribs, then dealt an uppercut to her jaw. The woman's eyes rolled back as she disappeared into the dust.

Terra hooked her arm under Dick's and helped him up. They stood back-to-back, facing the oncoming threats. Someone ran out of the cloud toward Dick at the same moment a man ran at Terra. They kicked, punched, twisted their bodies until they's erased the two threats.

"Which way?" Dick asked.

Terra, her direction lost, utilized APRIL's abilities to find the trees.

"This way," she declared, tugging on Dick's jacket.

They broke for the trees, accompanied by the angry sounds of the advancing mob. After a few feet, the trees came into sight. Terra had never been so relieved to see greenery. She passed into the bushes, Dick close behind her.

They only made it a short distance when APRIL warned, **Threat level: eighty-six percent. Ambush alert.**

Terra raised her weapon, pausing in her tracks. Dick bumped into her this time, sending her sprawling to the ground. By the time she picked herself up, over a dozen gunmen and women aimed their pistols at Terra and Dick.

"Lower your weapons!" a voice shouted.

They wore masks over the lower half of their faces, many with shaved heads, some with tight ponytails. Terra searched for the instigator of the command and found a familiar face staring back at her.

"You?" she asked.

"Me." The woman stepped forward, lowering her mask. It took Dick a few seconds to understand who he was looking at.

"Small world," Dick muttered.

CHAPTER EIGHTEEN

Terra glared at Harley, confusion written on her face.

"Surprised to see me?" Harley asked. "What did you expect to see, after fumbling down a fucking dumb waiter shaft and acting like nothing was amiss?"

Terra and Dick exchanged a glance.

"I thought we played it off pretty well," Dick offered.

Harley grinned. "Strange. I thought you were smarter than that." She pointed the gun at the house. "Inside. Now."

The group closed in, taking Terra and Dick by the arms. They saw no result in fighting off a dozen people with guns, so they complied as the dust cleared and they made their way back to the villa.

They passed Juniper on the way in, guilt riddling her gaze. She lowered her head, choosing not to make eye contact. Bill stood beside her with an apologetic expression.

"Your friends did well," Harley stated as they sat them both on the kitchen chairs and bound their hands with rope. "Perfect little songbirds chirping when asked."

Bill and Juniper remained outside the room, hidden from sight. Terra shook her head. "You're making a mistake."

"I don't think I am," Harley stated. "You're the one making a mistake. An AJS officer breaking and entering a private residence?" She tutted. "That's a sackable offense. Or, would be, were you currently on active duty."

The man beside Harley handed over a digital tablet. Harley scrolled down the screen, the light harshly accentuating her features. "AWOL from the AJS for almost a week. A raid down beneath the Laundr-O-Mat, and hasn't been seen since. Seems a strange coincidence to go on the run, doesn't it?"

Terra remained silent.

"I don't think you'll be very missed," Harley stated. "In fact, I think they'll be glad to have you back inside the station, except this time maybe behind bars for the crimes *you've* committed." She flashed a dark smile. "Or, perhaps, we can find another way to wipe your stain off the island."

"Windex," Dick offered. "That's always worked for me."

Harley didn't look impressed.

"Look," Dick stated. "You don't know what you're doing here. We're not alone in our objective. You take either of us out, and there are plenty more where we came from. As we speak, we're broadcasting to a trained network of operatives who will swarm down on you at the merest indication of danger."

Terra watched Dick, impressed. *See if they call our bluff.*

Dick continued. "As we speak, we're recording you, the footage streaming live to several secure servers that are storing the data. One wrong move, and it's over. You could kill us, but you can't stop the transmission."

"Oh, I know," Harley replied. She cocked her head and grinned. "Miss Terra Kris has the computer embedded inside her skull, doesn't she?" A few of Harley's comrades gave confused looks, clearly not involved in the knowledge.

"A sophisticated piece of gear designed by the hands of Atlantica's golden tech-heads. I'm aware of what you contain. I'm aware of the capabilities. It's unfortunate for you that my employer is also aware and is on his way to see you and to tinker with your wiring."

Terra's blood ran cold. "How is he going to do that? We've already severed all major connections with external controls."

"Tech is tech," Harley declared. "All it takes is a little know-how, and you can manipulate it without limits." She came closer, her warm breath heating Terra's cheeks. "Sit patiently, little duckling. The big man is on his way."

"Garcia wouldn't come here," Terra stated. "It wouldn't be worth the risk."

It was a long shot. Terra hoped that her announcement of Garcia as the kingpin would be highlighted or reflected in Harley's face. Instead, all that returned was a confident smile. "Close your eyes. Maybe get some rest. El Justicia will be here soon, and when he arrives, it'll likely mean your bye-bye. El Justicia doesn't like loose ends."

Harley whispered instructions to her nearest commander, then exited the room. She heard Harley muttering to Bill and Juniper outside. Then all went quiet.

Dick looked between the guards. "Okay, one or two guards I get, but isn't this a little excessive?"

The guards showed no sign of acknowledgment. Dick turned to Terra. "As deaf as they are stupid."

Terra smirked, her smile slipping when the room fell quiet once more, and they sat in silence.

APRIL. No pressure, but we need to figure a way out of this.

Working on it, Terra, APRIL replied. **Scanning databases and performing operational and situational analysis.**

Terra waited patiently as her vision filled with endless scrolling text and flashing imagery.

They waited for an hour in the relative quiet. While Terra waited for APRIL to offer some suggestion of escape, Dick hummed to himself, performing a medley of David Bowie songs that Terra remembered her father listening to years ago.

The humming seemed to annoy the guards, and as time wore on, their number thinned from the room. Harley appeared on occasion if only to offer a patronizing smirk. When Terra asked where their boss was, her reply was simply, "He'll be here when he gets here."

Still, APRIL scanned, pulling information that could be useful to the situation. It was only upon Harley's fourth appearance that the AI spoke up in Terra's head.

Harley Crawdad has a daughter.

Terra rolled her eyes. *Great. Who doesn't have a family?*

Information appeared in Terra's vision.

Ruby Crawdad, daughter of Harley Crawdad. Eighteen years old. Ruby Crawdad is currently serving a twenty-year sentence for her involvement in the murder of Robert Parkinson, an Atlantica attorney working the murder investigation of the head of Atlantica's Navy Fleet, Diana Benson.

That's a lot of information to digest, Terra stated.

Ruby Crawdad, APRIL continued, undeterred, **was suspected of direct involvement in the incident that led to Parkinson's death. They found a murder weapon with her prints on it, and though Ruby claimed she was innocent, she was found guilty of the charges, along with two of her friends.**

Damn, Terra thought. *That's dark.*

And also a false prosecution.

Terra's world jumped as she found herself inside the Atlantica

City Courtroom. Ruby Crawdad sat in the defender's seat, tears in her eyes. Her cropped red hair matched her red suit. In the seats behind her, Terra spotted Harley biting her lip and dabbing her eyes with tissues.

APRIL, where is this footage from?

It was illegal footage seized by the AJS. The originator of the content was David Turner, one of Ruby's close friends. A statement on AJS records indicates that he was performing his civil service to protect his friend. He received thirty-eight days in a cell for intrusion of public law process.

Why are you showing me this? Terra asked.

Because Ruby wasn't lying.

Ruby's voice magnified in Terra's ears. Her words were shaky, breathy. She stuttered, trying to catch her breath as she fought off the terrible charges pressed upon her. "I didn't do it. I promise. It wasn't me."

The judge, a large woman with deep-set eyes, turned her way. "Then would you like to tell us who did?"

Ruby shook her head.

The prosecuting lawyer raised a triumphant hand. "See! If you really were innocent, wouldn't you tell us the truth? Wouldn't you be able to give us the name of your accomplices? Wouldn't you be able to provide an alibi as to where you were and what you claim you did instead of ending the life of a man in his prime?"

"Settle down," the judge warned.

Ruby sobbed, then leaned toward the microphone. "I didn't do it."

The footage paused. APRIL zoomed in on the scared girl until she filled the screen. Data popped up around her face with the main headline reading: **Telling the truth.**

The footage vanished, and Terra reappeared in the kitchen. She sat there for a moment digesting the information as one of the gunmen raided Juniper's fridge and found himself and his comrade a can of Coke.

Terra glanced at the door, wondering what she could do with this information. Harley was around here somewhere. Wouldn't she want to know the truth about her daughter?

Another hour passed. The sun reached its zenith and the day grew warm.

The guards stationed themselves more sparsely around the house, encouraged by Terra's and Dick's lack of attempts to escape. When Harley next appeared in the room, examining her watch, Terra declared. "I need to pee."

Harley raised an eyebrow. "You can wait."

"Really?" Terra shook her head. "You think so? I haven't been since last night, and I need to go now. Would you rather I pissed myself and filled this room with the stink of urine?"

Harley considered this. She checked her phone. "Take her to the bathroom."

Hands grabbed Terra's arms.

Terra turned to find two men on either side of her. "No offense, but can I have a woman accompany me? I know what you guys are like the second you get a whiff of something that makes your loins stir."

One of the men smirked. Harley spotted this. "Any other requests, madame?" She rested her hands on the table and smirked. "I hardly think you're in any position to bargain."

Terra spat at her. Saliva pooled on Harley's cheek, a few splashes reaching her eye. Her face turned red, and she struck Terra with the flat of her hand. "You fucking bitch!"

Terra chuckled as the guys lifted her, hands untied. "Sorry, couldn't resist."

Harley swept around the table, pausing in front of Terra.

"I still need to go," Terra whined.

Harley smirked. "Then get your ass upstairs." She spun Terra, then pressed her gun into Terra's back. They made their way out of the room and to the stairs.

Halfway up the stairs, Terra paused. Harley shoved her, and Terra had to hold out her hands to stop her face from hitting the steps. "Oops. My bad," Harley crooned.

Terra pushed herself up again. When they made it to the bathroom, Harley waited by the open door.

Terra tried to close it.

"I don't think so," Harley stated.

"Really?" Terra asked.

"I know what happens," Harley explained. "Take your eyes off your hostage for one second, and that's all it takes to lose them. You could use the lid of the cistern to strike me. You could put shower gel in my eyes. You could climb out the window."

They both turned to the tiny porthole windows barely large enough for a ferret to run through. "You get my point."

"Fine," Terra replied. She sorted herself onto the toilet, using her jacket to cover her lap for some kind of dignity.

The two women stared at each other. Harley's eyes strayed when urine sounded in the toilet.

"You know…" Terra began. "We could always work out a deal, you and I. As you so rightly said, I'm AJS, which means I could work some cogs inside the machine that might benefit your cause."

Harley tilted her head. "Nice try. I have El Justicia for that. A man of his stature and power is plenty enough to keep me from finding myself behind bars for more years than I can count."

Terra finished and grabbed some toilet paper. "It's not enough for your daughter though, is it?"

Harley's expression froze. Her skin prickled. "What did you say to me?"

Terra continued nonchalantly. "Ruby is innocent. You know

that as well as I do, yet there she is, rotting behind bars, and only nineteen years old, too. It's a sad state of affairs not to be able to defend your only daughter from a lifetime of misery and abuse inside Atlantica's prison cells."

Harley took a step toward Terra, gun pointing at her face. "You tell me what you fucking know right now, or I'm painting these walls with your blood."

"That seems counterintuitive," Terra replied.

Harley grimaced, her phone vibrating in her pocket. She examined the screen, nostrils flaring. "Get up."

"Give me a second to sort myself out—" Terra started.

"Now," Harley commanded. "No bullshit. We need to go."

"Why?" Terra asked innocently enough.

"Because he's on his way," Harley replied.

CHAPTER NINETEEN

Terra walked to the stairs until a hand grabbed her collar and pulled her back.

"In here," Harley commanded, steering Terra toward a side room. Terra assumed this must be Juniper's and Bill's bedroom, given the decor and the scattering of family photos in small wooden frames.

Harley gently closed the door, her hardened expression fading to one of desperation. "Tell me what you know."

Terra met her gaze. "Ruby is innocent. She didn't have a thing to do with the murder of Robert Parkinson."

Harley's eyes shimmered. "I knew it. I fucking knew it all along. But how do you..."

"It doesn't matter," Terra replied. "What *does* matter is a nineteen-year-old girl is rotting in a jail cell, and she's innocent. More than that, one of the only people in this city who believes her and is willing to do something to prove that she's innocent is standing before you. Except I will likely be dead in a couple of minutes if I don't get out of here before El Justicia arrives."

Harley appeared suddenly torn. She glanced over her shoulder, then back to Terra. "I can't. If you escape, he'll kill me."

"Then come with me," Terra replied. "Come with *us*."

Harley raised an eyebrow.

"Dick's coming, too." Terra held her gaze.

"You're not serious?" Harley stated.

Terra didn't blink.

"Fuck…" Harley ran her hand through her hair. "Okay… okay…there has to be a way to make this happen…" She narrowed her eyes at Terra. "You're not bullshitting me?"

Terra raised her hands. "Ruby Crawdad, accused of involvement in the murder of Robert Parkinson, attorney of deceased Diana Benson? How would I know that if I didn't have information that could help?"

"Police records?" Harley replied.

Terra frowned. "Really? With what systems? I've been on the run for the last few hours, haven't I?"

Harley looked pained, trying to read Terra's face. Eventually, she decided. "We're short on time. If there's any hope of getting you out of here, you need to listen to every command I give you. To the letter. Do you understand?"

Terra nodded. "I do."

Harley let out a large sigh, running her hand once more through her hair. "Fuck. I can't believe we're about to do this…" She narrowed her eyes. "If you're lying, you're dead."

"If I'm lying," Terra replied. "We're probably both going to die."

Dick narrowed his eyes at the guard nearest to him. There were two of them now, which was a better situation than when eight had filled the kitchen. But with his hands bound and no weapon, there was little he could do to fight back.

"Cute beard," he muttered to the nearby guard, a man of about twenty years with a sparse crop of ginger hair on his face. "When you reach puberty, that'll really kick in."

The man's lip curled, fingers adjusting on his gun. He looked away.

"Don't worry," Dick continued. "Becoming a man isn't as bad as you think it is. You can drink all the liquor, smoke all the smokes, and get away with more shit than you ever could have dreamed. Especially in this city." He chuckled. "God, especially here. I guess that's why you're doing what you're doing, eh? Living the dream? Is this how you saw your life going?"

"Shut up," a voice warned from behind. Dick was aware of the second guard coming closer as he spoke. "Shut your fucking mouth."

"Or what?" Dick asked. "You'll tie me up and hold me captive?"

"We'll spray this room with your insides," the man replied.

Dick laughed. "I doubt that. If you wanted us dead, you wouldn't have waited hours for your boss to come, would you? You'd have killed us where we stood."

He drew a long breath. "No. If you wanted to, you could have killed us ages ago. But your boss wants to see us. Well, my money's on the fact he wants to see Terra. I'm caught in the middle of this shit. You know what I mean?

"I could be at home sipping on a smooth bottle of Blue Moon. Instead, I'm here sniffing the stale musk of a couple of has-beens who couldn't find their place in Atlantica so they had to settle for becoming some asshole's grunts." He shook his head. "A bad state of affairs—"

Something hard struck the back of Dick's head. For a moment, a burst of white light appeared in his vision, then faded. He looked up at the nearby guard who looked shocked at his comrade.

"Shut your fucking mouth," the voice from behind warned.

"Can't do that, friend," Dick replied. "Judging by the state of things, I only have a short time left to live. I want to air out all my dirty laundry the best I can and make the most of these last few breaths of oxygen."

Another crack in the back of the head, and Dick blinked at the pain.

"Easy, kid," Dick warned, heat flushing to his cheeks.

"Stand down, soldier," Harley commanded, sweeping into the room with Terra in tow. She pushed Terra into the chair, then commanded the men to keep their weapons trained on her. Harley crossed to a kitchen drawer and took something from inside that they couldn't see, though Dick could make an educated guess about the sharp, metal object she hid in her pocket.

The guard moved to tie Terra up again.

"Don't bother," Harley growled. "She's going to behave, aren't you, sweetheart?"

Terra narrowed her eyes, reluctantly nodding.

Dick sensed a change in the room that he was certain the others couldn't pick up. There was a vibe between the pair of them that he hadn't seen when Terra went upstairs. Outside, a car door slammed.

Dick's stomach dropped. Was he here at last? El Justicia, himself?

Harley grinned. "Oh, good. About time. The boss is here." She swept around the table and leaned toward Dick, whispering into his ear. "You better behave yourself. The pair of you. Your only hope of survival is to do exactly as we tell you to do."

As she spoke, Dick felt something slip into his hands. He gripped gently, the metal blade slicing into his palm.

"Got that?" Harley asked.

Dick nodded.

Terra sat patiently and glanced at Dick. She didn't say a word, but a sudden burst of adrenaline spiked through his body. Something *had* happened up there, and soon they would try to escape.

All he had to do was wait for the command.

And hope that the pre-pubescent ginger bearded boy wouldn't get a bullet in him before he had a chance to run.

Dick gently slid the blade against his bonds.

The front door squealed open. Terra heard it from down the hall.

Footsteps pounded the wooden floors, the sign of heavy boots. His shadow reached them long before his form did, and as he appeared in the kitchen, Terra's stomach curdled.

APRIL, are you recording this?

Terra waited for a response, but none came.

APRIL?

Ident...the...cannot...records...

Terra grimaced against the explosion of static sound that filled her head. APRIL was trying to speak to her, but she could only catch snatches of the conversation.

APRIL? What's happening?

The man stood at the head of the table, arms folded, looking down at them both. He wore a military combat vest, his arms exposed and glistening with sweat. Tattoos of tigers and snakes and dragons lined his biceps, but it wasn't this part that drew Terra.

The mask the man wore was jarring against the rest of his appearance. It was plain white, a simple latex cast that looked as if it was waiting for him to paint it. The mask covered his entire head, leaving only his eyes visible in the hollows. Eyes that Terra instantly recognized.

"Garcia," Terra stated.

The man behind the mask remained unfazed as if he hadn't heard Terra speak. He bore no firearm, only a utility belt with hidden items in the pockets. "Well, well, well... What do we have here?"

He rested his hands on the table, leaning over to look into Dick's and Terra's faces. The world was quiet around them, the air thick with tension. "A former cop and her investigator sidekick." Beneath the mask, Terra sensed, rather than saw, his grin. "Two thorns in my side ready to be dispatched in one stroke of the sword."

He stood to his full height, then reached for his mask. He pulled at the latex, Terra's eyes narrowing as she focused on his face and waited for what she knew was already true. *APRIL, are you recording this?*

A high whine of static was her response.

Terra's heart rate doubled.

The mask peeled off like a second layer of skin. The man beneath was slick with sweat, his balding head allowing large droplets to slide down his skull and drip off his nose. Moisture darkened his goatee, and keen eyes fixed on Terra as a triumphant smile peeled back his lips. "Officer Kris."

Terra narrowed her eyes. "Garcia."

Garcia grinned. "I find it a shame that we have to meet under such dire circumstances. You've been a pain in my ass since you first joined our division."

"Yeah, I have a habit of sniffing out scum and eradicating it from the face of the city," Terra replied. "Like a good cop should."

Garcia laughed. "Yes. You're certainly good at that. It's a shame, really. You could have done great things for our division. You could've climbed the ranks, accelerated your way to the top, made a keen mint for yourself if you only knew how to play the game."

"What game is that?" Dick asked. "I'm killer at Monopoly."

Garcia fixed him with a mirthful glance. "The Game of Atlantica." Garcia leaned back against the counter and folded his arms. "The greatest game on Earth."

Terra's lip curled. "The Atlantica Justice System isn't a force for corruption, Garcia. It's a force for good. The whole point of having an organization that can stop the bad guys is to make this city shine the way it should.

"Atlantica is a place of possibility, a place for good, and it's because of people like you that the rest of us can't realize the dream." She shook her head. "How many other crooked cops are out there doing what you do?"

"More than you can count," Garcia replied. "Of course, it wouldn't benefit me to list them all, but we all watch people like you closely."

"People like me?"

"Cops with wild dreams of an impossible world," Garcia replied. "Cops who grow up with dreams of a world free of crime. Children who have grown up on a diet of movies and songs that show a world that *could* be, not the world that is." He snorted derisively.

"Terra…Your parents did you no favors preparing you for this world. The AJS isn't a force for good. It's a force to turn a blind eye. Yeah, pick up the baby cases of asshole drug users and stop the hookers from roaming the streets, but leave the big sharks to their devices, and you'll be able to live happily.

"Everything would have been fine if you hadn't tried to turn me in. You'd be living your best life, feeling like you were making a difference." He wiped sweat off his nose. "You've made this really difficult for me."

"Good." Terra still tried to listen for APRIL but heard nothing. She shook her head to try and clear the static.

Garcia smirked. "In pain?"

"It's nothing," Terra replied.

Garcia laughed. "It's something." He took his mask from the counter and turned it inside out. A flat metal device adhered to the center of the skull. "A blocker. Specifically designed for the weapon inside you that you stole from us. This handy little gadget can block any frequencies from the OSCaR program within fifty feet."

He gave Terra a knowing look. "I'm sorry if I ruined the footage you were hoping to grab of me. Just means you can't run to the AJS and turn me in." He came closer, looming over Terra. He bent, his face close to hers. "I like you, Terra. You've got skill, you've got spunk. But, my God, if you don't get on my nerves. How about we make you a little deal, huh?"

He took his cell phone from his pocket and showed Terra the screen. The Satiata cash app was open with a seven-figure amount typed into the box. "Yours if you want it. Take a flight, get the fuck away from this island, and leave us be. I know how much you've always wanted to visit Europe, Asia, America... All yours now. Hop a flight, and get the fuck out of Atlantica. We don't need you here."

Terra imagined what it would be like, to finally leave the island and see all the sights she'd been longing to see. A born native of the island, Terra had longed to see the world, but duty and dedication to her career had always prevented her. How could she hop off to Spain or Brazil when there was so much here that needed dealing with first?

Her head flashed a montage of landmarks; the Eiffel Tower, the Pyramids of Giza, the Amazon rainforest, Bangkok, Dubai... What would it be like to be in a part of the world where justice was treasured, the law upheld, and private residences didn't create sanctuaries for criminals?

Then she recalled the Atlanticore in her back. It didn't change her decision, but her blood ran cold as she realized that it wouldn't matter if Garcia let her live after accepting the offer. She'd likely die as soon as she left the island. On top of that, Garcia would have evidence to blacken her family's name.

Terra shook her head. "No."

Garcia gave a knowing nod. "I thought you'd say that." His face looked pained. "Terra, I'm telling you that this island isn't for your kind. You're fifty years too late. If you want to save the world, go back and time travel to before the legislation protected the dark and the dirty. The world was a different place back then. Justice reigned supreme, but now…

"Now it's different. Atlantica isn't the island you think it is."

Terra considered this. "That doesn't mean it can't be."

Garcia gave Terra a pitying look. He nodded. "Very well. I knew that's what you'd choose, but I hate to say that I'm still disappointed." He extended his hand to the nearby guard. "Gun."

The man handed over his rifle. Garcia checked the magazine, chambered a bullet, and sighed. "I'm sorry, Terra. I'm sorry… whoever the fuck your friend is. This is the end of the line for you both."

He lined up the rifle, finger tensed on the trigger. "Goodbye."

Gunfire exploded. A voice called, "Now!" Terra kicked back in her chair and toppled to the floor.

CHAPTER TWENTY

Terra rolled to the side as gunfire rained around her.

The sound was deafening, interspersed with static from APRIL inside her head. She rolled beneath the table, using the thick wood as a shield. From here, she could see the legs of the guards and Garcia. Garcia had staggered back and slumped by the counter. His rifle lay on the floor.

Terra reached out with her foot and hooked the strap. She brought the gun toward her, barely able to hear Harley nearby calling for her to follow.

Terra shuffled back, working her way out from the table. She looked at Dick's chair, expecting to find him slumped over. But it was empty.

Blood slicked Dick's palm. As Terra kept Garcia distracted, Dick worked away at the bonds at his wrist, using small movements to sever the threads. He knew he needed to work faster. Terra was keeping him talking, but there was little time to spare.

Then the gunfire started.

Dick jerked his wrists, managing the final cut to free himself. As Terra dove back, he twisted to the side, running for the nearby guard. His shoulder folded into the man's stomach, winding him and crashing them both against the wall. The cupboards shook, crockery and unknown items crashing and breaking inside.

"Follow me," Harley called. Her face was creased, pistols raised as she covered the pair and shot at the guards pouring into the entrance. Garcia bent against the counter, face screwed in pain.

Terra scooted out from beneath the table, hunting for him.

"Up here, bright eyes," Dick announced.

Terra glanced his way, a smile momentarily appearing on her face.

"Enough of the reunion," Harley called, tossing Dick a pistol. "Cover yourselves. This way."

She ducked through a door behind her, and Terra and Dick followed. They made out the shouts of the other guards. A few ran to Garcia's side. They filled the halls ahead of them but fell when the three started shooting in their direction.

"We're surrounded," Terra called, spotting the guards approaching from the outside. "We'll never get out of here."

"Can't you use your AI friend?" Dick covered their six and fired at two shooters hiding in the doorway.

"It's compromised," Terra replied, the static beginning to grate on her now. Harley continued forward. "Enough chat. This way."

She took a hard left, clearing the way ahead of them. At the far side of the room was a door that led outside. Harley yanked it open, then ducked behind the door. "Shit."

"More of them?" Terra asked.

"Yep." Harley frowned. "This might have been a bad idea."

"Not the ideal time to figure that out, is it?" Terra asked.

Dick closed the door behind him. The wood instantly filled with bullet holes. "Why have we stopped?"

Harley drew a deep breath, gaze fixing on Terra. "You ready?"

"I think so." Terra wasn't so sure.

Harley gripped the door handle, then gave a swift tug. Bullets sprayed the wall beside her until gunfire came from above. "What fresh hell is this?" Harley asked.

"Run!" came Bill's voice from the floor above. "Now! Go!"

Harley, Terra, and Dick broke into the open, Harley leading them straight for one of the scattered SUVs. They picked off their attackers, Terra sparing a glance up at the window to see Bill and Juniper in neighboring windows firing down at the guards.

They reached one of the SUVs. Harley hopped in the driver's seat and fiddled with the wiring. A moment later, the engine rumbled to life.

The windows smashed. Terra and Dick ducked down in their seats. Harley pressed her foot to the gas, the wheels spinning on the dry and dusty ground.

Then the SUV was rolling. Engines roared to life around them. Terra spared a glance back at the house, dismay filling her stomach when a stray gunman turned to Bill and sent a bullet up at his window. Bill's figure flopped forward, then tumbled out of the window, coming to an abrupt stop as his body smashed into the ground.

"No…" Terra breathed.

"You might want to strap in," Harley barked as she jerked the steering wheel and fought the uneven road.

Terra looked at the safety belt, then to Dick. They both smirked. They twisted around in the back seat, keeping their heads low as they aimed their weapons at the chasing cars.

Bullets *dinged* off the SUV's frame. Terra let the rifle rip, catching the front tire of the closest car behind. Trees blurred by them, and birds took wing as chaos ensued. The damaged SUV veered off to the side and smashed into a tree, leaving a thick ribbon of smoke trailing into the sky.

Terra ducked, a bullet skimming over the top of her head.

Dick shouted, "This isn't what I had in mind when I said I'd accompany you to the manor!"

"What?" Terra called. "You didn't expect to climb down a dumb waiter, be held hostage in the middle of the jungle, then chased by SUVs? I thought you lived an exciting life."

Dick smirked. "There's exciting. Then there's…whatever this is."

Harley turned over her shoulder. "Enough of the sass, you two. If you could keep them off our back, you'll be doing us all a favor."

Terra aimed the rifle at the next SUV. She took out the windshield and the driver. A backseat passenger wrestled for the steering wheel, but Dick shot and took him out, too. The car skidded and rolled, causing a barricade to the other vehicles.

Gunfire followed them, but Harley managed to get some distance from the group. The jungle road curved sharply to the left, and they were out of sight.

Terra and Dick turned to the front, letting out a sigh of relief. Terra felt buzzed, her body filled with adrenaline and a whole mixture of biochemical cocktails that APRIL wasn't paying attention to. She held up a shaking hand, wondering whether it was the road or her body's reaction. *APRIL, you there?*

Reporting for duty, APRIL replied chirpily.

Dick was watching Terra closely. "You okay?"

"Yeah," Terra replied as APRIL began balancing the chemicals in her body. For a short while, Terra worried that Garcia's signal jamming would permanently affect APRIL. She was glad that wasn't the case. "Yeah, I'm fine."

Harley shook her head, looking at the pair in the rearview. "You guys know how to throw a party."

"Don't we know it," Dick replied. "There's a reason no one invites me to their birthdays anymore."

Despite the calm washing over Terra and the worry etched into Harley's brow, they all started laughing.

When they reached the edge of the forest, Harley slowed.

"What's going on?" Terra asked.

"I want to be sure there isn't an ambush waiting." Harley leaned so far over the steering wheel her nose nearly touched the glass.

The trees began to thin. On the other side, they made out the vast stretch of farmland that painted the landscape for miles around. Harley slowed to a crawl, then veered toward a dense crop of trees. "Fuck."

A cluster of three vehicles barred the way. A handful of men and women stood around, rifles strapped to their chests, cigarettes between their lips. If a memo came from the house they'd just left, they hadn't received it yet.

"How do we want to do this?" Dick asked.

Harley chewed her lip. "We have two options. The hard way, or the harder way."

"Both sound fun," Dick stated.

"We need to keep moving," Terra replied. "Is there space to ram straight by them?"

Harley considered this. "That would be the harder way. It's quicker but messier."

"The alternative?" Dick asked.

"I try and speak to them and get them to shift under the illusion that I'm still operating under Garcia's commands."

Dick and Terra looked at each other. "The harder way it is."

Harley nodded. "Have it your way."

Dick turned to Terra. "You going to tell me why she's helping us escape?"

"It's a long story," Terra replied. "Hopefully one that we'll have time for real soon."

"Let's hope," Harley stated as she stomped on the gas pedal and turned out onto the road.

They picked up speed rapidly, the SUV's engine raging as they sped toward the barricade. The guards turned at the sudden sound, staring ahead with curiosity that soon melted to panic. They jumped out of the way, shouting and hollering as the battered SUV poked its nose in the tight space between two of the blocking cars. They spun out of the way, slowing the progress of Harleys' SUV, but not enough to hold them back.

"Sorry, folks," Harley called. "Emergency meeting at HQ. Got to go!"

The men and women shot in answer.

Terra and Dick ducked back down.

"At some point, I'm going to be able to spend a day without fearing for my life," Terra stated. "And that day will come when Garcia's behind bars, and the AJS is a little cleaner than it currently is."

Dick shrugged. "You hope."

Terra looked at him.

"Why do you think I work solo?" Dick asked.

Harley laughed. "Not working solo right now, are you, champ?"

The sound of bullets quieted as Harley steered them along a thin strip of tarmac bordered by head-high crops.

"I don't like her," Dick replied. "She calls me out on my bullshit."

"About time someone did." Terra smirked.

"Where to?" Harley asked.

Terra thought about it. This was the first time she'd had a moment to think about what would come next after the escape. Several places sprang to mind, but only one that she thought would fit what they needed right now.

"East coast," Terra replied. "The Miriam Midnight Aquarium."

Dick raised an eyebrow. Harley gave her a concerned look in the rearview.

"Is now the time for leisure?" Harley asked.

"Just drive," Terra replied. "We'll find a place to dump the SUV en route."

Harley gave an agreeable nod, then focused on driving. Dick leaned over to Terra and whispered, "Seriously, what's with the fish?"

Terra smiled and looked out her window.

CHAPTER TWENTY-ONE

"This is bonkers," Harley replied. She put her hands on her hips and stared around the strange apartment, water flowing below them, fish dancing around in their brightly colored schools.

Dick looked below his feet. "I can't even begin to describe how uncomfortable this makes me."

"You don't like fish?" Terra smirked at finding a possible nub of discomfort for Dick.

"It's not that," Dick replied. "More that I don't like standing on glass above an indescribable volume of water. What if it cracks? What if it breaks?" He narrowed his eyes at the water. "There are people down there, can't they see you?"

Terra shook her head. "One-way glass. We can see them. They can't see us."

"I wouldn't trust that," Harley added. "Sounds like someone set you up to appear on some hidden camera porno channel."

Terra rolled her eyes. "It's fine. It's all above board. The guy who owns this place knows I'm from the AJS, so he's hardly going to fix me up and put himself in a position to spend a night behind bars." She motioned to the couch. "Please, take a seat."

Harley and Dick took positions on either side of the couch.

They sat far apart from each other, looking uncomfortable as they studied the space.

"How do they clean the glass?" Harley asked, choosing to watch an ocean sunfish sweep nearby.

"Divers, I presume," Terra replied nonchalantly. She opened the refrigerator and produced three beers. She chucked one to Dick, then one to Harley.

"You drink beer?" Dick asked.

"After today I do." Terra sat on the edge of the glass coffee table, face shadowing. She raised her bottle. "Here's to you, Bill."

Harley raised her bottle. Dick narrowed his eyebrows. "Bill dobbed us in, and you're praising him?"

"He helped us escape," Terra replied.

Harley nodded. "Don't judge everything by what you see. Bill didn't want to lead us to you, but he had no choice."

"Everyone has a choice," Dick replied.

"No." Harley shook her head, guilt flooding her features. "Not when I've got my pistols pointing at his face."

Dick's lip curled. "I don't like you."

Harley nodded. "I know."

Terra broke the tension. "Enough of this. We need to figure out a way forward. A lot happened last night, and thanks to Garcia's scrambler, I still have no evidence to pin him to the exact crime that he confessed to us in person."

"Yeah, what happened there?" Dick asked.

Harley looked between them. "Am I missing something?"

Terra narrowed her eyes, allowing APRIL to figure out if Harley was hiding anything or not.

Telling the truth.

Terra ran a hand across her face. "Thanks to Garcia, I've been fitted with a highly advanced artificial intelligence system specifically designed to assist Atlantica Justice Officers in their work. The technology is experimental, but saved my life after an incident that blasted me away from an exploding car. I almost lost motor and neuron function.

"Over the last few weeks, I've managed to sever the controls that link my internal database to any external influences, which Garcia doesn't like. It seems he's created a scrambler to prevent me from accessing APRIL when I'm in his proximity. Ordinarily, I can record and scan and identify anything around me as long as it's registered with the system, but in his presence, I was unable to."

"Hold on…" Harley replied. "APRIL?"

"Advanced Police Relationship Intelligence Liaison," Terra replied.

Harley's brow creased. "Didn't El Justicia say OSCaR?"

"Officer Security Companion and Report," Dick added with a smirk.

"Why so many acronyms?" Harley replied.

Terra thought about this. "OSCaR was the initial codename registered in the database. I don't know when they switched it to APRIL, but it certainly fits the bill a lot better. I stick with APRIL, though OSCaR keeps coming up again like a bad furball."

"I prefer it," Dick chipped in.

"Of course you do," Terra replied. "You're a sexist pig."

"Easy." Dick held up placating hands. "I'm nothing of the sort. If anything, I like the original name because it's clearly what the designers would have gone for. APRIL is an afterthought. OSCaR is the first."

"Well, it's not your decision." Terra sipped her beer. She made a sour face. "How do you drink this stuff?"

"Fast," Dick replied.

Harley chuckled.

"The point is, we're screwed," Terra continued. "We had him in our sights. We had him right there, and we have no evidence to pin on him, still." She shook her head. "This shit is impossible."

"Sounds defeatist," Dick stated.

Terra glared at him.

"Enough of *your* drama." Harley set her beer on the table. "You promised me you'd get my baby free. What's the deal with that? Who are you and what do you know about Ruby?"

Dick raised an eyebrow.

Terra fixed her gaze on Harley. "Ruby is innocent."

"I know," Harley replied. "But how do you?"

Terra described the courtroom footage she'd seen in her head, archived video held in the depths of the AJS database. Harley's face fell when Terra described the video. Tears pricked her eyes when Terra explained APRIL's lie detection scan, which determined Ruby told the truth.

"If they have technology like that in existence, why don't they use it in the courtroom?" Harley asked.

"Because this whole city is dirty," Dick replied. "You think they want people held accountable in court? No. If someone brings in the head benefactor of a social change conglomerate for cases of solicitation or sex trafficking, do you think they want him behind bars? No. They want him out there, providing money for good causes.

"Atlantica is designed to protect the corrupt. Ever since the private versus public debate at the end of the twentieth century, this has become a haven for scumbags. By employing lie detectors in the very place where they make decisions, they'd be betraying the whole damn point of Atlantica."

Terra threaded her fingers through her hair. "What's the fucking point in us trying?"

Dick gave her a strange look.

"Seriously," Terra replied before downing a large volume of her drink. "All this effort for what? So that the system can continue to breed filth? It's a Möbius strip of shit. It's endless.

"I've spent most of my life fighting for justice, and where has it got me? Here. On the run. Trying to bring down someone who sits in a seat that has power and influence. Someone who tried to kill me because I was digging around his business. Fuck…" She shook her head. "What's the point? Change doesn't happen here. We're always three steps behind."

Dick sat beside Terra. "Well, that's a pile of pessimistic bullshit."

"I mean it," Terra replied. "What's the point? What's the point with any of this. You've been in PI work for years, and you've seen the shit we *can't* deal with. How do you keep so upbeat?"

Dick glanced down at himself. "Me? Upbeat? I think you're looking at the wrong guy, Terra." They chuckled. "Look, this place is rigged against us, but that doesn't mean we don't make a difference. Think how much worse it would be if we weren't out there doing what we do. Think of the lives that would be lost if we sat in silence and let the assholes take over.

"The reason people still flock to this island is that there *is* hope here. There *is* a place to call home. Buried beneath all the shit is a jewel of a city. Sometimes it's down to the underdogs to go digging and find the buried treasure, y'know? Sometimes the littlest among us can make all the difference."

The room was quiet a moment, only the gentle *hum* of tank filters filling the air.

"You calling me little?" Terra asked.

"Stature-wise, yes." Dick laughed. "Heart-wise? No."

Terra looked into Dick's face. "I've never seen this side of you. You're usually a stone cliff face staring back at me. I didn't know you had a gooey center."

Dick scoffed, then sipped his beer. "Don't go telling everyone. It'll ruin my street cred."

Harley cleared her throat. "Hello?"

Terra nodded. "Right. Ruby is innocent, you can tell from the footage. APRIL's scan backs it up. With that combination, we can more than likely find a way to get Ruby out of that place."

"More than likely?" Harley asked. "That's not good enough."

Terra considered this. "It's a guarantee."

"How do we get started?" Harley asked.

"First things first," Terra replied. "You need to give us some information. If we hold any hope of getting through to the justice system, we need to get Garcia behind bars. You were working on the inside. You had a direct line to him. What have you got on him that we can use to bring him to justice?"

Harley glanced at her cell phone. Terra and Dick exchanged a glance.

"Shit," Dick muttered.

"Can he trace you on there?" Terra asked.

"No," Harley replied. She frowned. "At least, I don't think so. I turned the phone off the moment he came into the house."

"APRIL, can Garcia trace a phone that isn't on?" Terra asked.

Negative. Cell phones must be active to emit a signal or frequency.

"You need to keep that shit off." Terra pointed at the phone. "The minute you turn that on, he'll be onto us."

Dick's expression hardened.

"What?" Terra asked.

"Do we?" Dick looked at them each in turn, an idea forming on his face.

CHAPTER TWENTY-TWO

"I've got her." Slim stood in the doorway to Spencer's office, the heat of Gina's stare at the back of her head.

Tobias Spencer looked up from his computer screen, failing to hide the Internet tabs, which showed what appeared to graph the rises and fall of the stock market and brightly colored ads of naked women in compromising positions. "Hmmm?"

"Terra Kris," Slim replied. "I've got her. She called my cell. Asked me to meet her. I'm driving out to her location now."

A broad grin spread across Tobias' face. "Good girl, Newman. I knew I could count on you."

"Justice before mercy, sir," Slim replied.

A strange shadow fell across Spencer's face. "What did you just say?"

"Justice before..." Slim cut off as Spencer quickly stood and crossed over to her. His hand clamped across her throat as he pressed her against the wall.

"Are you trying to get yourself in the shit?" Spencer hissed.

Slim's eyes were full of innocence. "What did I do?"

Spencer examined her closely, then released his grip. "Word of advice. If you want that promotion, I'd avoid phrases like that.

That slogan was outlawed years ago when the island finally found its correct trajectory and set a course for freedom."

Slim raised an eyebrow. Spencer stepped back. Slim rubbed her throat.

"Sorry. I didn't know." Slim adjusted her uniform.

"Where did you pick it up from?" Spencer asked.

"I…" Slim considered this, too smart to give Spencer the truth. "I made it up. Thought it was appropriate."

Spencer returned to his chair. "Tell me what you know of Kris."

Slim outlined her conversation with Terra, detailing the meeting location that Terra gave her. She told Slim that she had the golden bullet, the thing that would bring Garcia to his knees. She needed Slim's help, and Slim was to come alone.

"Like that's going to happen," Spencer replied darkly. "You've done well coming to us. I'll assemble your team. You bring us Kris, and you've fast-tracked your way to the inner city. Captain Garcia will be most pleased with you."

Slim nodded. "Very well." She turned to leave, then stopped when Spencer spoke.

"Oh, and Slim," Spencer called.

Slim turned over her shoulder.

"Nice ass." He smirked, clearly proud of himself as he dialed a number and waited for someone to answer.

Slim walked past Gina, the receptionist's eyes boring into hers the whole way. She knew what the other woman was thinking. If Gina and Spencer were screwing, she wouldn't appreciate having any kind of competition for his affections.

Bile rose in Slim's throat. She composed herself and swallowed it, then headed out to speak to her team.

She had a big night ahead of her.

Imani sat in the quiet of her apartment, a wide grin on her face.

Finally...after all these months...

It was always great to hear from Terra, but that didn't throw away her skepticism. Years of training had honed Imani's skepticism to a keen edge. She knew never to trust anyone or anything and to make your decisions based on gut instinct and action.

Terra could have shit the bed again on this one.

Imani didn't think so. Terra had conviction in her voice. She had a plan, and that plan would finally bring about the end to Garcia's reign—if all went well.

The night before had been a waste, yet another dead end. Following Garcia had resulted in losing him and ending up trailing Spencer as he headed back to the AJS precinct where Leonie Black should be heading up the department. It was easy to lose a suspect when you couldn't see through glass.

All of that was about to change.

Imani flipped the APRIL glasses over in her hand, examining the smooth plastic texture. The lenses still had the protective film, and the fresh smell of new technology rose to meet her nostrils.

She exhaled slowly, feeling a sudden flutter of butterflies in her stomach. She knew what had happened when Terra had last worn these.

Would the same thing happen to her?

CHAPTER TWENTY-THREE

The suburbs were quiet and empty. Night had fallen, and the sleepy street basked in the glow of the streetlights.

Terra moved like a shadow, clinging to the darkness, accompanied by APRIL as she avoided detection and closed in on the house. She navigated her way to the back and looked in through the metal rails topping the red brick wall.

APRIL, scan for threats.

Scanning now.

Terra glanced around, able to see the hot red shapes of people in their houses. In the neighboring properties, she saw couples sitting on couches, some in bed, a few in their home gyms, and one or two in their offices. Across the road, out the front of the house, was a van with two people sitting inside, unmoving.

Terra knew they were there for her. Since she had gone missing from the AJS line of duty, she knew they'd stationed watchers at the front of her parent's house. She had to remain quiet and incognito if she were to make this happen successfully.

Terra scaled the wall.

She hopped into the garden, landing neatly behind a hedge.

The lawn stretched before her, a security light topping the back door. *APRIL, disable the security light.*

APRIL was quiet a moment, then announced, **Security light disabled.**

Terra's heart beat fast. *Shit. If I've been able to wield this power, what would happen if this kind of technology got into the hands of the wrong people?*

She sprinted across the lawn, still expecting the light to catch her in the act like some rowdy cat. Instead, she made her way to the house without incident. *Are we still in the clear?*

APRIL performed a scan. **Clear.**

Terra reached the back door and slid her key into the lock. She twisted the handle and let herself inside.

Navigating the dark of her house was a cinch. She'd lived in this place most of her life and knew every creak and contour of the villa. She passed through the back hallway and entered the kitchen, a familiar shadow waiting for her on a stool at the kitchen island.

Terra crossed over in silence, wrapping her arms around the figure. "Hi, Mum."

Another shadow moved nearby, more arms entering the embrace. "Hey, Dad."

Padding feet came down the stairs. Terra's blood ran cold as paws skittered across the tile. She hissed for Skooch to come toward her, hoping that in acknowledging the dog before any kind of surprise elicited a reaction, she could keep Skooch quiet. "Here, Skooch. Mama's home."

The dog sprinted at Terra, leaping into her waiting arms. Skooch smothered Terra's face in wet licks as the Papillon showed her affection and grunted. "Good doggo. Hey. Hey, there. Nice and quiet now, please."

"Terra, what the hell is going on?" Maria asked, her voice soft in the dark. "You've got us worried."

"Yeah," Michael added. "If you're in trouble, you need to tell us. We can help you."

"No," Terra replied. "You can't help. Not on this one. It's bigger than you could imagine."

Terra placed Skooch on the floor, the dog choosing to run circles around her feet.

"I wanted to check that you guys were okay," Terra offered. "And to say that…Tonight might possibly be one of the toughest missions of my life. I wanted to say that…I love you both very much. I hope I've done you both proud."

Maria's breath hitched. Michael rose from his chair and stood beside them both. He put his arms around Terra. "We've never not been proud of you, Terra. You don't have to think of your life as 'serving' us. We'd have loved you no matter what you grew up to get involved in. You're our little girl, and we'll always love you."

Maria's tone was different. "What are you doing tonight? Tell us what's going on. If we can help, then let us. You don't have to do anything alone."

"She's not alone, are you?" Michael replied for her.

Terra shook her head, then realized they wouldn't be able to see. "No. I'm not alone. And you can't help. This is something that I have to do on my own. You taught me how to hold my own in Atlantica. You taught me the value of fighting the big fight. I just want to let you know that the big fight has come, and no matter what the outcome, I love you both. And thank you."

Arms folded around Terra again. In the darkness, tears fell from Maria's cheeks. In the darkness, Skooch clawed at Terra's leg.

In the darkness, Terra knew that no matter what was to come her way, she was about to give her everything to serve the island that she loved.

CHAPTER TWENTY-FOUR

Terra watched from the balcony, looking down on the bustling street.

From four floors up, she could see Atlantica unfold beneath her. Neon lights from cars, restaurants, and clubs colored the ground. Headlights and street lights illuminated the world. Across from her, skyscrapers rose like giant monoliths into the foggy Atlantica sky.

The wind was crisp, prickling her flesh. Her heart was steady, and she didn't know if it was because of APRIL's meddling of her chemistry or her sense of inner calm.

"APRIL…" Terra murmured.

Yes, Terra?

Terra narrowed her eyes, honing in on a group of young adults down below, smiles on their faces, a skip in their step. "What happens in the event of my death?"

Death is considered by many to be the end. There are religious factions that believe in an afterlife. Religions such as Christianity—

"That's not what I meant," Terra interjected.

Apologies, Terra. Could you be more specific?

"What happens to you? When I die, what happens to your software?"

Under normal circumstances, electrical impulses sparked in neural communications power the OSCaR program. Synapses create micro electrical pulses that enable its functionality. In your case, a small piece of Atlanticore powers the system. In the event of your demise, the manufacturers assume that the program will shut down and become defunct. The Atlanticore may or may not change that. We don't know.

"Can they transplant you into another brain?" Terra questioned, unsure why it was bothering her so much to know.

In theory, this is possible, APRIL replied. **If the components are kept intact, there should be no reason why the hardware cannot be transplanted and powered inside another host.**

*Host...*Terra thought. *That's all I am.*

That's not all you are, APRIL replied, picking up on her thoughts. **You are a friend.**

Terra's ears pricked up. *A friend? To an AI? Now I've seen everything.*

"APRIL..." Terra started.

Yes, Terra.

"What are the odds of our plan working?" Terra rested her elbows on the balcony rail. If someone were to sneak up behind her now and shove her, there would be no way she'd survive the fall, even with APRIL to accompany her. No amount of tech could turn people into a god.

Based on the limited information I've collected, combining CCTV scans, biometrics of individuals involved, time signatures, and available resources, I'd settle you in at around thirty-three percent.

Terra nodded. "Yeah. I figured."

She looked up the street, staring out toward the west of the city, wishing she could see what was going on from where she stood without the need for technology. She imagined Dick sitting on the bench and waiting, a proxy to confuse and distract.

"Be careful out there, Dick." Terra drew a deep breath. "As much as I hate to admit this, I'm going to need you around for a little while longer."

Terra closed her eyes and let APRIL send her vision elsewhere. Her stomach twisted in knots as the junction came into view, a lone figure sitting shadowed on the bench.

The wooden bench numbed Dick's ass.

He sat patiently, waiting for the oncoming approach of the storm. They'd set their plan, but it was complex. Dick wondered what lay ahead of them and how far they could push their luck.

In the distance, AJS sirens blared.

Dick drew a long breath, then took a packet of cigarettes from his pocket. He tapped one out, then stuck it between his lips. He lit it and breathed in a thick plume of smoke.

"Just when I started to cut down…" he muttered.

People strode by, unaware of the investigator playing his part. Cars ripped by, and the smell of restaurant dining was in the air. Behind Dick stood a large golden statue of an elephant surrounded by three calves. The gold gleamed and caught the headlights of the cars, the elephant's trunk reaching for the bowler hat on its head.

Paid for by one of Atlantica's most influential Indian moguls, the statue depicted the cross between Indian and European cultural arts. "Bollywood meets Charlie Chaplin" was how they'd originally described the piece when erecting it over a decade ago.

The AJS sirens grew louder. Dick saw the first flashes of the cruisers as they cleared the block and closed in on his location. Five cruisers appeared, speeding closer. They zeroed in on him, and the closest cruiser screeched to a stop at the curb.

Officers poured from the doors, faces that Terra would have recognized, but Dick had no clue. A tall, dark woman strode toward Dick, her pistol trained before her. She looked around for someone she couldn't see before settling back on Dick.

"Terra Kris. Where is she?" the officer asked.

A man appeared from the cruiser behind her, a sweat-flop mess of a man with a cocky glint in his eye. "Newman. What's the problem? Where is she?"

Officer Newman turned over her shoulder, then scanned the surrounding area. She pointed her gun once more at Dick. "Have you seen Kris?"

Dick nodded. "Yeah. I've seen her."

Officer Newman waited for an answer that didn't come. "Where is she? The information you give will go a long way to helping the Atlantica Justice System."

"What if I don't want to help?" Dick smirked.

"Newman! What's the problem?" the smarmy officer called again, impatience coloring his face.

"Just a second," Newman called. She turned to Dick. "If you're withholding information that could be useful in helping us bring in a wanted criminal, we'll have to bring you in for obstruction of justice."

"I know." Dick replied flashed his badge. "I've been in this business a long while."

Newman cast a strange look at Dick, a smile whispering at the corners of her lips. She mouthed, "Is she safe?"

Dick gave a subtle nod.

"Newman!" the man called, growing more agitated as the other cops waited for something to occur. "What's the holdup—"

Gunfire erupted nearby. One of the cruiser's windows smashed. Bullets *dinged* off the metal, leaving small sparks in their wake. A car tire burst.

The cops ducked out of the way, finding shelter behind the cruisers. They looked for the source of the gunfire, eventually discovering the woman standing on a balcony in a nearby apartment building. Another few gunshots rang out before she disappeared back inside the building.

"10-71 on the sixth floor," an officer cried. "Suspect out of sight, armed and highly dangerous. All units respond."

Dick sat coolly on the bench, unaffected by the whole ordeal. He raised the cigarette to his mouth and took a satisfying draw. Officer Newman ducked by the side of her cruiser. She flashed a look at Dick, then grinned as he crossed his legs and exhaled a plume of smoke.

Harley ducked inside as a volley of bullets streamed toward the balcony.

The French doors shattered, leaving a trail of glittering glass. The bedroom was empty, the lights off. She ran for the door, knowing that she had very little time to execute her commands effectively.

This had all better be worth it.

She ran through the pristine kitchenette, then exited the apartment. When in the hall, she tore toward the stairwell and made her way up.

Her feet clapped on the hard tiles, echoing around the stairwell. After a moment, voices called up, more footsteps joining her as the AJS began their hunt.

She made it to the rooftop and opened the emergency exit. Gravel crunched underfoot as the night chill prickled her skin. There was a network of steel vents and tubes around her, and she navigated through the metallic labyrinth until she reached the lip of the building.

Her heart stopped.

The jump wasn't far, but the drop was substantial. The raised lip of the building gave her a perfect platform to make the leap, but this was a maneuver she hadn't been able to practice ahead of time.

"You've got this…" Harley muttered to herself. "For Ruby."

She took a few steps back, still able to hear the shouts of the AJS behind her. It was impossible to work out if they knew she was on the roof or if they'd go straight to the apartment. Either way, she had to jump, and she had to jump now.

She lowered her head and leaped.

The street was to the left of her as her form soared over the dark alley between buildings. She landed heavily, folding into a safety roll but jarring her shoulder, too. She sprinted toward the edge of this rooftop and made the second jump without hesitation.

Now at least two stories lower, and a couple of hundred feet away from the source of her original crime, Harley took a left and peeked out over the city.

The officers were swarming the building. AJS cruisers blocked the street. Lights flashed, and nosy neighbors poked their heads out to see what the fuss was.

Harley lined up her pistol and took a final shot at the cars. The trajectory would catch them off-guard, and hopefully, the single bullet would send them all into a state of confusion as she disappeared down the fire escape and into the shadows.

Her aim was true, bursting yet another tire.

Still got it.

Harley swung over the edge of the building and lowered herself to the fire escape. Her footsteps weren't quiet, but they were swift.

She touched down in the alley and ran to their meeting point.

Captain Tobias Spencer growled with delight as he emerged onto the sixth floor.

His minions were dotted around him, making way as he strode toward the apartment. They had her. They *must* have her, surely. Terra thought she had one up on them, firing down at the officers while they attempted their ambush.

"Where is she?" he barked as a couple of officers lowered their heads. They'd destroyed the room, glass littering the floor and holes in the ceiling from the AJS bullets. Spencer looked around the apartment as if waiting for the punchline to some joke. When he realized that there was no capture, his face grew red. "Are you fucking kidding me?"

"She ran upstairs and onto the roof, sir," a young officer with pronounced cheekbones stated. Spencer hadn't bothered to learn many names of the officers, knowing that his position would only be temporary. "Well, go and chase her, then."

"We did," the officer clarified. "We lost her."

Spencer nodded, eyes darkening. He swung his fist, catching the young recruit in the cheek and sending him sprawling to the floor. The other officers shuffled awkwardly.

"You *lost* her?" Spencer growled, already knowing what this would mean when he reported back to Garcia. "How the fuck could you lose her?"

The officer didn't answer. There was no point. Instead, he rubbed his swelling cheek and remained on the floor.

"Shit." Spencer walked to the window and looked out over the balcony. His eyes caught the stray man sitting on the bench, one hand in his pocket, the other playing with his cigarette. "Bring me that guy. I want him brought in for questioning."

Terra waited until she received the signal, one lone message from Dick Chambers with the word, "Done."

Terra smirked. *Good.*

She crossed to the dressing table and sat. Its surface held a handful of scattered colognes and pictures in frames. She picked up one of the frames and looked into the face of a juvenile Garcia. He had hair back then, the goatee yet to kick in. His eyes were full of light, his eyes free of lines.

Terra switched on the cell phone, then placed it on the vanity.

CHAPTER TWENTY-FIVE

Garcia's heart was racing.

He sat in his office, a clean, modern room with white walls and comfortable seating. His desk was grand, his computer one of the latest that Atlantica had to offer. The Tynamo logo sat in the middle of the reverse of the screen, illuminated in white. At the far side of the room, a coffee machine sat, and there was room in here to swing a cat, which made Garcia very happy.

He had worked his ass off to get here. Life as a Justice Officer for the Atlantica Justice System was tough. Each rise up the ranks was a trial by fire, and Garcia had earned his place here. With each promotion, the city had revealed a little bit more of itself to him, his job taking him to all four corners of Atlantica.

At first, he had gotten into service for the glory of it all. He loved the idea of sweeping the streets clean and earning recognition as a man who could get things done. His mother had died when he was only two years old, and his father raised him single-handedly, doing his best to rear an independent child who could handle himself.

Garcia learned the value of being tough. During his first few years on the AJS force, he broke the rules and got in trouble more than he cared to admit. His record showed several breaking and entering incidents and violating the public versus private rules of the city. It was frustrating. He wanted to get shit done. Why should a brick wall stand between Garcia and bringing a criminal to justice?

Over time, he learned how to play the game. His partners hated working with him, but they kept him in line. His superiors kept close eyes on him, giving him opportunities to lead as a way of teaching responsibility and trying to shape him into what they wanted to be.

And that's what he became…partly.

By the time Garcia earned the rank of captain, he'd already started networking with some of the scum within the city. Ink was taking off as the next big hit of the underground drug user world, and Garcia could see its impact almost immediately. On his final street mission, Garcia attended to a small group of ink users who had gotten *way* too high and were causing trouble in one of the public parks. Garcia took them down with ease—those who are high tend to have their wits barely about them—and ended up in talks with a woman who tried to beg for her freedom with offers of a *lot* of coin.

By this point in his life, Garcia had learned that the phrase "crime doesn't pay" also went both ways. Justice didn't pay, either, and as hard as he worked, he was tired of seeing other individuals around him grow their stocks and investments and become grossly rich.

Garcia was still living in his two-bedroom apartment, no girl-friend to his name, and no more hair on his head. He wanted more. When his father had passed away just one week prior, it filled Garcia with shame that he could barely cover the man's medical bills.

In the darkness of that park, Garcia made the drug-addled woman squawk. He found out further information about where the operation was running and set the woman free. His partner eyed him suspiciously when he asked where she had gone, and Garcia had no response.

One week later, his superiors promoted him to Captain.

His rank had several benefits, one of which was the opportunity to manipulate the departments and control the staffing. When calls came in, he could have his officers look the other way, as long as there was a reason to justify it. He worked hard, ensuring that he was getting shit done and that the powers above him would never think to bat an eyelid over his dealings within the AJS force.

One night, he visited the address stated by the lady in the park.

The place was a flea-bitten shack on the edges of town—broken timbers, cracked windows, the roof all but caved in. Garcia entered the property and walked in darkness, listening for activity.

A set of stairs led down to the basement level, and in the dark solitude of that tiny house, he found them.

The operation was basic, but it was still impressive. Flasks bubbled, liquids boiled, the smell of burning filled the air. As Garcia walked down the stairs, proudly displaying his AJS uniform, four pistols fixed their gaze on his chest.

He raised his hands. "I come in peace."

Skepticism crossed their faces. They glanced at each other.

Somehow, impossibly, Garcia managed to talk to them. The head of their group, a tiny man with a crop of crazed hair and a hooked nose named Alan Olsen, spoke to him, interested to hear what the cop had to say about what he could offer.

They came to an arrangement. Olsen and his team would create the product and sell it. Garcia would provide their protection. As long as distribution remained within his district, he could cover them.

Thus began one of the most successful drug operations Atlantica had ever seen. Garcia's bank account swelled instantly as the popularity of ink grew. Over the following months, his team dealt with the impact of the thriving trade, bringing in users and always avoiding any raid that could lead to the discovery of its manufacture.

As the operation grew, Garcia's team bought property across Atlantica, spreading their reach far and wide. The Laundr-O-Mat was one of many operations where ink was made in bulk and delivered to its customers. Though, as the operation grew, Garcia had grown more skittish.

Fernando Cross and Gary Clark were a means to an end. Garcia loved watching his income grow in his private bank accounts. The power of controlling his units filled him with joy, and late at night, he would look into the night sky and wish his father could see him now.

He moved to a new apartment, a luxury suite on East and Fifth. His evenings and downtime became a glorious concoction of strange women, cocktails, and card games.

His grip over the AJS only grew. His team was *good,* and they did as asked, no problem, never once batting an eye or drawing attention to any strange dealings Garcia found himself in.

He was far too careful for that.

Then, one day, his partner grew greedy.

Garcia had never wanted to be the sole operator of the ring. He was happy being a silent shepherd, keeping the sniffing hound dogs away. However, one dark and rainy night, Garcia had attended Kibble's Manor at the request of Alan Olsen. The other man claimed there was an issue with their distribution chain that needed addressing.

Olsen aged a lot in one year. His hair had turned from boyish blond to metallic gray. The bags beneath his eyes were heavy and dark, and his back showed signs of developing a hunch.

Garcia knew something was wrong the moment he walked into the room. There were too many of them there, men and women standing nearby, watching and waiting. Olsen gave

Garcia a speech about their financial arrangement and how since they'd grown to a mammoth monopoly, Garcia's share of the riches was far too extortionate. Garcia's lips thinned. The tension grew. Olsen's staff reached for their weapons.

Garcia was quicker on the draw. One well-aimed shot at Olsen's chest saw blood blossoming on the cotton of his shirt. A dozen guns aimed at Garcia, who threw his on the floor, then held up his hands, shouting, "If you shoot, your careers are over.

"I have dirt on each of you, written down in a private system that will activate the moment the AJS announces my death. Not only that, but none of you know the depths I've gone through to keep you safe from the law. One shot and this all ends. Your cash is gone, your life is gone, and all that you know will disintegrate before your eyes."

His heart raced. He expected at least one gun to fire, but after a round of exchanged looks, they lowered their weapons. They asked questions about what to do without Olsen, and it was then that Garcia picked up the torch to continue the operation.

It was difficult at first, picking up those threads. After a few months, things settled down. Garcia grew his team around him, operating as the head of the operation, ensuring that things carried on smoothly in the absence of Olsen. Or, so he thought...

It was late one night when he got the telephone call, a deep voice with a Texas twang dialing directly through to his cell phone, twisting all that Garcia thought he knew on his head.

There was no way out after that.

Not that he would want a way out, of course. With the amount of money that Garcia was making, the world opened to him. He kept his seat at the AJS, keeping up the facade of dutiful captain. From his seat in the AJS, he could watch over up-and-coming recruits. He could start grooming officers to work as his replacement.

That part of the operation turned out to be harder than he originally planned.

Spencer was great, but in no way was he "captain" material. He was a lap dog, not a leader. Imani Thomas and Terra Kris had shown promise, but their moral compasses were far too strong. Other officers had come and gone, and as time passed, Garcia grew more and more irritated. What was the point in having all of this cash if he couldn't go out and spend it?

Then the bitch started narrowing in on his operation. Terra reported Garcia to the powers above. That night had turned everything on the dime, raised Garcia's hackles, and demonstrated the fragility of his operation. Garcia could pack it all in and hide. He could take his hard-earned cash and retire, find somewhere in the city to be free of responsibility…

But he'd come too far, and he didn't want to hide. Now it was a game of pride.

Garcia stared at his computer screen, reading through Terra Kris' file. The information wasn't useful. So what that she had both her parents, one of them working within the forensic team of the AJS. He couldn't get to them…their home protected them. No doubt Terra would have warned them to be careful, too. How could he use them for leverage?

She was a great cop, and that was the problem. Terra knew how to work the system, and she got things done. More than that, Garcia's plans to remove Terra from the system had failed spectacularly. The glasses were supposed to babysit her and keep her every movement on his radar—that had failed.

The "accident" was supposed to take her out of the picture completely.

That had failed.

The installation of the AI was supposed to be the final babysitting effort. This cross-functioning experiment would see Terra under the AJS's ever-watchful eye while also trialing new software that the powers above were keen to explore.

That had failed, too.

Garcia growled as he stared into Terra's eyes on the screen.

The bitch was a problem that needed taking care of. If he didn't act fast, he knew things would only get worse. She was intelligent. She had skills. She had contacts, and now she had the whole fucking AJS database in her mind, coupled with abilities far beyond a typical officer...

And she had "right" on her side.

"Fuck..." Garcia mouthed as his cell phone lit up beside him. He picked it up and answered, his voice tired and gruff. "Garcia speaking."

A modulated voice returned on the other end, robotic and genderless in its sound. "Location triangulated."

Garcia raised an eyebrow. He knew this already. Spencer had updated him, told him that they'd located the bitch and would soon bring her to him. "I know. I have a team out there rounding her up as we speak."

A snort came down the line. "No. You haven't."

Garcia sat up, eyes fixing on the computer Terra as the voice detailed the information. His hands shook, rage swelling inside him. Through the glass door at the end of his office, he saw fellow officers walking around, the best of the best, heads deep in their current investigations.

Garcia ended the call, nostrils flaring. He opened the bottom drawer where his latex mask was. He slipped it into his pocket, then rose from his desk.

If a job wants doing, sometimes you've just got to do it yourself.

His eyes lingered once more on the digital image of Terra Kris. His lip curled.

He was so focused on his anger that he didn't watch the officer's eyes track him as he left the station.

CHAPTER TWENTY-SIX

Terra examined the luxury penthouse suite, strolling around in the dark. The place was minimalist and cold like Garcia. The only extravagances were in the huge, cinema-style TV screen, as well as several computer and video game consoles. The kitchen was pristine, larger than three typical kitchens, and Terra wondered if Garcia ever used this space to entertain others.

I doubt it. Would be a stupid maneuver to get too close to people in this place. Considering the line of work Garcia finds himself in.

She thought back through every interaction she had with Garcia. When she first arrived at the station, she had been in awe of the man. He was stationed several leagues above her, had the command of the AJS at his fingertips. Terra could shut her eyes and see herself in his position, and at first, that's why she thought there was such strange energy between the pair of them.

Garcia retreated from Terra, hiding behind layers of AJS bureaucracy, positioning other officers in front of her, dishing orders with a whisper and an unseen hand.

Only on a few occasions did Terra ever cross Garcia's path, and those were minimal. He was shrouded in mystery, and it wasn't until things started to unfold that she found herself drawn to him, keen to find out more about his life and what he did outside of his AJS role.

Part of her wished she'd never learned.

Part of her was glad she did.

Your heart rate is accelerating, APRIL offered. **Balancing biochemistry.**

"Thanks, APRIL," Terra replied, reaching for a photo frame that showed a young Garcia standing beside a man who couldn't have looked less impressed to be there if he tried. Garcia was beaming, a young recruit into the AJS. The man's brow was heavy, his eyes dead. If there was a more stark example of one-way love Terra had seen in her lifetime, she couldn't think of it. She wondered where that man was, what happened to him...

Garcia en route. Data jumping in three...two...one...

Terra groaned as she whirled into the eyes of the external city CCTV footage. Garcia hopped down the AJS stairs and headed to his vehicle. He was alone, which Terra was thankful for. If it was to come down to a showdown of wits and talent, she knew that she would come out on top every time. The wolf climbing the hill would always be hungrier than the wolf sitting on top.

She tracked the vehicle as it rolled down the city streets. She couldn't see inside, but she could imagine Garcia's face. He was coming for Terra, drawn by the signal emitted from Harley's phone.

It hadn't taken much for Terra to track down Garcia's private residence—a quick look into AJS staff records revealed all—but she had to admit that she was surprised at the lack of security built into this place. APRIL had performed a rudimentary scan and shut off the cameras at their source. Other than that, it was fair game inside the apartment.

Garcia's place wasn't far from the station, and soon APRIL cut off the camera feeds as Garcia exited his vehicle and made for the building. When the jingle of keys came from the front door, Terra ensured that she was standing in the hallway, waiting.

Garcia closed the door behind him, looking ghastly in the thin slivers of light that leaked through the windows of the nearby rooms. His bald head shone, his AJS gear looked far too small for a man who had gotten desk-lazy and grown something of a gut. Her eyes flickered to his pistol strapped around his waist, but he showed no sign of wanting to use it.

"Garcia," Terra stated flatly.

Garcia offered an amused smile. "Kris. What are you doing here? You know I could have you arrested for breaking and entering into a private residence—much worse since it's your former captain's, one of the seniors of the inner-city precinct." He shook his head.

Terra narrowed her eyes, mulling over her words. She had to admit that she was surprised he hadn't put his mask on. Then again, this was his house, and in the eyes of the law, *she* was in the wrong here.

"You tried to get rid of me," Terra stated. "That didn't work."

Garcia frowned, playing the professional actor. "What are you talking about? We've been worried sick about you, Terra. One minute you're recovering from severe bodily trauma, the next you've outed an ink operation, the next you're on the run."

He tilted his head, sincerity in his eyes. "Where have you been?" His eyes flashed to her pistol. "Why are you holding your pistol? Are you going to shoot me, Terra?"

Terra's jaw clenched. *Clever man, indeed. Playing the fool so video evidence has nothing on him. APRIL, are you still there?*

Affirmative, Terra.

Lie detect Garcia.

Garcia is telling the truth.

Terra's brow wrinkled. That couldn't be possible. *She* knew the truth, and Garcia was just playing games.

It hit Terra, then. Had Garcia programmed APRIL somehow not to detect his falsities? Had he installed a failsafe in case he ever found himself in such a situation as this?

APRIL, is Garcia telling the truth?

Affirmative.

A smirk appeared on Garcia's face as if he could tell Terra's inner struggle.

"You're a smart one," Terra announced.

Garcia narrowed his eyes, hands rising into the air as Terra brought her pistol up. "Terra, we can talk about this. You've been through a lot. The trauma to your body and mind is more than anything anyone on Atlantica has been through. We trialed experimental technology to give you a life, but clearly something has gone wrong. Let us help you."

He took a step forward. Terra took a step back.

"Please, Terra," Garcia continued, slowly advancing on her. "You're a good officer. You're just in a bad way. Let me help you. We can get you back up and running.

"Maybe we can find a way to remove the AI from your mind, give you your freedom back. All it would take is a call with the original manufacturer and some strings with the surgical team, and you could be free from all of this. Free from the turmoil and suffering that you're putting yourself through."

Terra backed into the stairs, nearly falling over. She adjusted, jabbing the gun in Garcia's direction. He stopped, hands steady in the air. "Please, Terra. You don't have to do this."

Terra looked into Garcia's eyes, momentarily drawn into the sincerity of his charade. Was she turning crazy? Was the software messing with her mind, making her see things and make decisions that weren't grounded in reality? It would make sense. No one could go through what she went through and come out without any kind of scarring.

"No…" Terra muttered.

Garcia tilted his head again. "I can help you."

He was lying, wasn't he? Hadn't Terra skirted around his operation and discovered whispers and breaths of Garcia surrounding the ink ring? Hadn't she invaded Kibble's Manor and shot down the elevator shaft and found herself in a stand-off with Garcia in the middle of the jungle?

"You're lying," Terra replied. "You're lying. I saw you out there. You tried to kill me."

"Am I?" Garcia took a step back as Terra jabbed the gun at him again. "Think about it, Terra. Recall the footage. Ask yourself what was really going on when you think that all happened? I've been in the office all day. I've been pulling AJS strings and attending to a homicide on Twenty-First. I've been nowhere near you."

APRIL, show me the footage of the ink operation from this morning.

Footage not found.

Terra frowned.

Show me 12:15 a.m.

Terra's mind went dark. She was in a bedroom, the lights off, only the dull red glare from an alarm clock keeping her company. From outside came the sounds of the city as Terra wrapped herself tightly in a bundle of duvets and snuggled into her snooze.

"No…" she breathed.

"See?" Garcia replied. "Whatever you think happened is nothing more than a fabrication of reality. The trauma does strange things to you. Couple that with the hardware installed in your mind, and you've got a recipe for hallucinations and misguided reality."

He lowered his arms, looking at Terra in pity. "We can fix this, you and I. We can bring you back to the force. Make you what you hoped to be. Help you make a *real* difference to Atlantica."

Terra held Garcia's gaze, searching her memory, and not that of APRIL. In her mind, she saw the table in Bill's house. She could feel the rope knots around her hands. She could smell the foliage, the humidity in the air.

Her stomach knotted in anger at the sight of Garcia removing his mask as though he was shedding a second skin, APRIL turning to disrupted static in her head. If he was capable of doing that…if what she knew to be real *was* real, what else was this man capable of?

"Bullshit," Terra grunted. "No." She advanced on Garcia until he retreated from her, fear in his eyes. Her pistol was inches from his face, finger tensing on the trigger. "No more games. You can try and get away with all of your shit, but I'm not falling for it. Confess. Confess and let the world know what it is you've done."

To her surprise, Garcia jumped at her. The weight of his body hit hers, and she fell backward, landing on her ass before his momentum forced her flat. Her head hit the hardwood floors. Sparks hopped in her vision. The next thing she knew, her head filled with painful static.

She opened her eyes. Garcia triumphantly straddled her body. He held his mask in his hand, a thumb on the metallic scrambler. His grin was shark-like, a rabid look in his eyes.

Terra realized what he'd done. If anyone were to review her footage, they would see a dutiful officer defending himself. Maybe the smack on the head would disrupt the circuitry anyway. She wouldn't have a defense to hold herself to.

Garcia had won.

Garcia twisted the pistol from Terra's hand and turned the gun on her.

CHAPTER TWENTY-SEVEN

Dick kept a level gaze as the officers approached him. His cigarette had burned to a nub, and he sent the final dregs away with a single flick of the finger.

"Please come with us, sir," a young officer with a developing mullet commanded, his shadow lengthening over Dick.

"No," Dick replied coolly.

Another officer joined the young buck, Newman, the officer who had first approached Dick when the team arrived on the scene. "What have you got to do with all of this?" she asked, gaze boring into Dick.

"I don't know what you mean." Dick drew a deep breath. "What's the problem, officers?"

"We'd like to bring you in for questioning," the young buck continued. "Please follow me into the cruiser, sir. We have some questions about what occurred here tonight."

"What?" Dick chuckled. "Some random gunman takes a few shots at you, and suddenly it's my fault? What do you think you're going to get from me? I'm an innocent bystander, sitting and watching the world go by." He dramatically checked his watch. "I've got places to go. People to see."

"Sir…" the young officer attempted.

Newman interrupted him. "Sir, your cooperation would be greatly appreciated. It doesn't seem like a coincidence that you're sitting in the place where we got a tip for a target to be, then a crazed gunman shoots at our units. We're lucky that no one got hurt or seriously injured here tonight."

Dick shrugged. "I don't play with coincidences or luck, either. I've been sitting here minding my business. Unless you have any real evidence that I'm in some way connected with what happened, you'll have to take me in kicking and screaming. As far as I was aware, this is Atlantica, and we have free rein to roam around in public spaces, no matter the hour or what kind of occurrences happen to take place nearby."

He scratched the back of his head. "That was strange though. Have your guys had any luck locating the perpetrator?"

Newman's jaw clenched. The officer's radio buzzed. Dick could faintly hear, "Bring him in, dammit!"

Newman sighed. "I'm sorry, sir. No more warnings. You're coming with us."

The woman approached Dick, hand hovering over her gun. Dick remained still, hands in his pockets. "You're making a mistake."

"I don't think so, sir." She took his wrists and slapped handcuffs on him. With the help of the young officer, she guided him toward the nearest cruiser. "You have the right to remain silent. Anything you say can and will be used against you in a court of law. You have the right to speak to an attorney, and to have an attorney present during any questioning. If you cannot afford a lawyer, one will be provided for you at government expense."

"What's my crime?" Dick asked. "You can't arrest me without stating the crime."

"Obstruction of justice," Newman growled, shoving his head into the back of the cruiser. She slammed the door behind him. When the young officer moved to the passenger seat, she stated,

"No. I've got this one. Tell the captain I'll bring him to the precinct, cell 4D."

"Yes, ma'am." The officer headed toward the apartment, where a man stared down from the balcony at the vehicles.

Dick adjusted himself in the back, attempting to make himself more comfortable. It was difficult trying to sit with your hands bound behind your back. "You're making a mistake," Dick declared.

"Shut up," Newman announced with a glance in her rearview. She hit the gas, then initiated the lights and siren. She sped from the scene, cars moving out of the way as she raced through the city toward the precinct.

Six blocks away from the scene, Newman cut the lights and siren. She merged with the traffic, taking a right and heading away from the station. She glanced in her rearview, checking that no one was behind her before glancing over her shoulder and giving Dick a wide grin. "You okay back there?"

Dick nodded, shifting his hands out of the cuffs that she hadn't fully secured. He rubbed his wrists, the skin pink where the metal had rubbed. "You could have been a little more gentle."

"I didn't fasten them," Newman replied.

"Sure seems like you did." Dick smiled. "Do you think we lost them?"

"I'd say so." Slim scanned the approaching streets. "Which way?"

"Left," Dick replied.

Newman signaled into the correct lane, then turned when the lights changed to green. The streets thinned into single carriageways, and as the neon lights of a lowly casino came into view, she turned down the side and into the quiet parking lot.

High rises surrounded them, trapping them in the parking lot like insects in glass jars. Newman found a space, then parked. She shut off the engine, and they sat for a moment in the dark.

"We're going to freak out a lot of addicts leaving the premises," Newman offered. "One sight of the AJS and those guys go nuts." She looked around the lot. "You sure they're coming?"

"Absolutely," Dick replied, hoping that everything would go to plan.

A drunk couple appeared down the alley, leaning heavily on each other as they laughed at a joke neither Dick nor Newman could hear. When they neared the back entrance, the man saw the cruiser and paused. The woman followed his gaze. Their laughter died as they shuffled quickly inside the premises.

Newman shook her head. "They know."

"They know what?" Dick asked.

"The moment they enter that building, we can't get to them." She sighed. "It's like when we were kids, and we'd play games of tag. There was always a safe house somewhere where the others couldn't get you, a place that made you invincible. That's all this city is—one big safe house to criminals. If we chase someone down the street and they hop inside a private building, they're suddenly immune. It's bullshit."

"You're preaching to the choir," Dick replied.

Newman glanced in the rearview. "You're a PI. The rules don't apply."

Dick raised his eyebrows.

"All right, I get you," she continued. "They *do* apply, but you get to care less."

"Right on," Dick replied.

While they were both staring at the back entrance to the casino, a loud knock came on the cruiser door.

Dick jumped, relaxing when the face stared in through the window and beamed. "You scared the shit out of me."

Harley climbed into the back of the car. Her neat ponytail was disturbed into scruffy wisps, and there was a flush in her cheeks. She gasped for air, chest heaving as she recovered from her run. "That was a lot farther than I figured it was."

Newman looked between the seats. *"You're* the gunman?" She turned to Dick. "Gun*man?*"

"I never said it was a man," Dick clarified. "That was you and your boys who assumed. I'd never be quite so sexist."

Harley looked confused.

Newman stepped past the moment. "I'm Officer Jenna Newman. Friends call me Slim. And you are?"

"Harley Crawdad," Harley replied.

"You never said you were Slim," Dick replied.

"I never said we were friends." Newman smirked. "Terra can call me that. Maybe you, too, Harley. Dick, we've got a long way to go."

Dick smiled. "Nice."

"Enough chin-wagging," Harley replied. "Shall we set off before the AJS realizes what the fuck has happened and comes after us?"

"Right." Newman shifted the vehicle into gear.

"Hold on." Dick leaned forward. "This vehicle is AJS property, right? Won't it be trackable by your guys? When they realize we're not at the station, they're going to come straight after us."

"Shit." Newman nodded. "You're right."

"Good catch." Harley turned to the window and scanned the cars in the parking lot. "Which ride you feeling?"

Dick smiled, following Harley's gaze.

Newman narrowed her eyes. "No. You can't be serious. I'm an Officer for Justice. I can't go around stealing cars."

"Well, you better turn a blind eye," Dick replied. "Because I'm about to break the law, and I don't think that after all we've been through tonight, you're going to want to arrest me."

Dick exited the vehicle despite Newman's protesting groans and complaints. He dug his hands in his pockets and strolled around the lot, moving toward the spots cast in the farthest reaches from the casino's neons.

There was a selection of vehicles up for grabs, some with

gleaming paintwork and engines that could make a dragon run in fear. A few looked considerably worse for wear which gave Dick the impression that their owners, while frequent casino attendees, didn't have the best luck and spent more money than they earned out.

Dick stood by a sleek black BMW that almost hid in the shadows. He approached the driver's side door and scanned his immediate vicinity to ensure that no one watched. Confident that he was alone, he crouched and produced a lock pick from his pocket. He jimmied the pick into the lock and leaned close, listening to the mechanisms, trying to find the sweet spot. It was tough and took longer than he liked, but finally, he heard the satisfying *click*.

He was about to open the door when the sound of footsteps met his ears. He shrank back, moving toward the wall and wedging himself between the bricks and the hood of the car. A woman stumbled nearby, grumbling to herself. From her demeanor, her trip to the casino didn't go well. She hiccupped, occasionally swinging her arms around her. Her heels clipped on the pavement as she closed in on a sleek-looking Mustang.

She climbed into the car and revved the engine. The headlights were blinding, and Dick hoped that he wouldn't catch her attention. She pulled the Mustang from its spot, only narrowly avoiding hitting several of the nearby vehicles, before driving out into the city streets. No doubt she'd experience a few near-misses and maybe an accident before she got home.

Dick returned to the BMW and climbed into the driver's seat. The panel was mostly digital, although there was a control box located under the steering column. Dick bent low after pulling a device from his pocket that would mimic the unique code stored in the key, then played with the wires until the car kicked into life. The headlights automatically switched on as he offered Ringo mental thanks. It hadn't been a cheap purchase back when he got it, but it had proved well worth the money.

He hit the gas and pulled out of the spot. When he lined up with the cruiser, he waved the others inside. Harley called shotgun, jumping into the passenger side. Newman begrudgingly climbed into the back.

"You ready to rock and roll?" Dick pulled out of the parking lot.

"As ready as I'll ever be," Newman replied without conviction.

"Where are we going?" Harley added. "Has Terra responded yet?"

Dick checked his cell phone as someone shouted behind them. There were no messages from Terra, but he still had the location she had sent over to them in the event of the plan going without a hitch. They had to meet her at Garcia's apartment.

"Hey! Hey!" Gunfire hit the wall beside them.

Dick checked the rearview, finding an obese man with a crooked tie running after them. Dick spotted an empty can of Coke in the cup holder and put two and two together. "Hold onto your hats," he stated.

He pulled out onto the street, cutting in front of a pickup truck and causing the driver to blare his horn. Another shot pinged off the ground, and Dick only hoped he would be right about the man, knowing that no matter how pissed off he was, the owner of the BMW wouldn't want to damage his beautiful little car.

CHAPTER TWENTY-EIGHT

"You've been a thorn in my side for far too long," Garcia growled, face contorted and twisted into a horrifying mess. "This ends today."

"Then fucking do it," Terra replied, meeting his crazed glare. "End it. Make it good because once I'm gone, there's going to be a whole investigation coming after your ass. You think I'm the only one who has the dirt on you? No. I'm not. You kill me, and you've got a whole ocean of bad out there to contend with. I'm just the fire starter. You're going to have to deal with the blaze."

Garcia's gaze intensified. "So be it."

Terra knew that was her moment to act. Garcia's intentions were sketched deep into his face, his finger squeezing the trigger. Terra felt the flood of adrenaline racing through her, her skin running cold as she fought against Garcia, twisting to the side as she brought her knee up to meet his groin.

The bullet fired. Warmth grew in Terra's cheek. A white-hot pain met her ear, but she had no time to pay attention to that now.

She threw Garcia off her, the man momentarily incapacitated

by her blow. She scrambled on the wooden flooring, finally managing to find her footing as she ran around the corner. Garcia shot after her, bullets catching the drywall and spraying clouds of dust.

Terra ran down the hallway, only knowing a little of the layout of this place. She remembered seeing a collection of weapons in what she assumed was Garcia's home office, and it was there she ran.

Her hand moved to her ear. It came back slick with blood. The hallway morphed, her sense of balance compromised as she navigated to the room. She ran up a set of stairs, aware of the crashing and sounds of the man giving chase.

Her head pounded. The world sounded like it was underwater. The pain intensified, and Terra only wished that APRIL was in action to help her. She had only had the AI for a few weeks, but it felt like a lifetime. She hesitated to admit that she needed it, but she did.

Using the wall for support, she made her way to the office. She closed the door loudly behind her, then scrambled for the guns. The wall held at least eight weapons, and she checked each in turn, looking for bullets, keen to see if they would be of any use to her.

She discarded a Ruger, an ancient Smith & Wesson, and a Sako, each bulletless. Her stomach dropped when she realized these were all for decoration, but that didn't stop her from taking the Winchester off the wall and aiming it at the door as Garcia crashed in after her.

A grin grew on his lips. "Please, Terra. You think I'd fall for that?"

Terra pulled the trigger. She knew it was pointless, but what else could she do. To her surprise, gunfire exploded, a series of bullets riddling the door beside Garcia.

Terra gasped. Garcia threw himself to the floor. A shadow appeared in the doorway behind him.

Terra beamed as Imani Thomas arrived, standing over Garcia, her Glock 99 aimed at the back of his head. "Keep your ass down and stay quiet, Captain."

Garcia had no choice but to remain still. He knew when his battle was up. Terra peeled herself away from the wall, looking at Imani as if she couldn't believe that she was there.

"Nice timing," she muttered, surprised at how breathless she was.

Imani didn't return the smile, a worried expression on her face. A pair of APRIL glasses hid her gaze. Terra was surprised to see them in her possession. "We've got to get going."

Terra nodded. "Let's handcuff this bastard and send him in." She moved to Garcia and crouched.

Imani stayed her with one hand. "No. We can't."

"What are you talking about?" Terra asked. "He tried to kill me. He's guilty as charged."

"You don't have evidence," Imani replied. "You have nothing to tie him to your accusations. Don't you realize what you're doing here? You're playing with fire."

Terra frowned. "Are you fucking kidding me? I've lost my ear. He shot my weapon at me. I'm not going to leave him here so we can lose him again. We take him into our custody, and we force the confession. I've seen him do it to plenty of perps. We can use his techniques to draw the confession."

"Terra, I can't," Imani complained.

"No. You can't," Terra confirmed. "But I can." Her face darkened, surprised at how much Imani's disappointment affected her. "I'm on the other side of the law right now. I might as well make the most of it. If I'm already in the shit, what's one more step down into the darkness if it's for a good cause?

"Garcia's a scumbag. He shouldn't be working for the AJS. He has a ring of inkers at his disposal, and he's using the AJS as cover to help them. This isn't right. This isn't how this is all supposed to work."

"Terra…" Imani breathed.

"No," Terra replied. "This is happening. This is ending. Here. Tonight. You can either be a part of this or not. Save your pride, save your career, see if I care. I'm making this happen, and you can't stop me."

Garcia wriggled beneath her. Terra smacked him on the back of the head with the Winchester, knocking him out. "What's it going to be?"

Imani hesitated a moment. Her serious expression broke into a smile as she shook her head and scoffed. "I've forgotten the fire that lives within you. It's nice to see that again. I've missed you."

"I've missed you, too," Terra replied. "Now help me cuff this motherfucker."

They worked together, fixing his hands into place and helping the unconscious Garcia to his feet. It was a struggle, each woman taking the crook of his arm and dragging him to the front of the apartment.

"You have a long fight ahead of you," Imani replied. "If I can help in any way, let me know. I'll do what I can while keeping up the guise of good cop."

Terra smiled. "Thank you. All I can do is keep this creep close and try to draw that confession." She looked over her shoulder, glad to see the mask lying on the floor, the chip only effective for a short distance. She looked at Imani's glasses. "New toy?"

Imani nodded. "You could say that. Pieces of shit, though. It stopped working the moment I entered the apartment. I thought they'd be better than that, judging by what you told me."

Terra paused. Imani jerked. Garcia flopped between them.

"What was that for?" Imani asked.

"The recordings," Terra replied. "Your glasses record your location and feed back to the main system. Aren't you worried about giving your location away? You freaked out when you first found out about my internal APRIL system."

Imani shook her head. "No. I'm not recording right now.

They stopped the moment I neared the building. They shouldn't capture anything suspicious. Well, until we get outside and they see that we've got Garcia in our custody."

Terra thought about this. "Wait here with Garcia. I'll bring your car around and get him inside before your glasses activate." She looked at Garcia doubtfully.

"Go," Imani encouraged. "I've got this." She tossed her keys to Terra. "Around the corner, across from the 7-Eleven."

Terra left Garcia and Imani together as she ran out into the street. She kept her wits about her, keeping a lookout for stray AJS that might have been alerted to where Garcia was going, but surprisingly no one was there. She hopped into Imani's cruiser, then drove around the corner, pulling up curbside in front of the apartment.

APRIL, you with me?

Affirmative, Terra. Your heart rate and biochemical levels are elevated. Balancing now.

Do what you've got to do.

A calm washed over Terra in an instant, her focus growing keen. She exited the vehicle and entered the building. The minute she did, the cold returned, APRIL disconnected from her system, and unable to keep her equilibrium.

Terra ran to Garcia's apartment. When she got there, she paused, confusion washing over her.

Imani was gone.

"Imani?" Terra called into the apartment. She looked down at the slumped form of Garcia. He was out cold, folded uncomfortably on the floor, chin tucked into his chest.

None of this made sense.

She called for Imani one more time. When no response came, she checked Garcia's heartbeat, then stood back.

"Where the hell are you?" There was no sign of a struggle. Nothing was out of place. Imani was just...gone.

Garcia grunted, head tilting to the side.

"Focus, Terra," she told herself, gathering her strength to lift Garcia. It took double the effort given that she was working solo, but soon enough she got Garcia down the elevator and out to the curb. They garnered a few funny looks along the way, but Terra waved these off with a casual, "One too many."

She shoved him in the cruiser's backseat and ensured she locked the doors. The partition between the front and back would be enough to stop Garcia from causing trouble when he woke. Terra was about to hit the gas when she looked back up at the apartment.

"Shit…" She couldn't leave. Not until she knew.

She locked the cruiser, then ran back inside the apartment. She sped around the rooms, the apartment blurring in her vision as her ear throbbed blood. She couldn't find Imani in any of the rooms.

Satisfied with her search but dissatisfied with the result, Terra returned to the cruiser. As she climbed into the driver's seat, she heard AJS sirens in the distance. She sighed, then hit the gas, speeding out into the street.

She navigated through the city. The roads were relatively quiet, but every few blocks she passed another cruiser. She kept her eyes fixed on the street, thankful that the AJS would believe her to be another cop out on the beat and wouldn't suspect her of having a senior captain in the back, battered and bruised.

Garcia remained unconscious, rolling around in the back as Terra took turns and closed in on her destination. She approached the city's east side, trying to work out what her next steps would be as she kept Garcia bunkered down in the safe house.

She wondered whether Leonie Black would be any help at all. At least she could keep a watchful eye on Garcia while she worked out her next move.

Lights flashed behind Terra.

She glanced in her rearview, expecting to see an AJS cruiser flashing red and blue. Instead, she spotted only the headlights of a large 4x4.

She frowned, then made a left.

The 4x4 followed her.

Terra watched the vehicle, trying to identify a driver. The truck was modern, its black body gleaming. The tires were large with thick treads, much more suited to driving in boggy terrain than the blacktop.

Terra took a right, moving away from her destination. The 4x4 closed in, headlights flashing again.

"The hell?" Terra replied, a bad feeling growing in her stomach.

She took a left, then another left, working around in a square to shake off the vehicle. After the second turning, the 4x4 continued straight, leaving Terra alone.

"Strange…" Terra frowned, working to recognize where she had driven to. She hooked a right at the traffic lights, then made her way to the coast. Ahead of her, the buildings peeled back to reveal the open ocean. At this time of night, the black stretch of waters appeared endless, not even the moon to cast a ghostly glow on the waters. She continued straight, knowing that she was only a couple of minutes from her destination.

The lights at the junction were green. Terra drove onto the crossroads.

Lights flashed to her right, blinding and bright. A horn blared. APRIL had enough time to call **Danger** in her head before the cruiser and the 4x4 collided. The bigger vehicle bashed the cruiser sideways, sending it rolling several times before it reached a standstill.

Terra's head wobbled, the cruiser upside down, her ponytail touching the ceiling. She looked out the broken window, blood spilling down her face, only to find two silhouetted figures striding toward her, backlit by the 4x4s headlights.

Terra opened her mouth to speak, but nothing came out. The edges of her vision grew blurry. Darkness took over.

All went black.

CHAPTER TWENTY-NINE

Terra ran.

The world was dark, pitch-black on either side. The floor was hard and smooth, her bare feet drummed their beat as she sprinted. Her arms pumped on either side, her gaze unfaltering. Air came and went in sharp bursts in her lungs, and all she knew was that she needed to keep going.

She needed to run.

The world slipped away beneath her. The road showed no end. Ahead of her was a flare of light the size of a dime. Her gaze pinned on the light, eyes unblinking. The rhythm was hers and hers alone, her body making music in the otherwise silent world.

She didn't think. She didn't need to, not now. Determination was her guide, and her faith was unwavering. The answers were ahead. All she had to do was keep doing what she was doing. She needed to trust the process. She needed to keep fighting.

A lone spark of recognition reached her. Terra's eyes darted to either side, confusion spreading on her brow.

The recognition faded. Her determination returned to the dime of light.

One foot in front of the other. Wasn't that all her life had ever been? Running one foot, then the next, following the treadmill of life as she attempted to climb the ladder?

No one responded. Terra lost her thoughts, laser-focused on the dime although she didn't know why. Run, run, run. That was all she needed to do. To fight, to run, to fight some more.

I haven't finished my work yet.

A beeping sounded. Rhythmic and regular. Voices mumbled, amplified in the darkness around her but indistinct, their tone reaching an almighty panic.

The beeping turned to a long whine, a high-pitched note running without end.

The note ran, but Terra stopped. She wanted to continue, but her body wouldn't let her.

Her chest rose and fell. The light grew brighter, or maybe it finally came closer.

Terra fell to her knees in the darkness and waited.

She waited.

CHAPTER THIRTY

A bad feeling grew in Dick's stomach as they reached the top of the stairs and found the open door.

"Shit…" Dick breathed.

They approached slowly, each with their weapons drawn. Dick led the way, Newman behind him, Harley bringing up the rear.

He nudged the door, ensuring that no one was behind and waiting for them. There were signs of a struggle, dark streaks on the floor where a pair of shoes had dragged across the hardwood.

"They were here," Newman stated.

"Tell me something we don't know," Dick replied.

"Did you know a male rabbit's testicles are in *front* of their penis?" Harley added.

Dick and Newman looked at her.

"What?" Harley replied. "You said to tell you something you don't know."

Dick turned his attention back to the apartment. "Newman, you look upstairs. Harley, you take the right-side rooms. I'll take the left."

They both nodded.

"Be careful," Dick added. "We don't know who or what could be waiting for us."

Dick strode along the hallway, investigating each room in turn. This apartment was clearly for show, each room pristine and uninhabited. It stank of a man who had more money than he did friends.

After examining all the rooms on his side, he bumped into Harley at the far side of the apartment. "Anything?"

"Nothing," Harley replied. "I don't get it. If she's not here, where is she? I thought she was going to keep you guys updated?"

"Yeah," Dick replied. "Me, too."

They headed upstairs, finding Newman on her way back from her rounds. "Nothing."

"Shit," Dick exclaimed. He scratched his head. "I don't understand."

"There are signs of a struggle," Newman offered. "Take those black streaks and the crooked pictures on the wall. Something happened here. I just don't know what."

"There was a bullet mark in the floor and more in the wall," Harley stated. "Dust on the floor. Someone got shot."

"Show me." Dick shook his head. "I can't believe you didn't tell us straight away."

Harley led him to a spot where a bullet had gouged the floor. Not far from there, drywall had exploded from the wall. White powder dusted the floor, and a bloodstain darkened and soaked into the wood.

"You said you didn't see anything," Dick stated.

"No people," Harley replied. "I thought we'd established signs of struggle."

Newman shuffled her feet. "Who's blood do you think it is?"

"I don't know," Dick replied. "Can't you AJS folks scan it and put it into the database?"

Newman nodded. "We could, but it would alert the AJS of our location."

Harley grunted.

Dick let out a growl of frustration. "We need to find her. She'd let us know where she'd gone if she was okay. She hasn't. We can only assume she's in trouble."

Newman nodded. "I don't know what to suggest."

Harley ran her hand through her hair. "One more sweep around the apartment?"

"Fine," Dick replied. "Let's take different routes this time. See if we can't find anything amiss that the other might have missed."

They reconverted a few moments later, disappointment on their faces. "This can't be a dead-end," Dick exclaimed.

"What would you normally do in this situation?" Newman asked. "You're a PI. What're your next steps?"

"Same as yours," Dick replied. "But considerably less legal. I'd take the blood samples and try to track down the perpetrators, working out if the blood was of the victim or the attacker."

Harley wandered around nearby, eyes caught by the pictures hanging on the wall. Most were abstract, consisting of strange combinations of color. Some were of vehicles—boats, yachts, supercars, and more. One drew her attention, showing a young Garcia. A smile stretched across his face as he shook hands with the mayor of the district, a medal around his neck.

She took a step closer, foot bumping into a small side table. A decorative vase wobbled precariously, the top-heavy plant almost tipping off its surface. She reached down and caught it, placing it back where it had stood.

Dick and Newman ignored her, deep in conversation about next steps.

Harley cocked her head. A tiny piece of paper caught her eye, sticking out from beneath the vase. She took the paper and read the scrawled handwriting on the front.

"Guys, you might want to see this," she declared.

Dick and Newman broke off their conversation, crossing to Harley. "What is it?"

"Here." Harley handed the paper to Dick.

Dick read the front, eyes widening, a grin on his face. "Where did you find this?"

Harley told him.

"We need to get going," Newman stated. "This has to be linked, right?"

Dick's eyes scanned the note again, a single address followed by the initials "I.T."

"Who's I.T.?" Harley asked.

"It's either interactive technology," Dick offered. "Or Terra's former justice partner, Imani Thomas. My money's on the latter."

"That's a hell of an assumption," Harley replied.

"It may be," Newman stated. "But it's all we've got. Come on, let's go."

CHAPTER THIRTY-ONE

Terra blinked as a shockwave of pain surged through her body.

She grunted, her back arching, causing another eruption of pain. There were hands on her body, fingers on her head, her wrists and legs and waist were bound. She knew all of this before she opened her eyes.

The light was intense. The shape of surgeons hovered above her like dark vultures with their claws in her mind. She didn't have a clue who these people were or what they were doing. All she knew was that she couldn't be here. They couldn't be here. She needed escape, to get out and away from whatever was happening.

She grimaced. A doctor leaned over her, blocking the light, a finger raised to her surgical mask. "Shhh. Remain calm please, Terra."

Terra didn't know how she knew, but these were bad people. A sudden attack of memory returned as she recalled the second major accident she'd had in a few weeks.

No. Not an accident. That shit was deliberate.

The 4x4 had sped toward her, crashing into the side of the cruiser. Terra had rolled with the vehicle, Garcia tumbling around in the back. Her head had smashed into the steering wheel. Blood had dripped onto the ceiling.

"Where am I?" Terra asked, straining against her bonds again. "Where am I!"

Terra tried to sit up. Hands pressed her shoulders down.

"Terra, you need to remain still if this is to work." The doctor spoke to her like a bratty child. "Please. We need your cooperation."

"Then tell me why I'm here!" Terra heard her words through the muffled blur of her shattered eardrum, dull and lost beneath sea waves. Her voice was drowsy, her consonants slurred. Was she under anesthetic? She had no idea.

A buzzing sounded, a saw blade whirring into motion. Terra's heart raced. *APRIL, help!*

No response came, only static. Terra heard the sound and the chill ran through her body. If there was no APRIL, that meant there was a disrupter nearby.

Either that or the mechanisms shattered in the crash.

"Shit…" Terra groaned.

"Making first incision," a steady voice stated above her.

"The hell you are," Terra growled back, wriggling as far as her bonds would allow. "Get off me."

The doctor rolled her eyes behind thick-lensed glasses. "I told you this wouldn't work. We need her out."

"We need her conscious if we're to know whether or not we're damaging the system," a voice replied.

Even under duress, Terra could identify Garcia anywhere. Anger surged through her. Every fiber of her being wanted to rip free of her bonds and lunge at the man who had ruined her life. She looked down, able to make out the top of his head. He leaned into view. "Terra. This is for your good. It's time that we fix you, once and for all."

"Fix me?" Terra asked. "This doesn't seem like fixing."

Garcia grinned. "You're right. Fixing isn't the correct word.

See, what you hold in your brain is far too valuable for us to lose by taking you out. Our team is going to dismantle the OSCaR system from your mind. That way you'll be free to return to your state before we used you as a guinea pig for our technologies."

Terra's breath grew rapid. "I was told I'd be dead without the AI."

Garcia feigned surprise. "Oh. Really? Well, that is a pity, isn't it?" He leaned over her, his musty breath reaching her nostrils. "You've served your purpose, Terra. It's time to say goodnight to Atlantica, once and for all."

Terra shook her head, fighting off the surgeons. They grew frustrated, looking at Garcia for help.

"No," Garcia replied. "We're not putting her out for this. We want Terra to live every last moment of her end. It's the least she deserves."

The surgeons had no argument to give. A pair of hands held Terra's face still. The smell of latex from the gloves was overwhelming. Terra's eyes stung with tears. The sound of the whirring blade drew closer. Terra felt the disturbance of air from the blade's movement.

In a thousand years of guessing, I never believed this would be the way I died, Terra thought.

You're not dead yet, a voice replied. Terra frowned. It sounded in her head, yet it wasn't APRIL's. Nuance and inflection replaced the robotic monotone delivery.

A human voice.

Stay with me, Terra. We're going to get you out of this.

The blade touched Terra's forehead. A fine pink mist accompanied a hot spike of pain. Terra opened her mouth and let out a yowl of pain.

Then the blade stopped. The light shut off and plunged Terra into darkness.

"What the hell?" Garcia growled. Hurried movements

sounded as doctors and surgeons moved around the room, looking for the source of the intrusion.

"The power's down," a voice stated.

"Well done for stating the fucking obvious," Garcia replied. "Fix it."

The hands let go of Terra's face. The bonds still held her, but now she could move her head and look around. Something viscous and thick rolled down her brow, and she tried to guide it away from her eyes.

The shuffling around Terra was disorientating. Lying there in the darkness, she had no idea where anyone was. All she knew was that someone had spoken to her, and the power had gone down.

If you're there, thank you.

No reply came.

Terra lay there for a few moments, listening to the sounds of the scuffling. From what she could tell, the power had gone off across the whole building. Nearby doctors powered on mini-flashlights to try and see the instruments around them and navigate around. Terra struggled against her bonds, expecting to find resistance. Instead, the clasps came open easily.

She raised her head in surprise. She moved her legs and found the clasps around her ankles were now free.

Shit...

Terra looked around. The nearest light source was at the other side of the room, where three doctors had gathered around a fuse box. "What happened to the emergency power?"

"I don't know," a voice replied. "This is impossible."

Terra groaned as she positioned herself upright. Pain shot out from her rib, and a tender examination with her hand told her that she'd broken it. Now, more than ever, she wished for APRIL's abilities to dish her organic pain relief.

She swung her legs off the operating table, bare feet touching tile. Her back grew cold as the hospital gown revealed her bare ass to the world. She stumbled away from the table, seeking the dark until she eventually leaned on the wall for support.

Garcia's voice was mixed among the chaos, demands, and shouts for technicians to fix the problem pronto. Terra drew a few deep, painful breaths, then tried to consider her next move.

Where is there to go, Terra? You don't know this place. You don't know these people. How are you going to get away?

She asked herself the question, and the answer came with the return of the voice. **There is a janitorial closet Six-and-a-half feet along the wall. Get inside, now.**

Terra psyched herself up and slid along the wall. Her hand found a round knob, and she eased open the closet door. She tucked herself inside, casting her in total darkness.

She felt around, trying to get her bearings. Shelving lined the small space. The handle of a broom nestled into her palm. The closet stank of bleach and cleaning supplies.

What now? Terra asked. When silence met her question, she added, *Please.*

Hold on…

The voice was calming, feminine. Terra wanted to state that she could do nothing *but* hold on. Each breath hurt her chest. Her knees shook as she fought to keep herself upright. Terra clung to the shelves for support as shouts raged from the operating room, Garcia now realizing that Terra was missing.

"How the hell could this happen!" His voice came, muffled only slightly by the door.

Activating night vision.

APRIL's voice came as a complete surprise to Terra. She expected the woman's voice, but she couldn't say that she was disappointed. The room lit up around her in shades of green and black, revealing rows of bleach bottles, cleaning supplies, as well as boxes of sanitized syringes and…

Scalpels.

Terra took a scalpel and looked for a pocket to deposit it in. Her gown was pocketless.

She rolled her eyes, then gripped it in her palm. *Am I going to have to fight my way out of this?*

Not if you're careful, APRIL replied. **Try not to bump your forehead, either. I haven't had enough time to do more than get the blood to start clotting.**

Arrows appeared in Terra's vision, pointing up to the entrance to a vent. Terra groaned. Her chest was already in agony, and now she had to climb and *crawl* through the air vents? What was this, a *Mission: Impossible* movie?

The shouts rose behind her. Knowing that she had no time to lose, Terra began her ascent.

Each rung up the shelving ladder was agony. She kept the scalpel in her hand, using the blade to help ease off the grate covering the vent. When she was high enough, she levered herself inside, hissing with pain as her rib touched the cold metal, feeling like a shard of glass was pressing into her lungs.

She shuffled, the pain so intense it was blinding. Her last moments of struggle saw her legs kicking, sending one of the bleach bottles crashing to the floor. She flipped over onto her back with great difficulty, then shuffled backward, one hand gripping her ribs, the other holding the knife.

All she could see was white. The vent was claustrophobic. A voice called to check the supply closet. She hoped they didn't look up before she was farther away.

Terra pushed as fast as her legs would carry her, navigating the first bend she came to with great difficulty, putting distance between herself and the terrifying medical scene she had awoken to.

CHAPTER THIRTY-TWO

They slowed as they approached the junction, the colossal building coming into view.

Dick had passed the Tynamo manufacturing plant a thousand times before, but like many of the strange intricacies of Atlantica, his brain had tuned it all out. The building was responsible for a large volume of Atlantica's technological exports, bringing a tremendous income into the city. The fact that it was an eyesore didn't cross the minds of the company's benefactors, who cared more about the bottom line than the impact the building had on the city skyline.

"AJS," Newman breathed as they rounded the corner and saw the collection of AJS cruisers surrounding the main entrance. "Damn, when you've got the AJS at your disposal you can do a lot to ensure that no one disturbs you when you're breaking the goddamn law."

"You think any of them are inside?" Dick asked.

"I doubt it," Newman replied. "If he invited them inside, they might see what horrors he's got to hide. He'll have set up Spencer to monitor the situation while he does what he needs to, especially after realizing that I never made it back to the station with you."

Harley shook her head. "You guys really shit the bed on this one, huh?"

Dick raised an eyebrow.

"Oh, come on," she replied. "You're telling me this is what happens when everything goes to plan? A cop and a PI on the run, looking for another cop that's...what? Been kidnapped?" She let out a long breath. "I'm starting to doubt my association with you, Dick Chambers."

"I never struck any deals with you," Dick replied. "Your business remains with Terra. You want your deal seen to; you help us find her and get her away from Garcia's clutches."

Harley chewed her lip.

"You okay?" Newman asked.

"I've seen what he's capable of," Harley replied. "You want to get that guy; you need to act quickly. You need to break in there and grab Terra—assuming she's even in there, of course. All we have is a scribbled fucking note telling us to come here. Can we trust Imani?"

Dick considered this. He had no prepared answer. He barely knew her.

"Thomas is a good cop," Newman replied. "I've come across her on a few occasions. She's one of the juggernauts in the higher divisions who you hear mentioned like a damn celebrity. She's good people. Her and Terra were a killer team. It sucks that the major separated them."

"What if they're not?" Harley asked. "What if they've reunited?"

"What if Thomas has turned crooked?" Dick asked.

Newman raised her eyebrows.

"We have to consider every angle," Dick stated.

They studied the cruisers for a short time, trying to work out their best approach. Now that they were here, they had no idea how to move forward. The building was huge. How were they supposed to find Terra inside such a huge space—assuming that she was there?

"She's in there," Newman replied as if reading Dick's mind. "If she wasn't, why would there be so many cops there?"

"Good call." Dick lit a cigarette, filling the car with smoke.

Newman coughed and waved. "Really? Not going to crack a window or anything?"

Dick shrugged. "Free country."

Newman opened her window, breathing in the chill night air. "Park around the back of the building. See if there's some way we can get closer and draw out some information from the other officers." She held up her radio.

Dick smiled. "Great idea."

He moved to the back of the building and found only more AJS cruisers. Instead, he moved to the nearest alley and parked there, able to see the building from where they sat.

It was then that the power went out, the large Tynamo sign fading from floodlight yellow to black.

"What was that?" Harley asked.

"You got me." Dick craned his neck to look high up for any kind of disturbance. Newman followed his gaze, suddenly jumping when her radio squawked to life.

A voice spoke through the static, clarity almost lost in the poor signal. Newman raised an eyebrow, confused about how the radio could have kicked in without her operating it manually.

"Listen to me," the voice stated, breathless and urgent. "You want your friend back, don't you? Then you'll have to listen to every word I'm about to say. Execute these commands, and you *might* stand a chance at bringing her out alive."

"Who is this?" Newman replied sharply.

The only reply was static.

CHAPTER THIRTY-THREE

Cool air circulated around Terra, chilling her skin and drying her sweat.

She lay on her back in the central fan room, embracing the gusts that blew her way. She had emerged from the ventilation shaft into the tiny operational space and closed her eyes for just a moment, allowing the pain to subside briefly and for Terra to collect her thoughts.

She barely remembered the journey, only knowing that she must keep moving. She didn't know which direction, and even if APRIL had been offering guidance, she wouldn't have been able to see it. While APRIL could balance her biochemistry and offer pain relief, there was a limit to its abilities.

Terra grumbled, feeling both too warm and too cold at the same time. When the fans had first kicked in, she had been shocked, surprised that the electricity had reestablished in the building, but now all she could do was lay there in pained calm and recover.

What the hell is going on?

Terra had no idea of where she was or how she got here. She was tired of feeling helpless, of having other people put her in these compromising conditions. She was fighting for her life, alone in a building filled with surgeons and Garcia, a broken rib, and technology inside her head over which she had no control.

At least APRIL had reactivated. That was a nice touch.

Hold on...

Terra dragged herself into a seated position. *How is that possible?*

She had been in Garcia's presence, and APRIL had been working...

An image flashed in Terra's head of Garcia's disrupter left on his apartment floor.

Terra's eyes widened. She had a chance to catch him finally. If she could get footage of what he was doing, the part he played in all of this, she might stand a chance of bringing him in.

Only, there were a couple of problems with that thinking. The first being that she had no idea where she was. The second being that she'd have to find Garcia on his home turf, and that would bring her dangerously close to potentially finding herself on the operating table again.

This time, she figured he might care less about having her conscious during the extraction.

Shit, shit, shit...

Terra moved a hand to her head. She was exhausted, even with APRIL's biochemical balancing. The remains of her ear had stopped bleeding but still throbbed for attention. Her forehead had stopped trying to drip blood in her eyes but was far from healed. Her rib was uncomfortable, and every movement reminded her that she was in pain.

APRIL, I need you now more than ever.

Anything to assist, Terra.

Terra opened her mouth, then closed it again. She didn't know who to trust. In the last few hours, APRIL had worked *for* Garcia and *against* him. Whatever networks were still accessing her head were playing with all that she knew.

Still, did she have much choice?

Get me out of here, APRIL.

Triangulating position, Terra. A map of Atlantica appeared in Terra's vision. She saw the hulking mass of the city, the rises and folds of the mountainous jungles, the golden coastlines. A series of indicators appeared, moving around the map as they tried to zero in on her location.

Terra watched closely, eager to know where she was. The indicators slowly aligned, closing on their coordinates. Eventually, a flashing arrow settled on the south side of town, not all that far from where Terra had originally been heading to find Corporal Black.

The building shown on the map was large and round, looking like a pimple on the surface of Atlantica. Terra had passed it before but never entered. She knew the building only to be one of Tynamo's production factories, a place where Atlantica's state-of-the-art TVs, screens, gadgets, and gizmos were assembled and delivered to stores and customers.

Then what are we doing inside?

The place was huge, easily three times the size of a football stadium. Terra asked APRIL to show her blueprints of the building and was pleased to find that APRIL located her position in the operations room on the map.

Terra's pleasure only lasted a moment as she realized how far she'd need to go to escape the building.

Fuck.

APRIL presented two options for Terra, each with limited chances of success. The first was to continue to navigate the ventilation shaft and work her way to the rooftop. There she would be able to either climb down into the city or hop onto the neighboring roof.

Although APRIL warned Terra that the longer she spent in ventilation, the higher her chances of capture. They already knew she was in there. The first place they'd be looking was above.

The second option was a route that wound through the corridors and saw Terra taking a series of stairwells or elevators. This was a much more public approach, and Terra knew that she'd draw a lot of eyes walking through the hallways in only a medical gown.

"I don't know…" Terra offered, fatigued and defeated.

You can do this, Terra, APRIL encouraged. **Upping painkillers to maximum dosage.**

Terra felt cold wash through her. The pain in her ribs and ear subsided a little, although it was still tough to move. "Thank you, APRIL."

You're welcome, Terra. Arrows appeared in her vision, a series of information showing Terra the two ways forward. **Where would you like to go?**

Terra weighed the two options in her mind, then proceeded to crawl through the vents.

The journey of a thousand miles starts with a single step.

Progress was slow. Terra shuffled on her back, using her bare feet to propel her along on her bare back and ass. After a short while, she was breathless, with no idea how far through the ventilation systems she had gone.

One hundred sixty-four feet remaining.

Damn. How big is this place?

Do you require an answer to that question?

Terra smirked. *You're learning.*

That's the benefit of an artificial intelligence system.

As she worked her way along, she caught snippets of activity through the vents. She passed grates giving a view into large rooms where workers were busy managing products along the assembly lines. Many had headphones in as they monitored the various electrical items they were assembling.

All of this in one building... Terra shook her head. *Insanity.*

When she made the final distance, Terra lowered herself into a small cubby hole area where she could sit upright. The ventilation shafts forked off in six directions, a hole to her side leading down and another leading up to the roof.

Terra looked up. The climb was an easy ten feet high before the vents spiked out in each direction again. She stood, her body shy of six feet tall as it was, but with her added arm length she could make eight feet of the journey with her fingertips.

She stretched her arm, then winced with pain.

How am I supposed to do this? she asked APRIL. *I can't climb that.*

There's always a way, Terra.

Terra looked around her, only able to see the chambers where the shafts disappeared. There were no props or platforms that she could see.

Well, since you're the smart one, why don't you find one for me?

Terra's arm stretched out and into the air of its own accord, led by her metallic hand.

Terra grimaced as pain shot through her.

Calculating pain nerve centers, APRIL announced.

Terra didn't like the sound of it.

Calibrating...

She drew her hand down. APRIL took control and raised her hand in the air. "APRIL, stop it," Terra hissed.

Calibration complete.

What are you doing?

Please take a seat, Terra.

Terra frowned. *Excuse me?*

Please take a seat.

Terra was dubious but obeyed. Her rib crunched as her stomach folded. She pressed her back to the steel walls and closed her eyes. *Okay. Sitting down. What's the plan?*

I'm going to attempt to locate the nervous system pathways that link directly to your areas of injury. Using these synaptic

pathways, I might be able to remove your pain sensors and erase your pain.

Terra lifted an eyebrow. "When you say 'might'…what do you mean?"

Nothing is foolproof, APRIL replied. **One wrong move might permanently damage your nerves and cause a permanent loss of feeling. One wrong move could lead to permanent paralysis, unfixable by modern medicine.**

You're not filling me with hope, APRIL.

Apologies, APRIL replied. **You can do this, Terra Kris.**

The phrase sounded so strange coming out of APRIL's metaphysical mouth that Terra had to stop herself from laughing.

Ouch, it hurts, she declared, clutching her rib.

That's why I would like to fix you. Do I have your permission, Terra?

Terra considered this. "Yes. Despite everything that has happened, I trust you. If you can fix this and get us out of here without breaking me further, I will find many ways to thank you."

I don't need thanks, APRIL stated. **This is all a part of my duty.**

Terra smirked, realizing how much APRIL sounded like she did when she was at her peak in the line of duty.

"Let's do this," Terra declared.

Close your eyes and relax, please.

Terra obeyed. For a moment, nothing happened, then she felt something moving inside her as if a creature was probing in her inner circuitry. Nerves were activated, sending signals of warmth, chill, pain, and pleasure in sporadic locations around her body. She laughed, then grimaced as her rib exploded in pain.

She rested her head against the metal walls as a sudden twitch of pain burst from her chest. She gasped, hand clutching her rib as she doubled over, face near her knees. "APRIL, you son of a bitch. That fucking hurt…"

She breathed, trying to calm herself.

Operation complete.

Terra frowned. If APRIL had completed it, why had it hurt so much?

She sat up, tentative as she experimented with the limitations of her body and the pain movement. To her surprise, although her rib still ground against the others, and the lump in her chest still showed that the rib was very much out of place, there was no pain.

"Whoa…that's weird," Terra exclaimed.

I can reverse the procedure if you like? APRIL asked.

"No!" Terra argued quickly. "No. It's fine. Keep it like this until we're somewhere safe, okay?"

Affirmative.

Terra drew a few deep breaths before standing once more, the ghost of pain still haunting her. However, she found that when she reached up with one arm, the pain was non-existent. She raised her other arm, only a short distance from the top of the ventilation shaft.

"Time to Miley Cyrus this bitch," Terra muttered as she jumped and used her knees to wedge herself into the gap.

Miley Cyrus…APRIL mused. **A possible reference to the 2009 Miley Cyrus hit, *The Climb*?**

"Right on," Terra grunted, fingers grasping for the lip of the shaft. Using her back and knees to shinny up, she finally managed to grab the lip and pull herself up.

Her rib shifted uncomfortably in her chest.

"APRIL?" Terra asked.

Yes, Terra.

"Is there a possibility that, by not being able to feel the rib moving, it could cause more permanent damage in my body?" Terra asked.

Affirmative, APRIL replied.

Terra sighed.

However, APRIL continued, surprising Terra to say anything more than a simple yes or no. **If you fail to make it out of this building, you'll be dead anyway. What have you got to lose?**

Terra smirked. "You make a fair point, AI."

Thank you, human.

Terra chuckled. Was the artificial intelligence beginning to learn sass?

She levered herself up the shaft and continued in the direction APRIL's arrow was pointing.

CHAPTER THIRTY-FOUR

The ventilation shafts were a labyrinth that Terra would never have been able to navigate without APRIL.

She twisted and turned, feeling like she was forever climbing without ever getting to the top. She had no idea how long she was in those shafts for, no idea how far she had ascended and traveled. As she progressed onward, occasionally catching glances of the rooms she passed and making every effort to remain silent, she found herself growing steadily warmer.

Has someone turned the heat up in here? Terra asked, resting her head and taking a moment to catch her breath. Her stomach rumbled, her head was beginning to throb, and as much as she trudged on, her muscles were weakening. *Or is it just me?*

Temperature has increased thirty-two percent since embarking into the ventilation system, APRIL replied. **Someone is likely tampering with the heat to flush you out of the vents.**

*And heat rises...*Terra thought. *Great.*

She closed her eyes, mouth dry, tongue feeling furry and rough at the same time. *How much farther is there to go?*

APRIL calculated the results, showing the images in the

blacks of her vision. **Two more stories to go until you reach the rooftop.**

Great... Terra thought, wondering if she had enough energy to get her there. *Let me rest, first.*

Momentum is very important, Terra. I advise that you keep moving.

Terra's lip curled. *Really?*

Affirmative.

Fine.

Terra continued onward. When she reached her final climb, she rose unsteadily onto her legs. Each movement happened as if in slow motion, each inch gained in ascension a Herculean effort. She imagined herself swimming through molasses, fighting through quicksand. As she pushed herself higher, fresh air licked her skin, fighting away the steadily increasing heat that rose around her and culminated in one fiery billow. Her fingers appeared first, then her head crowned. She pulled herself up and over the edge, her body slipping forward before crashing onto the pebbled surface of the rooftop.

She lay there for a long moment, eyes closed, letting the air refresh her skin. The city sang around her, car engines thrumming, AJS sirens, music beating out from nightclubs. The smell was colorful, now that she was away from the metallic, dry stink of the vents. Her body ached, her chest rose and fell with each heavy breath.

We did it.

You did it, APRIL replied. **Congratulations, Terra. Just a little bit further.**

Terra shook her head. *No thanks. I could happily sleep here.*

May I perform a scan first?

Terra drew a deep breath. *Fine.* She sat up, her arms shaking. Peeling open her eyelids, she was overwhelmed by the lights of the city. Above her, dark clouds rolled, and the first drops of a fresh shower fell onto her face.

APRIL scanned, filling her vision with thermal outlines of people sitting in the surrounding buildings. She turned to the front of the building and found a swarm of people sitting around in vehicles. **Performing data jump.**

Terra dry heaved, unprepared for this jump, her body and mind already weakened. She looked out from across the street at the fleet of AJS cruisers, her stomach sinking as APRIL jumped again, generating a full picture of the situation around the building. The AJS surrounded them. There was no hope of climbing down to safety. They'd have to find another way. They might have to jump.

I can't. I don't have the energy.

Terra protested as APRIL data jumped once more, sending her back into her own body. She moved her hand to her dizzy head, then almost threw up once more. "We had a deal," Terra complained.

Apologies, Terra. Based on the severity of the situation, I believed you'd be okay with me taking some liberties.

"Fine." She turned to her right, now checking out the second half of the rooftop. More orange glows confirmed men and women in the surrounding buildings, but it was the large, blazing outline of a nearby figure that made Terra's stomach drop. "You have *got* to be kidding me."

APRIL shut off thermal vision, and Garcia's figure came into view. All patience had worn from his expression. The gun was steady in his hand, eyes dark and murderous. "Really, Terra? Really? How are we still playing this game?"

Terra remained on the rough surface with no energy to pick herself up. "You tell me. You're the one still letting me play it. You appear at every turn I make as though you're stuck in my head and know my every move." She shook her head. "I can't take it anymore. Just end it, now. Do it. Put the bullet through my skull and finish what you started."

Garcia growled. "It's not that easy, Terra. You think I haven't dreamed about putting a bullet in your skull from the moment I first met you? You think I didn't know you'd be an issue from the moment I first looked into your eyes? If I could dispatch you straight away, I would, but you don't realize the game you're a part of. You don't understand the scale of what we're playing here.

"You and I, we're pawns, Terra. Playthings for a whole raft of invisible people who pull strings. That's all we are. That's all we'll ever be. It's bigger than ink. It's bigger than Atlantica. If I could kill you, I would, but I can't. That's the sad truth."

"So let me go," Terra replied.

"I can't do that either," Garcia replied. "You have treasure inside your head. Treasure that's too fragile to damage. I need it back." For the first time, Terra could see a hint of something strange in his eye. Was it fear? "Come. Let's end this. I'll remove OSCaR, and only then can I grant your wish."

Terra smirked. "No."

She couldn't believe she was saying it. After all the trouble she'd gotten into because of this AI embedded in her head, it seemed strange to her that she would be defending it. APRIL had brought her a second chance at life, a tool inside her mind that distinguished herself from all other cops and allowed her to perform impossible feats.

"I don't think you realize what you're saying," Garcia growled.

"I don't think you realize that I don't care anymore," Terra shot back. "I might not be able to pin you down on your ink rings or find a single shred of evidence that I can hold against you, but I will bring you down, no matter what it takes." She rose unsteadily to her feet, emboldening herself, even under the eye of the pistol.

Garcia scoffed. "Please, Terra. My ring is unbreakable. My alibi and defenses are solid."

"Not now." Terra tapped the side of her head. "You're on film, bitch."

"So what?" Garcia laughed. "You're not going anywhere. You can get whatever you want on me, but you're not broadcasting to anyone, not while my employer stays lodged in that pretty skull of yours."

Terra's throat went dry.

"That's right," Garcia continued. "No matter how much your crimson friend fiddles with our technology, you can't uproot the fundamentals. Tracking is part of the basic functionality of OSCaR. You alter the tracking, and you close the system. You shut down the system completely; you die."

He took great pleasure at Terra's pained face. "That's right. You and APRIL are one, and that means you'll forever be a slave to the manufacturers of this technology." He held his hands out, indicating the Tynamo building. "So, just give it up, Terra. It's over."

Terra took a step toward Garcia, stumbling. She folded onto one knee, grunting as her head lowered.

Garcia rolled his eyes. Behind him, several guards appeared on the rooftop, strolling toward the pair. Terra looked up, outnumbered and out of options. She held out a hand to Garcia. "Fine…Just…Could you help me up?"

Garcia grinned. "Of course." He lowered his pistol. "I'm glad you're coming around to my way of thinking—"

His words cut short as Terra took his wrist and pulled him toward her. Scalpel in her hand, she thrust the blade into the center of Garcia's chest. He gasped, the guards behind him momentarily confused, unable to see the blade.

Terra leaned toward Garcia's ear. "Go. Fuck. Yourself."

That's when the first shots fired.

CHAPTER THIRTY-FIVE

She twisted the blade, eliciting a pained yowl from Garcia. The guards drew their weapons as gunfire sounded from the surrounding buildings. Bullets *pinged* off the pebble-covered roof. A couple of the guards went down.

Garcia grimaced. "You bitch."

Terra twisted the blade again. He groaned. More shots fired. Terra flinched, though after a moment, she realized the bullets weren't coming for her.

She withdrew the blade, holding Garcia close to her and keeping him between herself and the guards. She didn't need to worry, though. The guards were turning their focus on their attackers, looking wildly around at the buildings surrounding the large round structure as they hunted for the source.

Is he going to be okay? Terra asked, holding Garcia close and hearing his pained breathing. The digital information was still a ghost in her vision, showing Terra where she would avoid doing permanent damage to Garcia and would merely wound him.

Your attack was accurate. Parker Garcia will make a full recovery, provided he receives medical care in... A digital timer appeared in the corner of Terra's vision, giving her plenty of time to navigate her situation.

Who the hell is firing? She searched for the sources herself. A number of the guards had fallen to the roof. Three remained, finding refuge behind the ventilation networks snaking along the roof. Metal *pinged* off metal. Something *hummed* in the distance.

Hide, Terra. Threat level one hundred percent.

Dragging Garcia with her, Terra moved out of the line of fire. She nestled herself behind a metal structure, then turned to the buildings. *APRIL, locate the shooters.*

APRIL scanned the surrounding buildings, soon highlighting three individuals located across three separate buildings. They were small, tucked away, only their heads and shooting hands in sight to avoid the return gunfire.

Identify.

APRIL zoomed in on each in turn. A weak smile spread across Terra's face as the legends appeared in her vision: John Chambers, Harley Crawdad, and Jenna "Slim" Newman.

The guards' return fire soon ceased as the trio picked off the final few. Terra turned to the place where they'd emerged, wondering if she'd be able to find a safe way back down.

"Oh, shit…" she muttered as APRIL triggered thermal vision and showed the outline of dozens more figures making their way through the building.

The humming grew louder.

Terra rested her head against the ventilation box. Garcia grumbled against her, unable to focus on anything but his blinding pain as he began to slip from consciousness.

Terra sighed, then looked out at the balconies. Dick Chambers appeared in full, waving at her, trying to shout something she couldn't hear. The buzz of traffic and that growing hum was too much to allow his words to carry.

"APRIL?" Terra huffed, her consciousness fading as her effort expenditure finally caught up with her.

Yes, Terra?

"Get me out of here, please." Terra's voice was weak, no more than a whisper.

Already working on it, Terra. Prepare to board.

"Prepare to…" Terra frowned, then turned to the sky as the humming grew to an almighty din. Lights flooded her vision. She shielded her stinging eyes with one hand, looking skyward at the approaching aircraft.

The black helicopter sped toward her, appearing through the cracks in the building. The air kicked out from its propellers stole the last of Terra's breaths. The craft landed delicately on the roof with barely any time to spare as Terra identified the horde of guards and AJS sprinting toward her.

Go. APRIL commanded.

Terra tried to get to her feet and found she couldn't.

Now, Terra. Up.

Terra tried again, this time getting some momentum. She found it odd that, after all they'd been through, APRIL couldn't physically lift her body. She had begun to wonder if there were any limits to APRIL's technology, and now she knew the truth. If she wanted this to happen, she was going to have to do this herself.

She rose shakily to her feet. She grabbed Garcia, slowly dragging him toward the aircraft. As she looked ahead, the outline of figures came into sight, silhouetted by the helicopter's bright lights. There was no label or logo on the aircraft. When Terra asked APRIL to identify those inside, the legends displayed only ?.

Terra gritted her teeth and let out one slow growl as she took the last ounces of her strength and half-ran, half-stumbled to the craft. Garcia was a dead weight behind her, but she knew he needed to come too. She wasn't letting him go this time. She finally had him in her grasp, and after everything, he wasn't going back on the streets.

A hand reached out to help her. They were strong. Terra was lifted into the chopper, her grip on Garcia slipping. Someone hopped down beside her, picking Garcia up and throwing him over their shoulder. Terra's assistant sat her on an empty seat. The person carrying Garcia threw him on the floor.

Shouts called from the exit to the rooftop. The helicopter lurched. Someone fired back. The helicopter rose into the air. Terra's eyes closed. She fell onto her side, instantly fading out of consciousness as the chopper fled the scene.

CHAPTER THIRTY-SIX

When Terra peeled her eyes open, many things assaulted her at once.

Her body was sore, muscles aching, throat dry, yet she lay in a level of comfort she hadn't experienced for some time. The room was white, so clinically clean and white that it stung her eyes and made her wonder for a moment whether she had died and gone to Heaven.

She groaned, slowly trying to push herself into a seated position, until her rib protested, erupting like hot lava in her chest, and she gave up the attempt. As memories slowly came back, Terra moved her hand to explore the parts of her body she knew to be damaged.

Her rib didn't stick out as it had, and there was a clean dressing on her chest. She felt for her ear and found an object where there shouldn't have been one, fleshy to the touch but devoid of any feeling. As she examined herself under the duvet, she realized that she was naked but that all of her wounds had been addressed and dealt with.

What the fuck is going on?

Do you want an answer to that, Terra?

APRIL's voice shocked Terra for a moment. The jump hurt her rib and aggravated her muscles. Barely able to keep her eyes open, she replied, "No. Not right now."

As you were, Terra Kris, APRIL replied.

Terra closed her eyes and slipped into an uneasy dream.

Terra stood motionless.

Her world was dark, pitch-black on either side. The floor was hard and smooth, her bare feet taking in the cool chill of a floor made of a material she couldn't determine. Her arms hung either side. Air came and went in steady billows in her lungs, and all that she knew was that she was safe.

Somehow, even just for a little while, she was safe.

The world appeared in black and white around her. The skyline of the city of Atlantica was beautiful, cutting across the horizon in an asymmetric display of architectural beauty. Her gaze pinned on the rising sun, appearing behind all the buildings and crowning its head. She heard her heart beating in her chest, and for the first time in a long time, she simply watched the world go by.

She sat, finding a bench waiting beside her. The sun rose, and the sun fell, and as Terra watched the cycle of the life of Atlantica, a feeling of certainty grew within her.

Things were going to be okay.

No matter what, she was going to keep fighting.

For, if she didn't, who else would?

She closed her eyes and took in the deepest, freshest breath she had for some time, aware that she was dreaming, knowing that once she woke up, the serenity of her bubble would pop, but for now, Atlantica was hers.

And that was pretty special indeed.

"How are you feeling?" a voice asked as Terra's eyes fought to open once more.

The fuzzy shape of Slim appeared at Terra's bedside, sitting on a perfectly white chair that blended in with the room.

"You couldn't tell them to turn the lights down a bit, could you?" Terra replied, testing her wounds with a soft hand. Already there was less pain in her chest, her ear didn't throb, and she found she could ease herself up into a mid-stage between laying and sitting.

Slim chuckled, glancing around the room. "It is a bit 'St Peter's Gate,' isn't it?"

"You could say that again," Terra replied.

"It is—" Slim began.

"Don't," Terra interrupted.

Slim grinned. "I learned from the best."

Terra tilted her head to the side, getting a full look at Slim. She noticed then that this was the first time she hadn't seen Jenna Newman in her AJS fatigues. Instead, she wore a plain black t-shirt and black cargo pants. She'd tied her hair back into a messy ponytail, and she looked more refreshed than Terra had seen her before.

"You look good," Terra stated.

"Thanks," Slim replied. "You look like shit."

Terra chuckled. "What happened? Where am I? Where are Dick and Harley?"

Slim looked over her shoulder as if debating whether someone would come in and tell her off for filling Terra in on what had happened.

"You're in a private facility," Slim replied. "It's not my place to tell you where, but the answers will come soon. As for what happened, there's a long story to that. No doubt they'll fill you in when they speak to you.

"As for Dick and Harley, well, Dick has returned to the city. He has a lot of business to attend to, and he didn't like the idea of getting into bed with an organization far above his station. He sends his best wishes and says to tell you that if you ever call him again to get involved in anything like this, he's going to shoot *you* in the ass."

Terra snorted, then held her healing rib in pain. "And Harley?" Terra asked, hating the idea that she might have dragged someone else into something larger than any of them could handle.

"Harley's fine," Slim replied. "Interesting character, that one. But she's here. She's eager to see you, but I'm sure you guys can catch up when you've rested more. She says you promised her something."

"I did," Terra replied. "I'll deliver. You tell her that much for me."

"Of course," Slim replied.

Terra studied her face, a wave of guilt instantly washing over her as the contrast between the Jenna Newman in the locker room and the Jenna Newman standing before her hit. "I'm sorry."

"Sorry for what?" Slim replied.

"I dragged you into this," Terra replied. "You had the opportunity to get everything that you ever wanted, to rise up the ranks of the AJS and make a difference. I took that from you. I'm sorry."

Slim laughed, waving a placating hand. "My first and last priority has always been the defense of this city. Justice is my compass. Morality is my shepherd. You really think I'd take an offer from a crooked cop like Garcia? Come on, do you really even know me?" She smirked. "Justice before mercy."

"Justice before mercy?" Terra contemplated the words. "I like that."

"I thought you might." Slim drew a long breath, then continued. "You put your head back and get some rest. Once you're in a better position to absorb everything, they'll bring you in and tell you all." She rose and smiled. "Rest up, Terra. You've done a great thing for Atlantica."

Terra's eyes widened, the most obvious question rising to her lips and coming out with sudden desperation. "Garcia!" She groaned as a spark of pain flashed through her body. "What happened to Garcia?"

"He's in custody," Slim replied. "The video footage from the OSCaR system—"

"APRIL," Terra corrected. "It's APRIL."

"The video footage from your APRIL system is enough to keep him with us," Slim replied. "The footage may not be perfect, but there were no blockers or disrupters, and we've potentially got just enough to hang a sentence on him for his crimes. He was stupid for thinking that you wouldn't escape and he wouldn't have to worry."

Terra frowned.

"What is it?" Slim asked.

"The APRIL system…" Terra sighed. "They can control it. I'm never going to be free of their clutches until this thing comes out of my head. As long as it stays embedded in my skull, I'm a liability."

"I wouldn't be so sure about that." Slim grinned. "Get some rest, Terra. Your world will open up soon enough."

CHAPTER THIRTY-SEVEN

Terra walked slowly down the corridor, a slight limp in her step.

Her recovery had gone well, but the ghosts of her encounter with Garcia and his team were still there. Her hearing had returned in her ear, but the rib was slow to heal. Even aided with APRIL's guidance, it would be a few more days until she was close to her normal self.

Her footsteps echoed down the clean white hallways. Slim had summoned her only a few minutes ago and now walked beside her, leading her toward the muted gray door at the end of the hall. They walked in silence, Terra's heart beating fast.

Slim knocked three times. A voice called, "Come in."

"Here you go, Terra," Slim offered. "Good luck."

Terra entered the room.

The contrast between this room and everything else she had seen was stark. While the walls were still an immaculate white, furniture made of dark oak filled the room. A desk sat in the center of the room. Photos were framed on the wall, filled with pictures from the seventies and eighties of people she'd never seen in her life. There were discarded weapons decorating the surfaces like trophies, and a vintage coffee machine sat on a side table near the desk.

A large woman sat behind the desk, her huge frame spilling over the chair. Seated beside her was a friendly face that Terra was happy to see.

"Thomas," she offered, nodding in Imani's direction.

"Hey, Terra," Imani smiled.

Slim closed the door behind her.

"I want to introduce you to a friend of mine," Imani stated. "Terra, this is Nora Asplin. Nora, meet—"

"Terra Kris," Nora finished eagerly, standing and offering her hand.

Terra took it, surprised by the enthusiasm of the greeting. "Nice to meet you."

"Nice to meet you, too," Nora replied with a broad grin on her face, head shaking as if she couldn't believe that she was meeting Terra for the first time. "Well, nice to meet you *officially* anyway."

Terra sat. "What's that supposed to mean?"

Nora considered this. "Long story. Maybe for another time. What I will say is that it is such an honor to meet the first subject of the APRIL restoration program. An officer with the caliber and skills able to make the bio AI work without a flaw... It really is rather impressive."

Terra frowned. "I don't understand."

Imani took over. "Terra, what you're about to hear is going to sound confusing at first—it certainly did for me. Stick with it because if you do, you're about to find that all of your wildest dreams of Atlantica are about to come true."

Terra frowned. She shook her hands in front of her face. "Hold on. I have questions *before* we've even started. Where the hell did you go, Thomas? You had Garcia. Then you were gone. I needed you out there." Frustration grew, and Terra found she couldn't help the words spilling from her mouth. "I needed my partner, and you were gone. I thought someone captured you. I thought someone took you. I went through all that shit solo because you *left* me."

"I needed to," Imani replied.

"And Harley? What about her daughter? What about Ruby?" Terra asked. "Is she okay? I promised her I'd free her. I promised I'd help."

"That's all being taken care of," Imani soothed. "She knows the score…Terra, that's not what you're here for. I'll answer all those questions in time. I will. But I need you to hear Nora out first." She turned to Nora, indicating that Terra should do the same.

"Terra," Nora began. "What I'm about to tell you may hurt to begin with, but I promise you, it's all been for the greater good."

Terra's nostrils flared. She debated arguing but saw no point. "I'm listening."

Nora nodded, the smile returning to her face. Her eyes danced to the memorabilia dotted around the room. "Tell me, Terra… What do you know about 'The Executioners?'"

Thank you for not only reading this story but our author notes here in the back. This book, I'm going to suggest that what this book mentions—AI and integration / tracking—is something that won't be a big deal in the future. Here is what I mean by that.

So, what happens to humanity when our vaunted integration with future technology allows everyone and everything to be tracked?

I'm not really sure.

It's not like different countries around the world (usually the more technically advanced and/or richer countries) already have the ability to track their citizens.

In the USA, we have the NSA, and we have NO idea what their capabilities are except that it is rumored to be capable of tracking all messages from anyone and everywhere. What we don't think NSA can do is have all cities under video surveillance like London, England.

We have not heard (yet) that the NSA can track even the emotions of people walking out in the streets, as I have seen profiled can be done in China (a highly technical ability considering it can be done IN REAL-TIME.)

Do the citizens seem upset?

Not really.

At least, when I was in Beijing, London, and New York I didn't notice anyone walking around casting furtive glances over their shoulders, and the populace in those three countries all seemed happy enough to me.

So, my unscientific research suggests it will be 'ho hum' on the worry-about-being-tracked-and followed front.

For those who are concerned with the future and private rights, perhaps investigate countries without the technical know-how and/or budget, or that frankly don't care about tracking the populace, and see what it will take to move to those countries.

If 2020 taught us anything, it's that technology can bite us, or it can release us to go to locales that aren't going to be putting up surveillance cameras anytime soon.

Ironically, it's those countries that are the least advanced that have the best chance to be out of the coming technology wars.

Hard to screw up a country's technological infrastructure if they don't have one.

(If you aren't from America, I encourage you to IGNORE what you see from Hollywood. A lot of that technology is NOT available to our police forces and forensic scientists.

Don't get me started with the NCIS's ability to use a one-megapixel camera and zoom into with sharpening to see minute details. Hell, my own camera on my laptop often can't get a good crisp image.

See you in *Terra Kris* 03!

If you haven't read the first two trilogies, go get them (just search for ATLANTICA on Amazon and Michael Anderle... SO MUCH GOOD STUFF!)

Ad Aeternitatem,

Michael Anderle

OTHER ATLANTICA BOOKS

John Chambers Books
Her Mother's Pendant (Book 1)
The Mystery Deepens (Book 2)
One Last Choice (Book 3)

Valentina Winters
The Red Countess (Book 1)
One Night to Kill (Book 2)
One Death Too Few (Book 3)

Terra Kris
She is the Law (Book 1)
Law or Justice (Book 2)
Justice Served (Book 3)

Santana Sokolov (Coming soon)

BOOKS BY MICHAEL ANDERLE

Sign up for the LMBPN email list to be notified of new releases and special deals!

https://lmbpn.com/email/

For a complete list of books by Michael Anderle, please visit:

www.lmbpn.com/ma-books/